"Zig's unsettling work peels back the white, middle class veneer so many of us recognize from suburban life ... compelling us to reflect on the hidden lives of those around us."
  – Andrew Pople
  2SER / Tuesday Book Club

"[Zig] has written this fabulous deliciously naughty book called *Just Another Week in Suburbia* ... with such humor and with such grace with such powers of beauty and observation that I really, really enjoyed it .... He does it so well."
  – Rob Minshull
  ABC Radio Brisbane

"*Just Another Week in Suburbia* is a hugely enjoyable novel which illuminates the extraordinary in the everyday, and the quirky in the quotidian."
  – Ryan O'Neill
  Their Brilliant Careers (Black Inc 2016)

"A stunningly polished psychological debut ruminating on issues of doubt, dissatisfaction, and temptation in even the most seemingly secure relationships. *Just Another Week in Suburbia* tells the intricate story of love's instability, the volatile nature of trust, and asks whether we can ever truly know another person. Zig masterfully delves into the fears and fixations within us all, showing how one small event can unhinge the human psyche."
  – NetGalley Roundup

"[Zig] has taken the somewhat monotonous elements of suburban life, the mistrust and fear which can develop between partners as well as the pressure of all those things left unsaid in a relationship and has packaged them up in one complex, tightly-laced character who we see unravel under the weight of his own psyche. It's a lot to go through and process in 300 odd pages, but it's an enjoyable read that will draw you in with its wit, and keep you there as the drama builds."
– Jenna Woods
GLAM Adelaide

"… a must read … a powerful novel that bristles with intelligence, and black humor … a dark, gritty read that explores the dark side of human nature … an engrossing novel, and one that leaves a lasting impression."
– Slap Happy Fun Time

"… engaging … honest and relatable. It was difficult to put down because the story was so compelling. I just had to know what happened next. At one point my heart was pounding, and I couldn't read fast enough … captivating."
– Jordan Reads Too Much

JUST ANOTHER WEEK IN SUBURBIA

LES ZIG

First published in 2017 by Pantera Press

This edition published in 2025 by ECG Press
www.ecgpress.com

Please send all permission queries to info@ecgpress.com

A Cataloging-in-Publication entry for this book is available from the National Library of Australia.

Cover: Rosie Giuliano (Instagram ~ the_rosie.g)

To Blaise,
whose strength,
support,
and encouragement
helped me to branch out on my own.

MONDAY

1.

Wallace's yapping wakes me just as I'm nodding off. Flipping onto my side, I bury my face in Jane's hair, hoping he shuts up.

He doesn't.

I drag myself into a sitting position. Sweat cools on my brow, so I wipe it away with my wrist. Damn belated summer has been unrelenting. The clock radio on Jane's bedside table glows with the lime of its digital numbers: 12:09am. It feels later.

Swiveling out of bed, I lock my feet into my slippers, and walk over to the window in my underwear, hoping I'll be able to *shhh* Wallace from up here. Unfortunately, he sounds like he's next door, which isn't good because my neighbor, Vic Booth, hates him in a way that makes me think some dog must've traumatized him when he was a kid.

Peeling back our curtains, I peek out. A street already cuts through the paddocks that unfold beyond our backyard, streetlights so bright they must use the bulbs from lighthouses. It's only a matter of time before new houses like our own go up. But that's all the suburb of Meadow is: uniformity.

In the Booths' yard, the beach table with the umbrella and banana lounges are blots of shadows, while light ripples across the pool. No sign of Wallace, though. Sometimes I worry he'll fall in the pool and drown. Instead of commiserating, Vic would probably charge us for the cleaning.

Grabbing my bathrobe from where it hangs on the back of the door, I stumble from the bedroom, and flick on the light in the landing. The first thing that greets me is the picture hanging at the top of the stairs of Jane and me on our wedding day. Jane – in her flowing dress, her hair elaborately braided – smiles at me like she's never known a harried thought in her life. I look mildly shocked, as if the photographer caught me unawares, an expression present in each of the six anniversary photos that chaperone me as I head downstairs. This was Jane's idea, to mark our coupling as we grew older. We're getting a seventh photo on Sunday morning, following a fancy dinner and a hotel room at the Sheraton in the city on Saturday night.

My slippers suction onto the floorboards as I reach the front door, squelching so noisily I'm sure they'll wake Jane. Unlocking the front door, I ease it open. The night's balminess strikes me. The heat's simmered in the air and made it sticky. It's meant to be hotter this week.

The street itself is quiet, except for the echoes of Wallace's excitement. The houses are silhouettes, trees in front of them small and still, silent tributes to the idealism of everyday middle-class suburbia. Everybody's bins are out. I've forgotten ours.

I go outside, grab the bins from around the side of the house, and wheel them to the nature strip while hissing for Wallace. The Booths live to our left. Wallace has his own doggy door, so he has the run of our backyard. It's meant to be contained, but there are pockets where he burrows under the fence. The Booths don't have a side gate like we do, so Wallace is free to explore their property, although he's been told repeatedly he shouldn't.

No fence separates our front yards. Our garages and driveways are mashed together. My Fiesta's parked on the nature strip. Our two-car garage is home to Jane's VW Beetle and seven years of crap we've accumulated. There's not much room for anything else.

"Wallace!" I say.

His yapping stops. I can imagine him cocking his head.

"Wallace!"

I hope he'll appear from somewhere else, but he comes sprinting from around the Booths' house and bounds across their yard – he's probably been chasing Silver, Vic's stupid cat. I open the security door and he struts in, a ball of white fluff with a black spot on his back, an irrepressible wire-haired fox terrier. We got him after our efforts to have a baby didn't work – not that he appreciates that.

"*Sshhh!*" I follow him in and lock the security and front doors.

Wallace peers at me as if to say, *What?* His little tail circles like a propeller, and his nose is dirty, so he must've burrowed under the fence.

I'm wide awake now, so instead of returning to bed, I go into the study and, as I turn on the light, stumble on something: Jane's handbag. When she's not forgetting it at work or in the car, she leaves it just inside the study door so she can scoop it up on the way out. Everything has spilled out. This isn't our first tangle. I leave the clean-up for later and sit on my recliner.

My sketchpad rests on my desk, my pencils fanned out haphazardly. I take my sketchpad onto my lap as Wallace tramps in, sniffs at the contents of Jane's bag, looks at me, then hops onto the couch. He has a basket in the laundry but has made that couch cushion his home. Circling the spot, he then flops down and stares at me, as if reproaching me for interrupting his fun.

I flick through my pad – lots of little sketches of fruit, furniture, and a couple of Wallace. Jane says they're okay, but wives are meant to say stuff like that. Beth, the art teacher at the school where I teach, says they're good. Of course, she could be humoring me, since she's also a friend. I used to draw lots. There wasn't much time once Jane and I got married. I've just taken it back up and my efforts don't enthuse me.

If only there was an inspiring landscape outside my window – something dramatically cliché, like waves crashing upon a precipice, maybe. But our yard's a big block of grass rimmed by a Coldstream wall, the big stones fitted neatly together. Recently, I've taken a sledgehammer to it because I want to put up something new – like everybody's done in the neighborhood – but there's a gulf between the theory and the practice.

I move to draw a line on my page, but know if I do it's because I want to commit to the pretense I'm sketching. Sometimes, pretense is all you have … and sometimes something else tempers it – fear, maybe. Fear that there'll be nothing *but* the pretense. I pull back. I don't want to dirty the page. The page is perfect empty.

Closing my eyes, I search for the tiredness to drive me back to bed, but there's nothing there. Once I'm awake, it takes a while to switch off – especially after I've taken a jaunt like the excursion to shut Wallace up. This is his fault. He lies curled up on the futon, chin on his paws, asleep. I should wake him.

Putting my pad on my desk, I decide to go back to bed. I can stay awake in there just as well as I can here. Anyway, there's the risk of eventually drifting off in my recliner, only to have to wake myself again to go back to my bedroom.

Kneeling by the spillage of Jane's handbag, I begin throwing things back in: purse, make-up, keys (which jingle – Wallace wakes, lifts his head, then hops down and saunters over to check out what I'm doing) … and then I stop.

A condom sits there – Four Seasons, glow in the dark. The corner of the wrapper is dog-eared. Maybe it's been battered inside Jane's bag, but it's likelier somebody started to tear it open.

Wallace peers at it, as if recognizing it's foreign. He looks at me, sniffs the packet, then looks back at me. I pick it up in a trembling hand. Jane and I don't use condoms – we haven't since before we were engaged.

Shooting to my feet, I storm up the stairs, Wallace trotting after me. The anniversary pictures flaunt our happiness, although we weren't always happy on the days they were taken – the first shortly after Dad died, the third only a fortnight after Jane miscarried, the fifth after we'd thrashed out a plan to save for IVF. I see the shock on my face over the course of the years, as well as some discomfort – a result of Jane dressing me in stiff suits and ties tight enough to noose me. That's the price of being immortalized. But now the shock not only mirrors what I'm feeling, but the potential for something much more insidious.

My steps slow as I reach the landing.

Falter as I reach the doorway.

Then stop. Wallace bumps into my ankles.

I don't know what to say. It seems obvious: *What's this condom doing in your handbag?* But it's not. It's like breaking bad news. There's the way you hear it in your head and the way it's said in the real world. The two rarely meet. And even when they do, you never want to know what comes next.

I sit on the bedside, condom clutched in my hand. Jane's still curled up, covers pulled to her chin. She sleeps in little silk boxers she buys to use as pajamas because she likes the way they feel. Even in winter, it's the boxers, so she's always hogging the covers because she gets cold. You'd think she'd put a T-shirt on. I asked her once why she didn't. She said she couldn't sleep in one. Instead, she drags the covers right up to her jaw. It's cute, in its own way, but God knows how she tolerates it in this heat.

Wallace sits at my feet oblivious to what's going on. I scratch his head absently. He waits for more attention, but when he doesn't get it, he must realize this isn't some new game we're playing, rises, and leaves.

I tear off my bathrobe, throw it aside, take off my slippers, and lie stiff alongside Jane, kicking the covers down to my ankles. There has to be a logical explanation that doesn't mean the worst for me, for us. Maybe she found it. Or bought it for somebody.

Maybe she was out for lunch and some high school brat wanted Jane to go into the chemist and buy her a condom because she was too embarrassed to do it herself, then ran off before collecting it. Do they even sell single condoms? The whole scenario's stupid.

It could just be that Jane's fucking somebody.

She works in an office with several guys. Her boss, Henry, is about fifty. I think one of the full-time coders, Barry, is in his forties. But the other one, the one with the funny name – Kip or Kai or something – is only twenty-five or so. Five years younger than Jane, though age means nothing. The rest of the staff are subcontractors, constantly in and out. I wouldn't know them if I bumped into them on the street.

Jane squishes up against me, her body warm, breath hot on my skin. Her hand slides up my belly and entwines in my chest hair. These are all trademark Jane mannerisms – *Janerisms* – which have always reconnected me to her, little bonds that tie us tighter together.

I want to know the truth.

But I'm afraid of what it might be.

2.

The clock radio wakes us at 6:25am. Jane slaps it off. Outside, the garbage truck heaves as it collects the bins, a herald that the working week has truly started.

Jane rolls onto me and snuggles close. I circle one arm around her and run my hand up and down her back. She kisses my jaw. I run my free hand through her hair. The shampoo she uses smells like roses, while the warmth of her skin is a comforting familiarity.

"I could do with another half hour," she says.

She kisses my chin, her big gray eyes locking onto mine as her crotch grinds into my morning erection. Her breasts flatten onto my chest, like she's melting into me and we're becoming one.

"You look tired," she says. "Wallace go off last night?"

Last night. The condom. I brought it with me. Clutched it in my hand. Thought I wouldn't sleep, but obviously did. Now where is it?

"Yeah, he—"

There's a flurry of little footsteps, then Wallace hurtles onto the bed. Jane sits up, straddled across my crotch and cradles Wallace to her naked chest, her skin as pale as his white fur. He licks her cheek, tail quivering.

"Were you a bad boy last night?" she asks. "Were you a bad boy?"

She babies Wallace and admonishes him for his foray into Vic's while I look frantically around for the condom. As she rocks Wallace, the cover slips back – her left shin stretches like a bridge right over the condom, her foot propped up on her toes. I shoot into a sitting position, nearly knocking Jane and Wallace backwards.

"What?" she says.

"Just …" And I don't know what comes next. I peck her on the lips.

Jane shakes her head and smiles. "I'm going to shower. You feed his majesty."

"Okay."

She kisses me, clambers off and deposits Wallace in my lap. I jerk my left leg over the condom just as Jane's line of vision falls on where it is – she frowns at me. I don't think she saw it. No, she hasn't, or she'd say something.

I scratch Wallace behind the ears and smile at Jane as if I'm doing nothing more than admiring her. But of course I do – that's never been in doubt. I watch her walk to the bathroom – watch her with rapt attention as if I'm privileged to see her semi-naked for the first time. She's lithe, legs perhaps a little thin, or at least she thinks so. Her hair bounces down to the middle of her back.

We first met at uni when I was nineteen. She was this shy girl who didn't talk much – at least not to me. I was studying teaching, she business. I don't think we exchanged more than a handful of words in all the time we were at school. It wasn't until a graduation party four years later that I bumped into her at the bar. We chatted, I grew infatuated. I timed my run of drinks to bump into her. The second time she remarked it was a coincidence. The third time she was onto me. The fourth time she asked if I wanted to sit with her and we talked. And talked.

Jane stretches in the bathroom – a yoga pose where she lifts one leg, and plants her foot against her knee, then lifts her arms above her head and presses her hands together. Yoga's something Jane used to do often but which, like a lot of things, fell away when we got busy making a life for ourselves. Now this is her last tie to it. She swaps which leg she has lifted, holds the pose – I think it's called "the tree" or something – then relaxes, pulls her boxers down and steps out of them. On her right buttock are two small bruises, no bigger than bottle tops. I wonder, are they the size of a thumb and fingertip? Was somebody clawing her too tight while fucking her? It would probably mean he was fucking her hard too.

Jane turns on the shower.

Steps into the water.

And becomes a blur to me.

I carry Wallace to the kitchen and empty a can of dog food into his bowl. He sniffs suspiciously at the food, then stares at me as if to say, *This is it?* Jane and I feed him too much from our own plates. He'd prefer steak or lasagna.

"Eat," I tell him.

He takes a bite, then turns his nose up. I try to coax him, digging a bit of food out with a spoon and mimicking eating it. He heads for his doggy door. I hear it flap open. Then, through our rear bay windows, I see him show up in our overgrown backyard, which reminds me of him getting into Vic's last night.

Following him out, I search the fence separating our house from the Booths'. I don't know what it was with the builders – the fence has to be at least ten feet high. I know Vic enjoys the privacy, but it makes me claustrophobic.

I search the base for where Wallace burrowed through, but it's the condom that's on my mind. Jane's given no indication she's cheating. She's never late home, always prompt when I text to check about dinner and things to do in the evening. Then there's this morning, climbing onto me the way she did. If there were someone else, would she still be so affectionate?

I should just ask her.

I will.

When she gets out of the shower.

I find the hole in the corner. It's one of Wallace's older ones, which he's re-excavated. I kick the dirt back in and stamp it with my slipper. Wallace watches me, trying to work out why I'm sealing something he's worked so hard on.

"You stay *here*," I tell him.

He spots a magpie on the other side of the yard feeding from the grass and sprints after it, barking.

I go to our second bathroom – designated my bathroom – undress, and stop as I'm about to enter the shower. Pull back. Take a deep breath. And become aware of my nudity, of my skin. Pale? Or pasty? Of my chest, or lack thereof; my stomach, with the first hint of a pot belly; my cock flaccid in a forest of pubic hair. Is it too small? *Unsatisfactory?* I once heard somewhere that 5.8 inches is average. I think that's about me, but maybe that's not enough. Maybe, after all this time, I don't please Jane.

Self-consciousness explodes, highlighting every inadequacy in my body. I caress my teeth with my tongue – they're straight, although there's a gap between the top two that I'm self-conscious about when I smile; run my hands through my hair, and feel the way it's already creeping back around my temples; pry my fingers into my ears, and remember that just last week, I found a few stray ear hairs that I plucked out with tweezers.

Am I – or have I become – undesirable? Was I always, but never knew it? Is it something Jane's discovered? Did she wake up one morning and conclude that she'd settled? She's never complained, although she wouldn't. Of course she wouldn't. I wouldn't, even if there were anything *to* say. There's not. She's perfect – well, she's perfect for me.

The condom sits on the bathroom sink.

Hey, hon, I stumbled on your handbag last night and this fell out.

Like I could be so glib.

Hey, hon, last night, Wallace was barking, so I got up. Anyway, after I let him in, I was still wide awake, so I went into the study to sketch. But I didn't see your bag and tripped on it. All your stuff spilled out. That's when I found this.

Still too succinct.

I won't get past the first line. Because what's at stake? Almost seven years of marriage, one miscarriage, slowly saving up for IVF, four years of trying to have a kid, a house (that we bought in anticipation of having a family) with a sizable mortgage, a life in the suburbs, Wallace, family, in-laws (and the loan we owe them), Christmases, other functions together – all of it. You build a community from a relationship. And then it can be lost, like a meteorite hit. Bye, bye, civilization.

All because of the answer to one question.

Of course, it could all be preserved with one answer.

But, right now, the only certainty is not knowing.

I shower, dress in jeans, a shirt, and a blazer, then go into the study and stand over Jane's handbag, holding the condom in my hand. I can't confront Jane about it. Not yet. I put the condom back in her bag. Retreat to the kitchen with the intention of making breakfast, then see it – Jane's phone, charging, plugged into a socket adjacent to the stove.

The question that arises is simple: *Should I or shouldn't I?* I've never looked through Jane's phone. Never. Even if I want a number, I ask her for it. But who knows what secrets her phone might hold?

I pick it up, hold my breath as I realize I'm crossing a line which can never be uncrossed, key in the passcode (my birthday), then flick through the messages. Nothing – messages with me, some with her best friend Sarah, a few with her mom, and that's it. I go through the call log. Nothing there either. Of course, she could've erased anything incriminating, but still, it's a relief to find nothing.

Putting the phone back, I make breakfast – two slices of toast and a cup of tea for me, just a coffee for Jane – and stand at the window. The morning's overcast, but it won't be long before the clouds break.

Jane comes in about fifteen minutes later. She always takes forever in the shower – an activity that's never drawn any curiosity from me, but which now has me wondering. Is she primping for somebody else? She wears a suit, the skirt tight around her hips. Her shirt is pinstriped, the first couple of buttons open to reveal her naked chest, but no cleavage. Her hair is pinned back. Her cheeks seem bright, but she wears no more or no less make-up than any other day.

She picks up the coffee I've left on the bench for her. Seven years has ingrained our routine. She sips on her coffee and goes through her satchel. I wonder what she does all day. She's the account manager at Web Myriad, which builds websites for big businesses. But I've never really known what she does on an hour-to-hour basis, outside of the basic understanding that she oversees the bookkeeping, invoicing, and payroll.

"We've got dinner tonight," she says.

"What?"

"Dinner."

"Dinner?"

"You okay? You seem a little out of it this morning."

I shrug.

"Dinner. Tonight. With Stephen and Renée."

"Oh. Okay."

"What do you think I should wear? That little red dress? Or my blue one?"

"Surprise me."

"You're hopeless."

I finish my toast. Throw the plate in the sink, wanting to be out of there.

"You're not going to wash up?"

"I'll do it later."

Jane already has the faucets blaring. She rolls up her sleeves. Grabs a sponge. "What's the rush?" she says.

"I need to get going."

"Early, isn't it?" Jane soaks a plate under the faucet.

"Stuart wants to address the staff about something or other."

"Oh."

Stuart is Stuart Piper, the school vice principal. The staff meet every morning at 8:45, but sometimes Stuart calls us in earlier – usually for something insignificant. Well, insignificant as far as the staff is concerned; for Stuart, *any* matter is consequential.

"Sorry, I forgot to tell you," I say.

"You sure you're okay?"

"Yeah."

I pick up my bag, the kitchen counter separating us. "What're you up to today?" I say, and inwardly cringe. It's a question I never ask.

"Usual," Jane says. "Lunch with Sarah today, too."

Sarah, her train wreck of a friend – always picking the wrong guys, always celebrating that they're the right one (finally), always breaking up ingloriously and crying on Jane's shoulder. They catch up almost weekly, but is Sarah an alibi? Not like Jane needs it – not for a lunch hour where she's never had to account for herself anyway.

"I should go," I say, starting for the hall.

"Hey!"

She purses her lips. I lean over the kitchen counter. The water gushes into the sink between us. I kiss her.

"Have a good day," she says.

"Thanks."

My feet are leaden down the hallway. Each step widens the separation between us. She's washing our cups. I keep moving. There's a crash. Hurried footsteps – Wallace come to see me off. He slides down the hall and leaps at my shins. He wants to get out.

I tramp to the front door, and swing it open. Sunlight hits me through a part in the clouds. Then the sounds of morning in the neighborhood, of people getting ready for work, for school, for whatever the day holds. This is me, re-entering the world just like I do every day, but now filled with uncertainty.

When I push open the security door, Wallace streams out, barking. Kids scream his name. It's Kirit and Pia Gupta, our neighbors to the right. They're only eight and seven, so understandably Wallace excites them. The kids are dressed in their burgundy school uniforms, backpacks slung over their shoulders. They kneel as Wallace greets them and pat him, scratching him behind the ears until he falls on his back so they can rub his belly. Their mother, Tarika, emerges from the house and walks toward her Lexus. She always smiles and waves at me – as she does now.

On the front curb, the bins stand empty. I want to get going, but if I leave them Jane will fetch them and really know something's wrong with me this morning. This is my job.

I put my bag down by the front step and go grab the bins.

"Hello, Casper!" Tarika says.

I wave and grab the bins.

"How're you this morning?" Tarika says.

"Good." I start wheeling the bins back. "You?"

"Good, thanks! It's going to be a beautiful day, isn't it?"

"It's going to be a hot one."

I deposit the bins in their usual place, around the side of our house.

"Come on, kids!" Tarika says, as she gets in her Lexus. Typically, the kids don't listen. Wallace is much more interesting.

I retrieve my bag, and head for my little black Fiesta.

"Hello, Casper!"

This comes from Vic's house – Vic's wife, Chloe, scrambling out of her red Mazda. She's tiny, her blonde hair in a topknot. It makes her look like the teenagers I teach. Her figure is taut in a purple and black leotard. When she's not working shifts as a nurse, she seems to split her time sunbathing by her pool, or doing aerobics or Pilates in the morning.

"How're you today?" she asks.

"Good," I tell her, because what else am I going to say? Chloe's friendly. Sometimes I get mixed signals from her, although that's probably just me. I don't read signals well.

"Oi, Gray!"

I stop as I reach for the door of my Fiesta. It's Vic, dressed in his greasy coveralls and wiping his hands on a hand towel – blackening it with each wipe – as he comes out the front door of his house. He's *big*. Not muscly big. Just solid big – the sort of guy who moves around like his duty is to block any light and joy in life. His crew cut makes him look militant.

"Your stupid dog was in here again last night chasing my cat," Vic says.

"I'm sorry," I say. And mean it. I tried to make friends with Vic when he first moved in four years ago. I even took my car to him to be serviced. But we have nothing in common. He's abrupt, and he overcharges. Jane's friends with Chloe, and they've gone out to movies together. But Jane can't stand Vic either. I don't know how Chloe does.

"I've warned you about your dog, Gray."

"He's a dog. You have a cat."

"I catch your dog in here again, I'm going to dropkick him out, okay?"

"He's ankle height."

"That's a good size to kick."

"Vic!" Chloe says as she approaches him. She pauses, like she wants to exchange a morning kiss. He ignores her. "He'll be fine, Casper!" she calls as she brushes past Vic into the house; he swats her hard on the butt and leaves a greasy handprint. She yelps playfully and jumps but doesn't stop. Vic points at me once. Chloe's words aren't going to contain him.

"Kids!" This from Tarika. "Now!" The kids jump up from Wallace, bid him their goodbyes, and get into the Lexus. Wallace gets up and shakes, straightening himself out.

"Go inside!" I tell him. I'm always worried I'll run him over on the way out.

"Wallace!" It's Jane, standing at the front door. Wallace bounds to her and leaps. She catches him and cradles him to her chest with one hand while waving goodbye to me with the other.

I open the door of my car. Across the street Josh and Karen Meyer are about to get into their car – they're a married couple in their twenties, just starting out like Jane and I were not that long ago. They wave to me, a simple acknowledgment of my presence.

I wave back. Slip into my car, start it up, depress the clutch. The radio blares. I leave it, look at my house flanked by Tarika's and Vic's. They're clones, but for the shades of brick. On the nature strips are tulipwoods – I think that's what they're called. The ones in front of Tarika's and Vic's houses are green, the one in front of ours a deep, rusty maroon.

My eyes flit from Vic on his doorstep watching me, to Tarika making sure her kids are buckled in, to Jane rocking Wallace. She grabs his paw and makes him wave goodbye. His furry face registers his disapproval, and he scowls, unimpressed.

I pull off the nature strip and drive away.

3.

Driving, all I can tell myself is *I should've asked, I should've asked, I should've asked*, although I know it's retrospective bravado. Everybody knows what they should've done after it's too late to do it.

I could turn around.

But I keep driving.

It's still early for school. I could hang out in the staff room, but there'll be other teachers there. I don't feel like the company – at least not that sort of company.

I wish I had the sort of friend I could bounce this off. Stephen used to fill that role. But now he's mine *and* Jane's friend. I can't trust him *not* to share anything I tell him with his wife Renée, who'll tell Jane.

Luke's the other option. He, Stephen, and I were inseparable as teenagers and into our early twenties. But I married, Stephen married, and Luke's still living the life of a sixteen-year-old. When you're a couple, your closest friends are almost always part of other couples.

That leaves Beth. Most of the faculty are older than us, so we became close by default. Then there's my drawing. She's always encouraging me, and she lives close, too, although she'd be on the way to school herself about now. I could call her, but I'm not sure I can tell her about this anyway.

I drive to The Corner – that's what the kids call it. It's actually the corner of Stark and Werner, which is about ten minutes' walk from school. There's a strip of shops – most of them fast food shops or cafes. Although they're not meant to leave during school hours, kids usually go to Hamburger Haven at lunch, which sells great cheap hamburgers. I bypass it and drive to Sofia's, and find a spot a few cars down from the entrance.

Sitting in the car, I try to make sense of my thoughts. People stream past, probably on the way to work. Kids from Meadow High – evident by their violet uniforms – amble by. Some vape, and a few even smoke. One kid from my English class, Dominic Carelli, pauses right in front of my car as he drags on his cigarette. He sees me through the windshield, then tilts his head upwards once in acknowledgment, totally unflustered – but that's Dom; at sixteen, he's not only one of these kids who thinks he has it all worked out, but he probably does.

On the actual corner of Stark and Werner is a thirty-something guy with a mini-mullet and a faded jean jacket, the collar pulled up. I don't know his name, but the consensus among the faculty and proprietors of the shops around here is that he sells pot or something. Sometimes, the proprietors call the cops to chase him away, but they mustn't ever find anything on him because he always comes back.

Jean Jacket says something to two sixteen-year-old girls from Meadow High – Bianca Orsino and Justine Gardiner. They're the school minxes – latest fashions, latest styles: Bianca dark and sultry, Justine bright and relaxed. They laugh and Bianca waves her hand, like she's dismissing him. Jean Jacket grins and says something else, oblivious as a sleaze in a bar trying lines on all the women.

As if sensing my derision, Jean Jacket looks at me. I turn away but feel his scrutiny. I wait; the sensation remains. Sure enough, he *is* still looking at me. He takes a step toward me.

I get out of the car and scurry into Sofia's. It's bigger than it looks from the outside. Photos from local artists hang on the walls, and checked tablecloths cover the tables. A brick archway leads to a back section. It used to be another shopfront, but Sofia's did so well they rented it, broke through, and fitted it for their own patrons.

I approach the counter in the corner. A customer's just leaving with a takeaway coffee cup and a paper bag that probably contains donuts.

Caroline – who owns and runs Sofia's with her husband Leon – is so tiny, she must have trouble seeing over the counter. At first glance, she could be mistaken for a child, right down to the energy she radiates. But lines are creeping through her make-up, and her hands are worn and veined – reward for a lifetime in the service industry.

"Good morning, Casper!" she says. "How're you?"

"I'm good, thanks."

"And Jane?"

"Jane's great."

"Pass on my regards."

"Sure."

"What can I get you?"

I scan the shelves of donuts, croissants, and other pastries. Everything's too sweet. I look at the menu on the wall above Caroline, although I know everything Sofia's serves, so I don't need to read it, but I do it all the same, trying to decide between the various teas, lattes, cappuccinos, and milkshakes, only to take a bottled water from the fridge.

"And a chocolate donut," I say.

Caroline deposits my donut into a small white bag. "Don't usually see you here for breakfast."

I pass her a ten-dollar bill, shrug, and offer a nothing smile.

"You okay?" Caroline hands me my change.

"Yeah. Didn't sleep well."

"It's the heat."

"Yeah." I stuff the change into my pocket, take my donut and water. "I should get to school. See ya."

"Bye, Casper. Have a great day."

I leave Sofia's. Jean Jacket's waiting outside the door.

"Hey, buddy, saw you checking me out," he says.

I don't answer. Return to my car.

"Want to buy?" Jean Jacket asks. He probably approached initially with a mind to sell, but he's picked up he can toy with me.

I get into my car, and throw my purchases onto the passenger seat. Jean Jacket laughs. He pops something into his mouth and chews. For an instant, I want to put the car in drive and run him over.

Backing out of the spot, I drive to school.

4.

I sit in my car in the school's parking lot. Kids amble past, pausing briefly, trying to work out why I'm sitting there. Others joke and laugh. I'll become the topic of speculation in recess conversations.

Mr. Gray was sitting in his car before school.

Do you think he's doing something? Like drugs?

He looked like crap to me.

I take out my phone and tap the screen like I'm using an app. That should shut up gossip – the smallest rumors embellish into the most extraordinary stories when teenagers are involved, although I'm amazed I'm worried about that at a time like this.

A knock at my window startles me. I jump and the phone falls out of my hands, bounces on my lap, and hits the floor. It's Beth. She told me once her maternal grandmother was a Filipino, a heritage that teases her features – the big, dark eyes, the latte complexion, and the small, pursed lips – into something almost unclassifiably exotric.

She smiles. "Sorry!"

I retrieve my phone, grab my bag, and get out of the car. Beth's car, a little red Hyundai Getz, is parked opposite mine.

"You okay?" Beth says.

"I was thinking about today's lesson plan."

"You're late for the staff meeting."

I check the time on my phone. 8:51am. "So are you."

"I wanted to talk to you."

"Something wrong?"

Beth never greets me at my car. She's usually the center of attention in the staff room. Everybody has a crush on her; it's not just that she's pretty, but she has a mesmerizing quality that makes people trust her. It helps, too, that she's such a patient listener.

"I wanted to catch you while the others aren't around," she says as we stroll toward the school.

"What is it?"

"Can I talk to you during lunch? Maybe we could go to Sofia's."

"Is everything okay?"

"Nothing to be concerned about – I need a man's opinion on something." Beth laughs, then gives me a brief half embrace. "Sorry – I didn't mean to sound like a drama queen. It's nothing major, really. I don't think it is, anyway."

"You sure?"

Beth nods. "So, lunch?"

"Okay. Do you want to meet there or drive up together?"

"I'll meet you at my car, okay?"

"Okay."

Kids filter into my classroom late. They're so unconcerned. But that's growing up. You're born and don't have a care in the world. They accumulate. The world teaches you to worry, whether you need to or not. At some point, it becomes habit.

Bianca and Justine saunter in, laughing. Then Anthony Tselikas, hulking and sullen, eyes unashamedly fixed on Bianca's rear. Then Dom Carelli. He grins at me. He could've been a sitcom character in the 70s.

"Hey, Mr. Gray," he says, pointing at me with this underhanded flourish.

"Good morning, Dom," I say. "Please sit down."

I take attendance to commence my English class, calling through twenty-five names. Then I reach into my bag, which sits at the foot of my desk like an obedient dog, but freeze. For several seconds I forget why I've reached in there. All I see is clutter – homework I've marked, exercise books, and novels. Kids wait expectantly. Some shift in their seats. Others exchange sidelong glances. Justine whispers something behind her hand to Bianca. Bianca fights to contain a laugh. Another student – Maya Ino – has a book in her hands: *The Catcher in the Rye*. She sits upright, at attention, and holds the book straight so I can see the cover.

That's it.

I pluck my tattered copy of *Catcher* from my bag. "Everybody finished this?"

Maya shoots up her hand. "I have, Mr. Gray."

Some of the kids behind her roll their eyes. Others titter. Poor Maya. It doesn't pay to excel in school when you're a teen – not unless you want to become a pariah.

For the next thirty minutes, we talk about *Catcher*. It's pleasing to see kids like Dom (who I had to belabor into reading the book) and Anthony (who comes from a family where his father and two older brothers all have criminal records for repeated misdemeanors, and everybody expects him to go the same way) and Eric Duff (poor old Eric, who's ridiculed throughout school – despite being funny and intelligent – because he's overweight) get involved, appreciating Holden's irreverence and rebellion.

It also helps distract me. Pockets of chatter fire up, then flare into a cacophony. Usually, I'd refocus them to the main conversation. But right now, I welcome it.

The door opens and Stuart Piper, the vice principal, comes in. He's a thin man, his features too sharp. He dresses in awful brown suits and tan shirts, the shoulders and elbows too pointed, and wears rectangular spectacles that are always sliding down his ski slope of a nose. He thinks he's funny and knowledgeable and connects with the kids, but he doesn't even connect with the adults.

"Mr. Gray, could I see you outside for a moment?" he asks.

"Sure." I get up, look at the kids. "For the next ten minutes, I want you to work on your own *Catcher*. Start a story about a journey you've taken and write about the things that've happened to you."

"Does it have to be true?" Justine asks.

"It can be whatever you like. Excuse me."

I follow Stuart out. His eyes narrow under eyebrows so bushy they look like a pair of caterpillars performing yoga. I wonder when Stuart became irrelevant – if he ever was relevant. How do people like him sidle through the world with such confidence and aplomb?

"Look, Casper, I didn't want to embarrass you in front of your class; you're one of my best teachers. But what's going on in there?"

"What do you mean?"

"The noise! Don't you realize how noisy your class is?"

"Really? Sorry. We were discussing *Catcher*."

"With so many people talking, I don't know how you were discussing anything. Seems many of them were talking among themselves."

"But they were talking about *Catcher*."

"Okay," Stuart says in a tone indicating it's not okay and he doesn't believe my explanation. "Maybe keep it down a bit, huh?"

"Sure. Sorry."

Silence. I wait to be dismissed, the way Stuart would dismiss one of the kids. He's impossible to escape once he starts up. The kids joke about it. I'm sure he won't hold me up when I have a class to teach, but he stands there not saying a thing.

"I should—" I begin.

"You weren't at the staff meeting this morning."

"I had some personal issues," I say.

Stuart claps my shoulder with long fingers that are surprisingly strong, then gives me an assuring shake, although the gesture's so forced it's robotic. "Everything all right?"

"Yep."

"You know you can call on me if you ever need somebody to talk to."

"Thanks."

"You have my number."

"I appreciate that."

"Okay." Stuart winks at me. "You best get back in there."

I reach for the door.

"Casper?"

"Yes?"

"Let's remember the volume."

"Sure."

I get back into the classroom. Typically, given there's been no supervision, conversation has resumed. I clap my hands. "Can we keep it down, please?" I ask, sure that the kids will connect my discipline with Stuart's intrusion. But it doesn't matter given the kids don't think any more of Stuart than I do.

I sit back at my desk and open my notebook. I want to undertake my own exercise, but I can't stop contemplating what Jane might be doing now. Absently, I scribble a big cartoon cock across the lined page. I rip the page from the notebook, scrunch it up, and throw it in my bin. Kids giggle. Others frown. The bell rings.

"I'd like everybody to finish that by next week – one thousand words!"

There are lots of groans, although Maya beams.

"If you can't finish that, then one thousand words on why you couldn't."

Kids laugh. Some will take up the challenge, either because they want to prove how rebellious they are, or because it's a challenge to look at something from a lateral perspective.

Sometimes, I hope I'll discover some great talent among them, and be able to nurture them into something better.

But right now, I want class, and the day, to be over.

Composition is next, so I give the kids some pointless busy work as I silently rehearse how I'll approach Jane. If the condom's still in her bag, I can pretend I tripped on the bag tonight and found it then. If it's not, I'll have to tell her I found it yesterday but didn't know how to approach her, although … well, if the condom's not there anymore, that might mean it's been used.

I have to excuse myself and leave the room as the prospect makes my eyes mist. I don't know what'd be worse: that she's fucking somebody or she's fallen in love with somebody. I guess we're recoverable if it's the former – if that's something I could find in myself to do. Plain lust means no emotional attachment, although it suggests I'm deficient in some way. Love means something else entirely – a more complete deficiency.

When the bell rings, I head for the staff room, but bump into Shirley Crecy, the history teacher. Shirley's a sixty-four-year-old doddering sort whose house is probably overflowing with cats. She's meant to have yard duty at recess, but I offer to do it for her. I tell her I want to stretch my legs, but the truth is I don't want to be in the staff room.

I picture it: the teachers sitting around the main tables, "the round table" Stuart once christened it, although the tables have been arranged in a rectangle; almost without exception, everybody will have a coffee. The staff room reeks of it, although the coffee drinkers never notice it.

Jerry Logan, the math teacher, will regale whoever's unfortunate enough to be sitting next to him with his weekend's adventures. Stan Doyle – one of the other English teachers – given a bit of prodding, will lament his unhappy marriage. Olivia Harding, the language teacher, seems a woman of the world, well-traveled and multilingual. She is the latter, although it comes from listening to language lessons on her phone. There are others – Max Loughlin, the sports teacher, who talks only about football; Ed Welling, the accounting teacher, who thinks himself such a financial maestro, he advises everybody on how to handle their money, despite living in a one-bedroom flat and driving a twenty-year-old car. On and on they go. Right now, I don't want to be part of them.

Shirley accepts my offer. "If ever you need a breather, Casper," she says, "you need only ask."

"Thanks, Shirley."

I make my way out to find the morning clouds are all but gone and I can taste the heat simmering. The kids, as always, have broken into groups – some play sport or other games, some sit and talk, some disappear into the toilets to smoke. They're so free. This is their reserve.

The school comprises two main buildings running parallel to one another, with courtyards and the canteen intersecting them. At either end are the locker rooms. They sit in their own buildings, and have concrete floors and shutters. Out the front, grass stretches from one end of the property to the other, where the parking lot is. Out the back are play areas – the school's gym, outdoor basketball and tennis courts, and enclosed courtyards where they can play other games. Behind them is the school's soccer field.

I wander around the back where kids play ball sports or chase each other. Sitting in the net of the goals at one end of the soccer field are Bianca, Justine, and Dom, exchanging a cigarette. I should make the journey to tell them to stop, but today it seems so insignificant.

Next, I backtrack around one of the main buildings. Some of the younger kids comment they saw me sitting in my car this morning, like they caught me doing something I shouldn't have been doing. I tell them I was installing an app on my phone. Luckily they don't chase up the lie because if they asked what app, I wouldn't know what to tell them.

I keep going, passing one set of locker rooms. Through the entry, I see Deidre Kent and David Jenkins. David is leaning against the lockers in a pose probably meant to be suave. Hell, David's sixteen, built like a tank, and champion of the football team – he *is* suave. Deidre, pivoting on the balls of her feet, hands locked in front of her, giggles at whatever he's saying.

From what I know, Deidre is the girlfriend of Kieran Nolan, who's also on the football team. Looks like she's moved on. Or maybe she hasn't, but she's about to.

Walking on, I think about relationships. My parents were married for twenty years before Mom died of cancer. They seemed happy, although they argued lots, and after Mom died, Dad slowly drank himself into oblivion. Jane's parents have been married for over forty years. They don't argue much – well, not that we see, but Jane says that's the way they actually are – and still express a closeness you'd expect from a new relationship. I wonder if any of them ever strayed.

I take my phone out of my pocket and type a message to Jane – *Hey, what're you up to?* – but don't send it. Jane and I don't exchange messages like that anymore. We used to – little check-ins to reconnect. She found it sweet when I did that. But, rightly or wrongly, young love matures and those little gestures become increasingly infrequent.

I put the phone back in my pocket and long for a beer, even now at 11:20am. Maybe for lunch I'll suggest to Beth we go to The Andion – a bar across the road from The Corner – although who knows what she'd think of me drinking so early? I strike the idea.

The bell rings, so I hurry to class.

I have a free period next and use it to correct English papers, although I read the same paragraphs over and over. But at least the staff room gives me some privacy, and when other teachers come in and see me huddled over the papers, they commend me for my industry and leave me alone.

At 12:10, I pack everything into my bag and hurry to the parking lot. I throw my bag and blazer onto the back seat, then lean against Beth's Hyundai Getz. The car's dirty, the back panel dented, and the back seat is crammed with art supplies, but there's something unashamedly chipper about it.

When the bell rings, kids spill from the school building like it's regurgitating them. Beth smiles and waves as she scoots over.

"You ready?" she says.

"Yep."

We get into her car and she drives us down to The Corner. Beth's quiet along the way. Whatever she wants to talk about must be more serious than she let on, and it's only now that I realize that in all the time I've known her, she's never appeared anything but upbeat.

She pulls into the same spot I had this morning just as a car vacates it. My eyes rove down the street but Jean Jacket's not there.

We walk into Sofia's and order toasted focaccias and milkshakes that are made in actual stainless steel cups. Beth has caramel while I have vanilla. Caroline's husband, Leon, makes them. He's big and grizzled, with the squashed nose of a boxer – not that I know if he ever boxed.

"You gonna eat here or go back to school?" Leon asks, sliding our milkshakes across the counter. He puts his arm around Caroline, swallowing her in his bulk. She gives me my change, then pops a straw in each milkshake.

"You kidding?" Beth says. "It's a relief to get out of the asylum for a bit."

Leon gives us a number – eight – to take to our table. "I don't know how you do it," he says. "I dread going home to ours."

"Leon!" Caroline says.

Leon kisses Caroline on the cheek. His mouth is like a plunger. Caroline laughs and shakes. I almost shudder as I unwittingly visualize the two of them having sex, Caroline's small legs splayed as Leon's huge, hairy backside bounces up and down.

I pick up our milkshakes while Beth grabs our number and leads us to a table in the corner by the archway and facing the window, although the view is only of The Andion across the road. We sit down and she sips her milkshake, like she wants to occupy her mouth because she doesn't want to get into why she brought me here.

"You all right?" I ask.

Beth takes a deep breath, then lets it out slowly. "I would've killed for a beer," she says.

Now she tells me.

"I don't know why I'm so nervous," she says. "Feels like I'm on a first date or something." She takes another sip from her milkshake – she's already halfway through it. "How's the drawing?"

"It's okay."

"Just okay?"

"I've done some more little things."

"I'd love to see anything new. You should bring them in," Beth says. "Or I can drop by."

Drop by? Beth's never been to my house. Strange that she'd invite herself. Now I wonder if she's got me out here to admit feelings for me. Who knows how these things work or where they start?

"I'm still … um …"

"What?"

I shrug. "I'm looking for my masterpiece. I've drawn lots of simple stuff. I'm looking for something bigger."

"A breakthrough."

"Yeah."

"Do you think I'm attractive?"

I freeze in the motion of taking the first sip from my milkshake. One of the waitresses comes over with our focaccias. She's in a cream uniform and doesn't look old enough to be out of high school herself.

"Ham, cheese, no tomato?" she asks.

"Mine," I say, my eyes still on Beth. She's gone back to sucking on her milkshake.

The waitress puts the focaccias down in front of each of us, then leaves, which means I now have to handle Beth.

She's never previously shown any interest in me. Our friendship has really been one that's existed at school and school functions. She has a long-time boyfriend, some lawyer named Roger, whom she's lived with for the two years or so. He came to the last school Christmas party, and proceeded to look down on everything and everybody. Beth said (somewhat apologetically) he was preoccupied with some civil suit he was working on (and later won big time). I think he thought we were beneath him.

"Beth ..." I say, then I don't know what's next. *I'm flattered.* Or, *I'm married.* Or both. I don't know. But I have to say something, have to stamp this out before it gets even more uncomfortable – if that's possible. "Beth," I say again, "I'm ..."

"It's Roger," Beth says. "We've been together seven years. And look." She holds up her left hand, and wriggles her naked fingers. "Nothing. Not a wedding ring, not even an engagement ring." She smiles forlornly. "I don't mean to sound desperate. Do I sound desperate?"

I'm still getting over the blunder I almost made. "No, not at all," I say, although I don't know if my answer was loud enough to cross the table. I take a bite of my focaccia.

"It's not like I want to get married straight away. But I want to know we're heading in the same direction. For a while, I was dropping hints, you know, about getting engaged. Lately, I've been a lot more blunt, saying we should plan for the future."

"What's Roger say?"

"He gets angry."

She falls silent. I wait for Beth to elaborate.

"Dominant."

"Dominant? Does he ... hurt you?"

"No!" she says, but the exclamation feels forced. She takes a moment to compose herself. "He's dominant in that he expects things to be his way," she goes on much too quickly. "He says we have plenty of time. And we do, I guess. But I feel like he's keeping me at bay. Almost like he's weighing up his options."

Given my impression of Roger, it wouldn't surprise me if that were true.

"So, I'm wondering, am I attractive? Maybe I repulse him."

"If you repulse him, he's blind."

"Then maybe it's not my looks. Maybe *I* repulse him."

"Beth, you know neither of those are true. You're gorgeous – and I'm not talking about your looks, or not specifically about your looks. It's just you … being you. Everybody loves you. Every boy at school has a crush on you."

"That's nice of you to say."

"It's true. You live together – doesn't that count for something?"

Beth rolls her eyes. "You wouldn't believe the world war I fought to get that to happen."

"Maybe Roger is more focused on other things."

"Like?" Beth looks at me sharply, like I've hit upon something that she doesn't want to face.

"His career."

"Oh. I guess."

"I've only met him a couple of times, and he came across as very career oriented. I'd be surprised if you didn't realize that."

"I do. But, sometimes, I wonder …"

"What?"

"Maybe there's somebody else. Somebody on the side. Or *somebodies*."

I put my focaccia down. "Has he given you reason to believe that?"

"He works late sometimes, but I know he's working. He always has truckloads of paperwork, and colleagues are always coming by to go over stuff." Beth brushes at her eyes. There are no tears – it's a preemptive brush to reinforce herself. "I hate being so suspicious and insecure. Does Jane ever make you feel like that?"

Everything almost spills out – and there's no reason to hold it back. I could ask Beth's opinion the way she asked mine. But I don't. I don't want to condemn Jane without evidence, I don't want to blow anything out of proportion and – I find the truth is – I most definitely don't want to articulate something I'm not ready to confront myself.

Yet.

"No," I say. "I mean, I'll get jealous if we're out and some guy gives her attention, but you reconnect. There's that bond. It's like … I don't know. Submarine radar. You *ping* to get the signal back. God, that was stupid."

Beth laughs, reaches across the table and touches my hand. "No, I understand, and it makes sense. That's what I don't have with Roger. That reconnect. It's an uphill climb."

"I don't know what to tell you, Beth. Wait, I do as far as there being *nothing* wrong with you. If Roger isn't on your timetable, it's got nothing to do with you. It's him. Don't doubt yourself."

"Then that makes me doubt *him*." Beth picks up her focaccia for the first time. "A partner shouldn't make you feel like that, should they?"

As Beth stares at me with those huge brown eyes, the world opens up to me. She's right. A partner shouldn't make you feel like that.

"You know what?" she says. "I'm going to get it out in the open. There's no point stewing, is there?"

She's right.

I have to face Jane.

5.

I have another spare period after lunch, so I use it to correct more homework. It's inexorable, but it's better doing it here than dragging it home. Then I power through my last class – another English class.

When the bell rings, I'm out of the classroom before the kids are. I hurry to the parking lot before anybody can delay me. A sickly sweet smell greets me inside my car – the donut I bought at Sofia's this morning. It's melted in the heat; a ring of chocolate smears the paper bag. The bottle of water I also bought has become hot to touch.

As I drive, I again rehearse how I'm going to approach Jane, casting appraising glances of my performance in the rear-view mirror. It's too hard. Words are too hard. And yet, somehow, I teach English. All thoughts of what I might say scatter as I approach my house and see Vic – still in his grease-stained navy coveralls – peering under the hood of his car. Music blares from the radio, an old hard rock band I can't identify. A Cooper's sits on the roof of the car alongside a couple of empties.

I pull into my driveway and reverse onto the nature strip. Vic doesn't move. Taking a deep breath, I grab my water and donut, and get out of my car. From inside the garage, Wallace barks. The moment he hears my or Jane's car, he runs from the backyard and into the garage to greet us. There's something to be said about Wallace's enthusiasm. I take a step toward the garage door, not bothering to look at Vic or exchange a greeting.

Usually, he wouldn't either.

Usually.

"Your dog was yapping all day," he says from under the hood.

"You didn't go to work today, Vic?"

"What's that supposed to mean?" Vic draws himself up, like his girth is meant to intimidate me – unfortunately, it does.

"I'm just saying—"

"What're you just saying?" Vic grabs his beer, takes a swig, and leans back against his car. It's like he wants to give me ammunition to pick him apart – because he knows I won't.

"I was curious because you said you heard Wallace all day."

"You were curious?"

"I … well …" And I don't know where to go from here because there's nowhere *to* go from here. He'll mock anything I offer.

Vic takes another swig of his beer, although his eyes never leave me. Then he snorts, places his beer back on the roof of his car, and sticks his head back under the hood.

I walk around the garage and open the door. Wallace leaps at me over and over until I catch him and cradle him to my chest. He licks my chin and his tail thumps my arm. I nuzzle his head and wonder what to do next.

It's 3:35. Jane won't be home until about 6:00. Even if she were here now, I'm sure I wouldn't confront her. Not after what happened with Vic; it's deflated my nerve – although that's an excuse. Like with so many things, I'm much braver in my imagination than I am in real life.

I get moving, knowing I have to keep myself busy.

I toss out the donut and put the bottle of water in the fridge. Next, I refill Wallace's food and water bowls, brush Wallace, hand strip him of loose fur (a necessity), then brush him again. He fidgets, unhappy with his grooming, but I reward him with a biscuit when I'm done. Then I take him outside so I can mow the lawn. Vic glares at me throughout. Tough. Mowing the lawn is life. And he *should* be at work. So I take my time.

Wallace watches from the front doorstep. At one point, he gets up and crosses toward Vic's house, sniffing at the boundary that separates the properties. Vic tenses, another dog protecting his territory. He's preparing to fight. I whistle to Wallace, and he looks at me as if to say, *What? I'm not doing anything wrong.*

"Wallace!" I say.

He comes back, none too happy.

I finish mowing the front lawn, refill the mower from the petrol canister we keep in the garage, then do the backyard – a much harder job because it's three times the area of the front lawn. By the time I'm finished, I'm soaked in sweat and my back and shoulders ache but I keep going because the activity has driven everything from my mind. I empty the cuttings into the environmental bin and wash the mower, leaving it out in the sun to dry.

Usually, I might take a break – even lie on the grass and rest in the sun. But, for now, I need to move.

I grab the sledgehammer from the garage and go out to the rear wall, feeling Herculean. Every house in the estate originally had a Coldstream wall like this, chunks of rock fitted together like children's building blocks. It's a nice wall, but just not very suitable for the estate. Everybody got rid of theirs – Vic brought in a bulldozer – and then replaced it. Jane and I are the last holdovers.

I swing the sledgehammer at the wall. The impact jars up into my shoulders. I think I've been shaken from my skin. There would be so many better ways to do this. The three or four times I've tried this before, I've ended up with blistered palms, sore muscles, and the sense that the wall's mocking me. Maybe that's why I want to demolish it with my own hands – or at least with the sledgehammer in my hands.

Within twenty minutes, I'm puffing and unable to swing the sledgehammer anymore. The wall *should* yield, but it stands tall, while I've got nothing left.

Dropping the sledgehammer, I sit, that mix of freshly mowed lawn and the mower's petrol fumes still thick in the air. It's a good smell, the smell of everything being right in a household – even when it's not.

I lie back and look up at the sky. Wallace comes over, sniffs me, and licks at the sweat on my forehead. I laugh and pat him. He lies beside me and rests his chin on his paws. He sighs. I scratch him behind the ears.

For a little while, we stay as we are, and everything's peaceful.

Finally, I get up, put the sledgehammer and lawnmower away, and go inside.

I grab a beer from the fridge and sit in my study. Wallace hops up on the couch, does his little circle, then lies down.

"You need to learn to be quiet," I say.

Wallace blinks, like he's trying to understand.

"Quiet." I emphasize it long and slow.

Wallace decides it mustn't be important and sighs.

Grabbing my sketchpad, I put it on my lap, flicking again through the sketches. They *are* okay. Beth wouldn't humor me. If they were crap, she would've found some encouraging way to let me down – the way we encourage the kids at school when their efforts are good but their work isn't. I wish I could progress to something more advanced.

I drum my pencil on the blank page, beer in my right hand, and wait for inspiration to hit.

Nothing.

I try to imagine things I could draw as I take another swig of beer. Sometimes that motivates me and frees up my creativity. Not now. I finish the beer, busting for a whiz, but keep sitting there trying to come up with an idea.

The front door opens, closes. Jane's keys jingle. Wallace springs from the couch, runs out. Then I hear Jane greeting him. Moments later, Wallace trots back into the study, spins in the doorway, and barks once, as if to tell Jane, *He's in here.* Jane enters, and plants her hands on her hips.

"You're not ready?" she says.

"Ready?" I blink.

"Dinner. With Stephen and Renée. *Remember?* Or are you too busy," Jane indicates my blank page with a thrust of her chin, "working on the masterpiece?"

"I guess I forgot."

"Maybe it's time to think of something else."

"Crochet?"

"What've you been doing?"

"I mowed the lawn and tried to knock down the wall."

"How'd that go?"

"The lawn's cut but the wall's still there."

Jane shakes her head once, comes over, and kisses the top of my head. "You smell," she says. "Go shower. I need to shower, too. Half an hour. *Don't* be late."

My eyes go to the spot inside the doorway. It's bare.

"Hey," I say.

"What?"

"Where's your bag?"

"Shit. I left it at work."

"Do you want to stop by and get it?"

"It's okay. It can stay there until tomorrow."

"Are you sure?"

"Yeah. I've really got to shower. We're going to be late." Jane kisses me again, then runs upstairs.

I think about Jane needing to shower. I know the comment is innocent – she wants to be fresh for dinner with friends. But I can't help considering all the sordid possibilities.

I'm drying myself after my shower when the doorbell rings. I know Jane won't get it. She'll still be washing her hair. The doorbell rings again. I run naked across the landing into our bedroom. Jane's laid clothes out for me on the bed – a pastel blue shirt and gray slacks. I grab my robe and wrestle it on as I hurtle downstairs. Wallace is already at the front door, yapping.

"Sshhh!" I say, opening the door.

It's Jane's workmate – Kai or Kip or whatever it is. I've only met him a couple of times and he's made little impression on me, but now I study him, measure him up as a threat – he's a scarecrow that's come to life and decided everything has to be black, from his oversized shirt, to the pants that hang from his non-existent hips. His hair stands up unnaturally, so either he uses a lot of gunk or stuck a fork in a socket. In his hands is Jane's handbag.

"I'm Kai," he says, mistaking my silence for lack of recognition. "Kai Bardy." He has a faint accent – Jane told me he was French or Belgian or something. Or maybe he's just conceited.

"Sorry," I say. "I remember you. Just surprised to see you."

"Jane forgot her bag. Did I catch you at a bad time?"

Wallace keeps barking.

"Wallace!" I say.

"Cute little dog," Kai says.

Wallace barks at him. I scoop Wallace up and pat his head. He wriggles in my hands but stops barking. I open the security door and take the handbag. "We're getting ready to go out."

"Sorry, I didn't mean to disturb you," Kai says. He reaches out to rub Wallace's head, but Wallace growls at him. Kai pulls his hand back.

"I guess he doesn't know you," I say.

"Honey, who is it?" Jane calls from the second floor. Her footsteps approach. Then she peers over the balustrade, a towel around her head, her robe tied tight, but her right leg poking too provocatively through its slit – although it's no more provocative than some of her evening dresses. But this is a robe, so it seems *wrong* for that much leg to be exposed. Wallace's tail shakes and he barks once at her, speculatively, as if to say, *Check this out!*

"Hey, Jane," Kai says. "I was bringing your bag back."

"Oh, thanks. You didn't have to do that."

"I don't live far."

I try to gauge if there's anything more to their communication than what I'm seeing or hearing – a subtext, an underlying tone. But I can't tell. I never can.

"I'm sorry – you caught us at a bad time," Jane says. "We were getting ready to go out."

"Casper was saying," Kai says. "I'll leave you to it."

"Thanks for the bag!"

"I'll see you tomorrow."

"See ya!"

"Casper," Kai says to me.

"Bye."

I close the door on him. Jane disappears from the balustrade. Her footsteps thump back through our bedroom and into the bathroom.

I take her handbag into the study, put it on the floor, then almost walk away. Almost. I kneel and rifle through it, finding the condom immediately. Wallace sniffs at it. I study it, checking its creases. For a moment, I fear it's a different one but, no, it has the same dog-ear.

I really need to clear this up.

I stuff the condom into the bag and go finish dressing.

6.

Jane drives us to dinner, eyes fixed on the road in that way she concentrates whenever she's driving, her brow furrowing. She's in her little red dress cut straight across her chest and must be wearing a push-up bra because her small boobs are thrust upright. Her legs stretch out from the short, frilly hem. She looks good – she always does to me. But I can't be as flattering about her perfume, something like ripened strawberries. She's used it for years – a dab on each side of her neck. She loves it. I've never told her how cloying I find it. You never tell your partner those sorts of things.

"How was lunch?" I ask.

Jane smirks, like that sums it all up with Sarah. Usually it does.

"That good?"

"Have I told you she's got a new guy?"

"Is he the one?"

We're always joking about Sarah's love life because she's always discovering soulmates, and every time it's "for real this time". Everybody sees the disasters she's walking into but her.

"She thinks he is," Jane says.

"Thinks. That's new for Sarah."

"She wants us to meet him. Dinner, Friday."

"Really?"

"Yep. She wants us to be the judge."

"Great." Dinner's usually later in Sarah's itinerary, and every time I cringe through the whole meal. Sarah always wants me to befriend her latest boyfriend, too, like if we became best friends then we could do stuff as couples all the time, and I could go out with him and play golf or something. "When?"

"Six-thirty at The Palace for drinks. Then dinner at seven."

The Palace is a bar and grill down the road from Jane's work.

"You going to come home or should I meet you there?" I ask.

"I'll meet you there. We have a presentation at five. Hopefully, it won't run overtime."

"It better not run overtime. You're not leaving me alone with Sarah and … what's his name?"

"Alex."

I'll forget it by Friday. "You're not leaving me with them, so make sure you're there on time. I can meet you at work and we can walk down."

"Sure."

"What time?"

"Presentation will be about half an hour. So, about six?"

"Okay." I fall quiet. Watch the road. "How was work?"

"Usual."

"Usual?"

"Henry thinks he scored a caterer today. Mancini's. Do a lot of corporate gigs and celebrity weddings. Barry and Kai are meeting with them to help outline what they want. I'm guessing it'll include a blog. Everybody wants to blog nowadays, like everybody has something so important to tell us. For caterers. Can you believe that? What're they going to blog about?"

"I'm sure there's something interesting in catering world. Recipes. Stuff like that."

"Or maybe they'll pump themselves up by telling us which soapy star's engagement they're catering. How was your day?"

We used to share everything. But then everything became the same. Then we started sharing only the oddities. Now I don't recall doing that as much either.

"I had lunch with Beth today."

"Yeah? Did you go to Sofia's?"

"Yeah. Beth's worried that Roger's cheating on her."

Unblinking, I study Jane. No reaction.

"Why does she think that?" she asks.

"She wants to take the relationship to another level and he's not budging."

"I really don't like him."

"You've only met him once."

Jane bounces one shoulder in a gesture equivalent to a shrug. "He's really handsome—"

"Really handsome?"

"In a way. But then there's something about him. Something, I don't know, *cavalier*."

"He's arrogant."

"Yeah, I guess."

Jane's jaw sets – she's building herself up to something.

"Can I tell you something without you getting upset?" she says.

I tense. "Sure."

"I think he hit on me at your staff Christmas party."

"Are you for real?"

"I *think*."

"What does *think* mean?"

"We were talking – I told him I worked in web design, and he started going on about wanting his own website, so I gave him my card."

"You gave him your card?"

"It was a reflex. But then he really began to flirt."

"What did he do?"

"He complimented my dress, my hair, said you were a very lucky man – you know, to have me."

I'm unsure how to take this. Jane's manner is straightforward – she could be telling me about the weather.

"Then he asked if I wanted to see his car because he'd leased a Porsche or something."

"Why didn't you tell me?"

"At the time, I didn't think anything of it. I thought it was one of those superficial conversations you have. It wasn't until later that I started wondering if I should've read more into it, but by then, there was no point saying anything. It's not like we bump into Roger on a regular basis."

"You should've told me."

"Are you upset?"

"I'm just saying you should've told me."

"What would it have accomplished?"

I don't know. It's not like I would've confronted Roger. I would've wanted to, would've wanted to indignantly accost him and demand to know how he could dare make an advance on my wife, but I probably wouldn't have had the courage to actually do that. Jane knows that, too.

She puts a hand on my knee, squeezes. "He flattered me because he's a bore. And it's not like I went to see his car. I told him I wasn't interested. Then Beth joined us. He even told her he was telling me about his car and had offered to show it to me. That's why I thought I'd overreacted."

"Where was I?"

"Getting drinks."

I remember that. I came back with wines for Jane and Beth, a beer for myself. Roger hadn't wanted anything, like drinks served in plastic cups were beneath him. He'd taken Beth and left not long afterwards. It should be a *nothing* thing, so small and dismissible. But it makes me think about the things Jane keeps from me.

"Hey, we okay?" she asks.

"Sure," I say.

The Noble Temple is an Asian restaurant with hardwood floors and a stylish bar. The tables are crammed together – although there isn't much of a crowd, given it's a Monday night – and a stage with a karaoke machine occupies the furthest corner. A plump middle-aged man sings Chicago's "Hard Habit to Break" to an equally plump ash-blonde woman who giggles girlishly at a nearby table. Just as a waitress comes over to seat us, Jane gets a text from Renée saying they're running fifteen minutes late, so Jane tells the waitress we'll wait at the bar until our friends arrive.

We grab drinks – me a Corona, Jane a red wine – and I put my arm around Jane's waist, wondering if anybody else has held her this way. Jane sways and watches the plump guy finish his song. He plonks down from the stage and his partner pops up to hug him. Jane places her hands in the middle of my chest.

"Let's go sing a song!" she says.

"God no."

"Come on!" Jane tugs my wrists.

I survey the patrons – there can't be more than ten or fifteen people in here, but I have zero singing talent. Jane can carry a tune as long as it's not too demanding, and years ago she used to do karaoke regularly. I'd join her if I'd had enough to drink. But she sees now I'm going to be immovable, so she downs her red wine in one gulp, plants the glass dramatically on the bar, raises on her tiptoes, and kisses me on the lips.

"You're such a wimp," she says, then flees to the stage and cycles through the alternatives on the karaoke machine, before a song kicks off – backing vocals with a slow, building tempo that takes me a while to recognize as The Partridge Family's "I Think I Love You".

Jane smiles like she's going to laugh her way through it, but settles into a rhythm, bouncing around as she does a great job with the vocals, pointing at me and wiggling her hips whenever she hits the chorus. It feels like it's just me and her, and the spotlight she shines on me makes me forget my doubts – she wouldn't be doing this if something were going on. Would she? *Would* she?

The other guys in the restaurant watch her with appreciation – even the plump middle-aged man who'd serenaded his partner only earlier. Jane has *something*, this almost aristocratic sex appeal. I can see the lust in other men's eyes, *hear* their thoughts, because that's what *we* do. We fantasize.

It's not such a dismissible aside because it does make me realize that some men not only see Jane like this, but try to act on it – just like Roger did. It's a sickening thought, one that stirs up insecurity and jealousy and nausea. Men always think they're a chance with women, irrespective of how improbable (if not outright unrealistic) that chance is.

That's when Stephen and Renée find me, although I don't immediately recognize them – nobody's seen much of them since the baby was born. Stephen used to be fit, but now his stomach hangs over his belt and shadows mark his eyes like mascara. Renée looks great given she had the baby only six months ago. She's a gym junky and was hitting the treadmill hard even when she was carrying, but she must've really upped the ante once she squeezed the baby out. I wonder if she has the baby on an exercise regime.

We sway in unison, like we're at a concert, and Stephen even grabs a nearby candle and holds it over his head, waving it until the waitress comes over and politely reprimands him. When Jane finishes her song, the few people in the Noble Temple applaud and cheer – a few too vociferously. Jane trots back and I hug her – unwittingly so tightly that she mocks a gasp – and we all tell her how great she was.

"It was nothing," she says.

The waitress returns and because the night's warm, we decide to sit outside on the balcony, which has the glorious view of Main Street traffic. After all the pleasantries are over with, and Renée and Stephen apologize for being late (they say they're always late nowadays), we settle down and order more drinks – another Corona for me, and red wines for everyone else.

Then, it's the baby. It's all the talk for the first fifteen minutes. Stephen and Renée show us a ton of pictures while they lament they never get any sleep, are constantly stressed whether they're doing the right things, and never have time for themselves. Jane coos and talks nonstop about how beautiful he is. I say nothing new and just agree with Jane.

"This is the first night we've been out since he was born," Renée says.

"So he's … what?" I say. "Home alone, watching a few movies?"

"Casper!" Jane slaps me on the thigh as Stephen and Renée laugh.

"He's with my parents," Stephen says.

"He's so sweet," Renée says. "Such an angel."

"You wouldn't believe the lungs on him, though."

Are they as good as Wallace's? I almost ask, but know that won't go over well. For right now, their son is perfect. Everything he does is perfect. They wouldn't appreciate him being compared to a dog, even one as cool as Wallace.

The waitress comes over and asks if we're ready to order. We scan the menus. Jane puts a hand on mine.

"They have calamari," she says.

Stephen snorts. "That still all you ever have?"

Jane arches her brows. "We were out a couple of weeks ago, and he got a bad batch. He was vomiting all night."

Renée winces. "You poor thing," she says.

"It wasn't pretty," Jane says and pinches her nose. "Well?"

I scout the menu, checking the price of each meal – a habit I fell into when we started saving for IVF. Jane orders the king prawns – one of the more expensive dishes – while Renée orders the seafood and bean curd hotpot, and Stephen a sautéed beef eye fillet. I do find calamari, but it's some chili calamari type that sounds too exotic for me.

"I can be different," I say, although I keep looking for something conventional. "Chicken Teriyaki, thanks."

Jane rubs my hand and laughs.

"So …" Renée says, once the waitress has gone.

"So?" I ask.

"How're … you know?" Stephen says.

I do know and I hate the tiptoeing. Renée and Stephen met at our wedding. They dated, had a long engagement, and married a couple of years later. Because of that, there's a guiltiness about their questioning, almost like they're apologetic about beating us to the baby-making.

"Are you still trying?" Renée asks.

Jane casts a shy glance in my direction. This always comes up – and not just with new parents who want to impose parenthood on everybody. Because Jane and I have been married for six years, everybody expects that we should have an assembly line going. A few friends, like Stephen and Renée, know we've had problems. We used to talk to them about it often enough.

"Well, it's not like we've stopped having sex," I say, taking a swig of beer.

But the baby-making, yes – having sex when Jane's ovulating; her drinking foul herbal brews meant to help with fertility; the positions meant to increase the chances of conception; and even Jane lying there after sex with her legs up, as if that'd turn my sperm into guided missiles to seed her eggs.

"Now, if it happens, it happens," I say.

Renée squeezes Jane's hand. "It'll happen for you. I know it will."

Jane wipes her eyes. The silence is too long. Stephen and Renée must think me heartless, not consoling Jane, but I don't know what to do. When she miscarried, I tried to hold her, but she said she didn't want to be touched, locked herself in the bathroom, and sobbed. The next night, she crawled into me and I held her. I'm never sure of the etiquette.

"I saw Luke!" Stephen says too loudly, breaking the silence. "I bumped into him at the market yesterday. He said we should catch up."

"Yeah, that would be good," I say.

"He told me to tell you to drop him a line."

"Sure."

Jane looks at me with brimming eyes. She's so pretty and vulnerable, her face laden with disappointment. It's times like these I notice how ingrained it's become in her, this absence. It makes her prematurely old, and I want to save her from that, from that crushing expectation.

I hold out my arm and she leans into me.

I sink into bed while Jane's in the bathroom.

I need to make a decision. I should ask. But I'm beyond *shoulds* now. I *will* or I *won't*. And if it's the latter, I have to accept that this is a secret that may never be uncovered – unless Jane is cheating, and one day surprises me by telling me she's leaving me. Of course, it's impossible to *not know*. It's like living with a lump and not knowing whether it's cancerous. But, equally, discovering that as a reality is terrifying.

Jane comes out of the bathroom, and slips into bed behind me. She spoons me, her body warm. Her pubic hair presses into my buttock – she's come to bed without her little boxers.

Her arm curls around me. I turn and her mouth lands on mine. Her lips are cold. She tastes of the two red wines she had at dinner – red wine always makes her frisky. Her hand slides down my belly and into my underwear. She grabs hold of my cock, and strokes me.

"What're you doing?" I say when she breaks the kiss.

"You don't know?"

She trails kisses down my chest and stomach – her hair a contrail that tickles me – and then pulls down my underwear and takes me in her mouth. I hiss as she swallows me whole. She runs her mouth up and down the length of my cock, first so quickly that it feels like I'm going to explode, then slowing and tightening until I arch my back and grip the sheets.

Releasing me, she runs kisses back up my stomach, over my chest, my neck. Her tongue parts my lips. I run my hands down her back and cup the swell of her buttocks. She sits up and straddles me. I squeeze her breasts and her distended nipples. She guides me into her. She is so wet. She isn't always, but now I slip into her. She grinds into me, swiveling her hips and tilting her head until her breasts push into my hands and her hair falls back.

Our rhythm is comfortable and familiar, and I feel myself ready to come. This position always gets me going easily. But I know Jane is nowhere near ready. I feel it in her body. Hear it in her soft cries.

I sit up, lock my arms around her, and kiss her. My tongue wrestles hers and all I can think now is how much I hate red wine, although I've never told her this. I taste it in her mouth, on her tongue, and on her breath.

I push forward until she yields, and falls onto her back. Hooking one of her legs over my shoulder, her other on my bicep, I thrust deeper into her. My knees slip from under me and my feet tangle in the covers. I brace my knees and thrust. Jane whimpers in my ear, tells me it feels good. My hands find her breasts again as my butt pistons back and forth, but my knees keep slipping.

I slow. Stop.

"What?" Jane says in my ear.

"I'm slipping."

"Out?"

"My knees."

"What?"

I sit up, pull her up, kiss her and relish the feeling of her body against mine. She kneels in front of me, and gets on her hands. Her butt thrusts out toward me. She has a great butt, and I've fantasized sometimes about sex that way, but we've never experimented. That's the way married life goes – or ours has. Maybe that's what's wrong with me. I always take the unadventurous option.

Grabbing her hips, I enter her from behind, although my attention is fixed on the hourglass of her hips as they contour into her narrow waist. A sheen gleams on the arch of her back.

Jane's buttocks quiver and her breasts bounce. The sound of colliding flesh is a metronome in the bedroom. Her cries grow louder. I wish I could make her scream, like in the porn that Stephen, Luke, and I used to watch, so I can be certain what I'm doing is exciting and satisfying her. But those reactions don't seem to happen in real life, and married sex becomes measured sex.

I see those two bruises on her right buttock. My pace slows. My hand hovers above the bruises – my thumb and forefinger. They would be a perfect fit, if that's what caused the bruises.

But they're not mine because Jane and I haven't done it this way recently.

Then, in the doorway, I see Wallace sitting there, watching us, his head cocked as if he's trying to figure out what's going on. Or maybe he knows and is trying to figure out how to throw a bucket of water on us.

Jane propels her butt back into me, and I drive myself into her over and over. The pain in my shoulder from trying to sledgehammer the wall screams but I don't stop, even as I feel ready to blow. Jane lifts herself until her back is pressed against my chest. I keep thrusting, one hand squeezing her bouncing breasts in turn, the fingers of my other hand hopefully finding her clit. Her cheek nuzzles against my lips.

We feel so connected, so unified, and the only delineation that comes is when her body grows rigid. All sounds from her cease. A guttural moan escapes my lips as I come. My hips stutter, slow. It's the only time that we've ever come so close. Usually, I'm first, although there are times I don't come at all.

Jane and I collapse, still welded together, our heads by the right corner at the foot of the bed. Our chests heave and the sweat cools on our bodies. I feel chilled, and know Jane will, too, so drag the cover over us.

We stay like that and I kiss her ear. She pushes against me, although it's not like we can get any closer. My arms embrace her as my deflating erection slips from her.

Jane smiles – a small, contented smile. "I love you."

I blurt out the question before I can stop myself. "How much?"

"Out of ten?" Her smile broadens and she kisses me on the nose. "Six, maybe seven when you take out the garbage." Then there's nothing but the chorus of our breathing falling into sync as we hold one another.

And, eventually, we sleep.

TUESDAY

7.

The clock radio's alarm wakes us. Jane tries to swat it off, but we're sleeping the wrong way. She buries her head under my chin, trying to escape the morning. I fold my arm around her, enjoying how idyllic our relationship is in this moment. The clock radio continues to buzz. Welcome back to reality.

"Do we have to get up?" Jane says.

"Somebody's gonna have to switch off the alarm," I say.

"How long before it shuts itself off?"

"About fifteen minutes, I think."

Wallace jumps up onto the bed, licks Jane's forehead.

"Wallace, get the alarm," she says.

Wallace continues to lick her.

She sits up and pats Wallace. Her hair is disheveled, but there's always been something sexier about her that way. I place my hand on her back, enjoying the feel of her warm skin under my fingertips. She smiles at me. Her breasts look so inviting. Already, I feel myself stirring.

"I should shower," she says.

She switches off the alarm, then walks into the bathroom. I stare at her butt as she does her morning stretches, her lean form taut. As she holds her tree pose, I have the unbidden thought that she's a monument to our marriage, to our life together. Then the thought evaporates as she releases the pose, gets in the shower, and closes her eyes as the water runs through her hair.

Wallace's mouth hangs open like he's laughing.

"What?" I say.

Downstairs, I fill Wallace's food and water bowls. I call for him but he doesn't answer, so I walk to the rear windows and look out to the backyard. The sky's blue – not even a wisp of a cloud. It's going to be another hot day. A gray cat stands in the middle of the yard – Vic's cat Silver.

Wallace emerges from the side of the house, completely unawares. He sees Silver. Stops. Then breaks into a sprint. Silver bounds for the fence, balances on the top, and hisses at Wallace. Wallace leaps around the base, barking until Silver jumps back into Vic's yard.

I feel like marching to Vic's front door and complaining about his stupid cat being in our yard. It's the perfect salvo in the battle of one-up-pet-ship.

Wallace patrols the fence to make sure Silver's not coming back, then canters to the back door. Moments later, he bursts through the doggy door and comes into the house. I kneel, rub him, and tell him what a good boy he is, although he gives me a look like he doesn't know why I'm so happy.

It doesn't matter. It's a beautiful day.

As I absently make breakfast, I convince myself there's a harmless explanation for the condom. There *can't* be anything insidious given how normally Jane's behaving toward me, and yet doubts still flood my mind. I butter the toast, the knife digging into the bread.

She could've had a fling. It could be over. Or she could've thought about it, but never went through with it. Either way, last night might be her attempt to reconnect with me, although she does spontaneously initiate sex; seven years of marriage hasn't blunted that – it's just lessened it.

I eat and decide that I'm not going through another day of this. Dumping the plates in the sink, I go into the study and take a seat at my desk. Wallace jumps onto the couch. Jane's running late; I hear her thumping around upstairs.

Taking my sketchpad onto my lap, I hold a pencil above the blank page, but all I can think about are the different approaches I can use with Jane. None of them sound right in my head. I'll wing it – if I can. I want to be diplomatic, but I'm scared of the way things will come out.

Jane comes down the stairs, hidden behind a bundle of sheets – of course, she's changed our sheets since we made a mess last night. I should've changed them myself. I hear her toss them into the washing machine, then the machine begin to whir. She's a blur as she crosses the study, but she senses me, stops, and comes in. She's in another business suit, although this one has slacks. Her shirt is plain, and the slightest bit transparent so I can detect her bra is pink.

"Hey," she says. "You drawing?"

I shrug.

"How's it going?"

I shrug again.

"It shouldn't be this hard, should it?"

"Listen, I don't know how to say this …"

And that's become more than the truth. Do I tell her I stumbled upon the condom the other night or that I just found it? All my overthinking hasn't prepared me for this simple point. This is what actors experience with stage fright – rehearsals can't truly prepare them for the real thing.

"What?" she asks.

"I was coming in here and I tripped on your handbag."

Her jaw sets in that way it does when she's bracing herself for something.

"A condom fell out," I say.

There are no other indications of anything untoward. She smiles, but doesn't laugh it off, like she knows that's the wrong reaction.

"It's Sarah's," she says.

"Yeah?"

"Sarah met me at work so we could go to lunch. We stopped at the chemist because I needed tampons. Sarah wanted condoms for her and Alex. She was goofing around and opened the box to … show me they were glow in the dark. I put the box in my bag because she didn't have anywhere to carry them during lunch. I guess one fell out."

It's a stupid story, but the truth often is. Still, there's something treacherous about finding a condom. Maybe some people would brush it off. But for me, it's like a lipstick stain on a collar. This isn't just about our relationship, about *us*, but about the life we've been building together.

"This was yesterday?" I ask.

I'm sure Jane pauses for a millisecond longer than she should. "Last week," she says. She steps up to me, takes her phone out of her pocket, and thrusts it at me. Her expression is stony. "You can call Sarah if you like."

She could've arranged for Sarah to be her alibi. Or Sarah might do it automatically out of friendship. Stephen would. Well, he might. Luke definitely would – not that I'd ever need either. Of course, I should trust Jane instead of picking holes in her explanation. That's going to lead to a vicious cycle of doubt.

Jane hurries out.

Wallace looks at her, at me, then follows her.

I go into the kitchen. Jane stands at the bench, her back to me. I embrace her from behind.

She's unresponsive.

I kiss her cheek. "I'm sorry."

She turns in my arms, holds me limply, her chest heaving – she's trying to *not* cry. I run my hand up and down her back.

We stand there for a while.

I see Silver is back in the yard.

We kiss on the front doorstep, the neighborhood unfurling around us as it does every morning. Then Jane goes into the garage. I pick up Wallace. Kirit and Pia call out a greeting to him, and I move his paw to wave at them. Their mother greets me. I smile, then wave at her. Across the street, Josh and Karen get into their car. They wave. I hold up a hand back.

The garage door opens and Jane pulls out. She pauses in the drive. I wave to her. Her window rolls down. She holds up a hand. Then smiles.

She drives off up the street.

I take Wallace and put him in the backyard. Silver's nowhere to be seen. Then I lock up the house and walk to my car. Vic, outside in his coveralls, is about to get into his.

"Your dog was barking again, Gray," he says.

"Your cat was in my yard," I say. "Twice."

"It's a cat."

I stand there, unsure how to address the double standard. Vic snorts, then hops into his car. He starts the engine and revs it, grinning at me. Chloe emerges from the front door. She's in her leotard again and covered in sweat.

"What're you doing?" she calls to Vic.

Vic cocks his head and puts a finger to his ear to indicate he can't hear her. Then he pulls out of the drive. His tires screech on the road as he accelerates away.

Chloe looks at me almost apologetically.

I get into my car.

8.

I park in the school parking lot and sit in the car again, fiddling with my phone. Sweat streams down my face and into my collar. It's 8:47 – I'm already running late for the staff meeting. I should hurry, especially after missing yesterday's. But I don't. I roll the window down and relish what little breeze there is.

Jane's explanation gnaws at me – I don't know if it's unease, or something to do with her story about Sarah and Alex. Then it hits me. Jane said Sarah bought the condoms *last week* for her and Alex, but Jane only told me about Alex yesterday, like she had just found out about Alex yesterday. A feeling of sick elation surges inside me, like I've caught Jane out. I squelch it down. It's possible Jane knew about Alex earlier and didn't tell me – it's not like I show interest in Sarah's love life. I rub my temple, trying to remember what Jane said exactly. She asked if she'd told me Sarah had a new guy. It's ambiguous – it could mean she knew earlier and was only now getting around to telling me, or she found out yesterday. Or maybe she only told me about it yesterday because Sarah was proposing catching-up for dinner. Here's something I never would've thought twice about previously. I'm paranoid, and this possibility nags me with fresh vigor. This whole thing should've been settled. I wish Beth would come out and greet me – today, I'm ready to spill everything. I will, too, the moment I can pull her aside, because I really need an objective opinion on this.

But right now it's just kids, walking past on their way into the school. Some gawk at me. I smile weakly at them, wave at the ones I know, then continue to play with my phone like I'm doing something important.

Maybe I could do something important with it. I *could* ring Sarah, like Jane dared me to. Of course, Sarah would relay any conversation we had back to Jane, even if I begged her not to. I try to think of ways I could ask Sarah discreetly, but no such way exists.

What I should do is trust Jane.

That's all it comes down to.

Stuart is waiting for me at the front doors to the school. He points to his naked left wrist. I'm sure he usually wears a watch. Maybe he took it off, like pointing at his naked wrist would be a more emphatic condemnation, like he can keep track of time even *without* a watch.

"You missed another morning staff meeting," he says.

"I'm sorry."

"Is there something I need to know about?"

"Like what?"

"You tell me."

"I have a lot on at the moment and it's getting a bit on top of me. But don't worry, I'll sort it out."

"I would hate for your personal life to affect your teaching."

"It won't."

Stuart doesn't blink.

"It hasn't."

"I went through an ugly divorce early in my career, Casper. I made sure it never affected my work."

The way he treats work is probably *why* he went through an ugly divorce. I can see him sitting at the dinner table, lecturing some faceless woman because her fork's clanging against her plate, or because she's talking too much and he's deemed that dinner is solely for eating.

"I'm not going through a divorce," I say. "It's just … *stuff*."

"Stuff? The point remains that we need to keep our personal and professional lives separate."

"It's really not a problem."

Stuart says nothing, eyes peering at me over the frames of spectacles that have slid down his nose. I wait again – as I did yesterday – to be dismissed. No such luck. Stuart's one of the world's great pausers.

"Does this involve Beth?" he asks.

"Beth?"

"She wasn't at the staff meeting yesterday either. And she's not here today."

"She's not here?"

"No."

"I don't know anything about that."

"You're going to have to take her art class, third period."

I don't know anything about art, almost spills from my lips.

"Okay," I say.

"You better get to class."

I reach for the door.

"Casper?"

I stop, brace myself.

"Let's not make a habit of this, okay?"

I bite back several retorts. "It won't happen again."

Hurrying down the hallway, I take my phone out of my pocket and message Beth: *You okay?*

I put my phone on silent and get to class – Remedial English. We're reading Robert Cormier's *I am the Cheese*. I give the kids the job of reading several chapters to occupy half an hour because my mind is elsewhere, vacillating between Jane and Beth.

I think about what Jane must be doing at work, how she must be feeling about me after the way things unfolded this morning. Suspicions are normal. If the positions were reversed, Jane would have them, and she wouldn't be gracious about wanting answers. Still, I take out my phone, text her, *Sorry*, and put the phone on my desk.

Then there's Beth, who was going to confront Roger. Now she's not here today. Surely that's not coincidence, but what could it mean? She might've learned that Roger was cheating on her and is home right now in tears. Or he could've grown violent. Maybe he hit her, and she has a bruise she can't show at school. Of course, just because Roger's a prick doesn't mean he's violent.

That's when it occurs to me I should've asked Stuart *why* Beth couldn't make it in today. She would've given a reason.

My phone vibrates on the desk. The whole class looks up, some of the kids startled. Others titter.

"Keep reading, please," I say.
The kids get back to it. Relief washes over me – finally, an explanation from Beth. I snatch up the phone. But it's Jane.

It's okay.

X.

I send her three kisses in reply.

When the period's over, I try to catch Stuart, but he's nowhere to be found, so I get to my next class – Humanities. I leave my phone on the desk throughout.

At recess, I try to ring Beth twice, but the phone rings out to her voicemail.

I hurry into the staff room. The other teachers are there, but not Stuart, so I head to administration. The principal, Charlotte Hetrick, sits in her office, sifting through paperwork. She would seem an unremarkable woman if not for her gravitas – she might be the manifestation of centuries of public education forged into this ineffable emblem.

She smiles at me, although the smile contains little recognition. I could be anybody. It's a reflex, an effort to acknowledge her staff with some comradeship. I smile back, sure it looks more like a grimace, then dart across to Stuart's office.

Which is empty.

He must have playground duty – or be on duty, even if he's not assigned it. Stuart does that sometimes. He's hardly magnanimous, though. I think he lurks around corners and eavesdrops on the kids to keep abreast of attitudes in the school – not that he'd admit to that.

I find him circling in front of the school, patrolling the lawns and exchanging greetings with some of the kids playing football, while others are sitting in groups.

"Excuse me, Stuart."

"Casper. I must commend you."

"Why?"

"Disgraceful!"

"What?"

We're passing the lockers. Deidre Kent and David Jenkins are in there, standing close, holding hands. David had been leaning in to kiss Deidre. Stuart fixes his gaze on David. Deidre bows her head. David takes a step back from Deidre.

I. Am. Watching, Stuart mouths, pointing his finger at them with each word.

"They're just …"

Stuart glares at me, and I decide *not* to tell him that they're just teenagers.

"You were saying?" I prompt him.

"I was going to commend you," Stuart says as we walk on. "Your classes were quiet this morning."

One relatively noisy class yesterday and he goes on like that's the norm.

"Thanks," I say.

"Is there something I can do for you?"

"Beth – did she say why she couldn't come in today?"

"Look at that!"

We're around the back of the school now. Through all the kids on the courtyards, we see the triumvirate of Dom, Bianca, and Justine approaching from the soccer field.

"They've probably been smoking if they've been sitting out there," Stuart says. "They certainly weren't playing soccer."

"Sometimes the kids go out there to sit."

"Their uniforms are a travesty."

I don't see anything wrong with them – they're not dirty or disheveled, although Dom doesn't have one side of his shirt tucked in.

"Have the girls hemmed their skirts?"

"I don't know, Stuart. They look normal to me."

"They most certainly do not."

"Stuart, about Beth—"

"She has a stomach bug, Casper."

"Really?"

"That's what her partner told me."

"You didn't talk to her?"

"I am certain those skirts are shorter than regulation."

"Stuart?"

"No, I didn't speak to her. Her partner said she was pitched over the toilet. Gastro's a nasty business, isn't it?"

"Yeah."

Stuart rips his attention from Bianca and Justine. "Why are you so curious, Casper?"

"I was just … wondering."

Stuart is unmoving. I need something to satisfy him. He's putting two and two together and coming up with all sorts of wrong answers. The bell rings. Kids haul themselves up. Stuart checks his watch – the anal bastard has it on now – and nods, as if everything is going according to schedule.

"Don't forget the art class," he says.

When I get to class, I take my phone out and leave it on Beth's desk. The kids stare quizzically at me, probably wondering how capable I am of filling in. They have sketchpads like mine planted in front of them and are waiting expectantly, which means I need to come up with a plan. I haven't given a single thought to what to teach, nor have I tracked down any of Beth's notes.

"Where's Ms. Buckley?" Bianca asks.

"She's sick today, so you have me," I say.

"What do you know about art?" Dom asks.

"I've picked up a bit here and there. Let's try this: I want you to reach into your bags and take out one item. It can be a drink, a snack, your lunch – anything."

The kids rifle through their bags. Most of them take out the first thing they grab – either a pencil case or a book. Some look for something unique, as if that'll hold them in better stead.

"Now, put whatever you've grabbed in front of you," I say, "and look at it. Study it. Look at the object's texture, look at its corners and facets, look at the way it's made up of shades and light. Close your eyes and see it in your mind. Feel it, the way it occupies space."

I scan the class. Everybody has their eyes closed. Some aren't taking the exercise too seriously, but others are concentrating.

"Now, open your eyes and draw your object."

"That's it?" Justine says.

"It's about the way you imagined the object in your head, the way you interpreted it, and the way you're going to express it. Not the way it actually looks."

Some of the kids get to work immediately. Others know this is filler and screw around, chatting and joking. I caution them to keep it down. Last thing I need is Stuart in here.

I do a round of the room to make sure the kids are undertaking the task, but my attention keeps wandering to my phone. I sit at Beth's desk and check for messages – nothing. I lean back, fidgeting. Kids glance at me. It's not difficult to tell something's wrong. I must look like an idiot, sitting here, clueless, so I take out my notebook, flip it open, and drum my pen.

The lined page of my notebook challenges me – empty like the blank page of my sketchpad, like the chasm I feel growing between Jane and me. Her explanation should be the bridge, but it isn't. I imagine myself plummeting. Hitting the bottom, I jolt. My chair screeches against the floor. Kids look at me again. This is the last place I want to be. I fixate on the pad, and drum my pen harder, like I'm trying to pound some inspiration from it. The breathing of the kids is too heavy. The sound of pencils scribbling across sketchpads is a cacophony of inhumane squeals. Their attention is too damning.

I half rise, planning to excuse myself for a bit, but in the process I see Bianca, sitting in front of me, head bowed as she sketches an apple. Her lustrous black hair falls over half her face – similar to the way Jane's hair can cover her face. She is Jane, from many years ago – unsullied by hand, by thought, or by suspicion, beaming with hopefulness for the future, the way she was when I first met her, before the pressures of setting up our future and constantly trying to have a baby marked her with the responsibilities, realities, and burdens of everyday life. Bianca's visible eye is large, make-up not entirely disguising the shadowy crescent beneath. Her lashes are upturned and dark – too much mascara. Exactly like Jane at that graduation party.

As I sit, my pen comes down on the page. The first stroke is almost automatic, the second like a misstep on a slippery slope. Then there is nothing but my ballpoint scratching against the lined page. My anxiousness dissipates into calmness that isolates me from the kids as they whisper behind their hands, trying to work out what I'm doing. Even when the bell rings and kids pack up around me, I keep drawing.

"Whoa, Mr. Gray!"

It's Dom, who – on his way out – has caught sight of my sketch. Now, because Dom's endorsed me and he's about the coolest kid in school, the other kids crowd around. Their gasps flatter me.

"You're an artist, Mr. Gray!" Justine says.

"That's incredible, Mr. Gray," Maya says. "I wish you'd drawn me."

"Should've drawn her as a centerfold, Mr. Gray," says Anthony Tselikas.

"Don't be a creep all your life, Anthony!" Bianca says.

Anthony leers at her.

I'm worried Bianca might be uncomfortable about me drawing her, but the picture transfixes her. Up close now, I see she's wearing more make-up than she should. Typical teen, in a hurry to grow up. My sketch of her has greater maturity – perhaps Bianca, ten years down the line, after she's graduated, found work, and started to think about what she wants to do with the rest of her life. Perhaps it's not even Bianca, but Jane I've drawn by proxy. My sketch condemns me for my distrust. I tear it out, wanting to be done with it, and thrust it unthinkingly at Bianca.

"There you go."

She reaches for it, but Dom cuts her off. "Sign it, Mr. Gray."

I scribble my name in the corner (some of the kids cheering) and shove the picture into Bianca's hands. She takes a chemistry textbook out of her bag, opens it, and carefully places the picture in the middle. Then she closes the book and puts it inside her bag.

"Thanks, Mr. Gray," she says, smiling shyly.

She's gorgeous then – not in a sexual way, although she's obviously pretty. But there're none of the pressures of adult life in her face, none of the confusion about trying to decipher relationships or indecision within herself. I'm sure she – and all the other kids – feel all those things, but at this stage they are adjuncts to their lives, instead of the core. I envy her. *Them.*

"Okay, everybody, off to lunch."

The kids filter out, some of them still talking in disbelief about my sketch, like teachers are incapable of anything – of any life – outside teaching.

I sit in my car and close my eyes until the flightiness seeps from my body. My shallow breathing grows steady, and the tension in my shoulders relaxes.

Beth. I should call her. I pick up my phone and ring her. Voicemail. I try again. Voicemail again. Something's wrong. It's too coincidental she's unreachable the day after she said she was going to confront Roger.

I want to ring Jane, and ask her advice. But this feels like an evening conversation, something we'd discuss over dinner.

Beth wasn't at school today.

No?

I'm worried. She was going to confront Roger yesterday.

You think something happened?

I'm worried he made something happen to her.

I'm being melodramatic and wonder how concerned I'd be if I didn't desperately want to speak to her. If I didn't need her advice, would her absence be a blip on my radar? This is more about me than her. But then something else arises – some pang of uncertainty. No, we're friends. I *would* be concerned – maybe not as much as I am now, but after what she told me yesterday, about telling me Roger could get *dominant*, I would definitely be concerned.

Looking at my phone, I scroll through the contacts, trying to find an alternative … Luke. Stephen said Luke wanted to catch up. Yesterday I ruled him out, but now he's my only option.

I text him. Luke's hopeless at getting back to anybody with texts. So I leave my fate in the hands of providence.

Hey, want to catch up for a beer?

He responds almost immediately: *Working today. Tomorrow?*

We go back and forth, thrashing out the details. Initially, Luke suggests catching up late. I explain that's impossible on a weekday because I work the next day and I'm married, and that it's only going to be a couple of drinks, not a night out. Luke's single so he doesn't have to worry about his other half, and he works shifts at several different bars so his hours are all over the place. He comes back to me with 4:00pm tomorrow at The Andion. I tell him 4:15, as I have bus duty.

I can't believe it's come to relying on Luke for relationship advice.

I open the door, thrust a foot out.
Jerk it back in.
Close the door.
And start the car.

9.

Beth's house – well, Roger's house, which she moved into – sits in Greenbrook, a big suburb right next door to Meadow. Greenbrook's all hills and trees, the houses older, the bricks ugly shades of brown and tan (I'm not sure when they were ever fashionable). Many of the houses are double story, although they're utilitarian more than anything else. The yards are huge and filled with greenery, most of it overgrown.

I pull into the driveway, hop out of the car, and run up the steps to the front door. The bell – this strikingly new thing that's been screwed in a little crooked – echoes through the house. I wait for footsteps but there's nothing. I ring the doorbell again, then knock on the door. Still nothing.

There are lots of reasons Beth might not be answering. She could be sleeping. Or too sick to get up. Or she could be embarrassed to show herself because Roger's backhanded her.

I don't know why the latter presents as such a threat. The truth is, I know *so little* about Beth's relationship with Roger. She hardly ever talks about him, and he's only shown once to a school function. On Monday mornings in the staff room, I don't recall anybody asking Beth how her weekend was with Roger whereas I get asked about myself and Jane all the time.

A car pulls up to the curb – a silver Porsche with sparkling rims. Roger gets out. He looks like he models his whole appearance on flashy lawyers in films – the tailor-made suit, the fancy shoes, lustrous hair that bounces with every step. Only the image doesn't quite work because he's so lanky, with big sunken eyes that are strangely doleful yet captivating. Despite the heat, he's not sweating.

He comes up the stairs, two at a time, a plastic bag containing boxes of fast food hanging from his wrist – I see the lid on top of the biggest box has a logo for Cloud's Fried Chicken.

"Can I help you?" he asks.

"I'm from the school," I say.

"School?"

"Where Beth teaches." I put my hand out. "Casper."

Roger clenches my hand, shakes it, squeezes tighter, and doesn't let go. His brows are manicured thin and sharp, possibly to make his head more aerodynamic when he walks.

"Oh, we met at the thing last year," he says.

"Yeah." He's still got my hand. "The thing."

"What're you doing here?"

"I was a bit worried about Beth, so I thought I'd see how she is."

"She's got gastro."

"Can I talk to her?"

"She's probably sleeping."

"Just for a minute."

"I really don't know …"

"I won't be long."

Roger releases my hand, and puts his on his hip. "Is there a reason you're being pushy?"

"Pushy?"

"Yeah, pushy."

"Sorry, I didn't mean to. It's … well … we have a staff meeting after school she was meant to speak at." Good old staff meetings. They can get me out of anything. And if he thinks I'm being pushy, he's being pushy right back. I don't like it – don't like his dismissiveness. "I've got to cover for her," I tell him. "So I wanted her input."

"I'll get her. Wait here." Roger waggles his finger at me the way I would at Wallace, then opens the door. The first thing I notice is a whirring coming from somewhere, soft but distinct. Then it's the long hardwood hallway that stretches out before us. "Beth, honey!" he calls. "I brought you some lunch."

He walks to the end of the hallway, opens one of the doors, and disappears. I strain my ears and hear bedsprings. He must be rousing her from bed. Conversation follows, too muffled to make out. I fold my arms across my chest, expecting to see Beth pop out, but there's nothing. I lean in through the front door, try to find an angle where I can see through the open bedroom door, but it's impossible. A mirror hanging in the hallway shows the bedroom. I lean further inside, slip, then steady myself against the wall.

The whirring stops.

I stop.

In the reflection, I see Beth rise out of bed. Roger, holding her robe open, obscures her, but it's evident she's naked. She gets up, and guides her hands into the sleeves of the robe. Roger folds it around her. It's such a caring gesture that it doesn't seem like him. She ties the robe around her waist, brushes Roger off – like she almost shoves him away – and heads for the door. I retreat back to the doorstep.

"Hey, Casper," Beth says as she comes down the hallway. Roger stands in the bedroom doorway, like a bouncer minding the entrance to some exclusive club.

"Hey, Beth."

She takes one little step after another, like an old woman with arthritic hips, and keeps her arms folded across her chest. Her hair is messed up, she's not wearing make-up, and crescents sit under her big eyes. She looks exhausted. But not sick.

"What're you doing here?" Beth asks when she gets to the door. She smiles a little smile that's the same old Beth, but for the tiredness.

"I thought, you know …" I don't know what to say, not with Roger standing there. "We've got the staff meeting this afternoon. I had to take your art class. Is there anything you want me to put across?"

The request must sound like the stupidest thing in the world, but she gets that it's for Roger's benefit.

"Can you let Stuart know we need more art supplies?" Beth says. "Especially paints. There's hardly any left, and only a few colors, like red and black. I also need to note Bianca's attendance because she's been ditching. The last few weeks she's missed. I thought she and Dom must have something going because he wasn't there the first time. The second time it was just her. But I did see her at school on that day."

Roger doesn't move. The prick.

"Okay, so that's it?"

"I can … I can cover the rest of the stuff when I'm in again."

"I tried to call …"

"Sorry. I've got my phone on silent."

"So is it settling?"

"Settling?"

"I told him about your gastro," Roger says quickly.

"Yeah," Beth says, although there's a flicker of irritation in her face. "It's settling."

"So you'll be in tomorrow?"

"Yeah."

"Okay." I want to say more, wish we could slip away, but Roger's not moving. "I'll see you tomorrow."

"Bye, Casper."

"Roger."

Roger lifts his chin at me by way of acknowledgment.

I head down the steps.

I get in my car, start the engine, but sit there. Tomorrow, I'll have to ask Beth what all that was about. She wasn't marked – at least not that I saw – but something's going on. She doesn't have gastro – Roger wouldn't be bringing her fried chicken if she did. I hope I haven't caused more problems for her.

Putting the car into reverse, I pull away from Roger's house, and drive back to school.

10.

I'm distracted through my remaining classes and, in the staff meeting after school, I sit mutely while Stuart drones on. He talks about being watchful of kids smoking and vaping, of kids going to The Corner at lunch (we all see them, but nobody but Stuart cares), and attendances. He goes on – not for the first time – to talk about how we need to develop relationships with the kids so that they feel we're their confidantes, and yet maintain boundaries at all costs.

When he's done at 4:45pm – he should've been finished fifteen minutes earlier – he asks if anybody has anything to add. I relay Beth's messages about the paint and Bianca, but that's it. Even if the others had anything to say, they just want this meeting to be over.

Stuart dismisses us and I go home.

11.

As I turn into my street, I'm worried Vic will be outside and there'll be some new issue with Wallace. Vic's gotten worse over the years. Now everything about Wallace bothers him. But as I pull into my drive and reverse onto my nature strip, I see Vic's not there, although Chloe is, emerging out of her car, dressed in her nurse's slacks and shirt.

"Hey, Casper," she says as I get out of my car.

"Hi, Chloe."

As usual, Wallace begins yapping in the garage.

"Had a good day?" Chloe asks.

"It's been survivable."

"That good?"

I shrug. Wallace's barking gets more insistent. He knows I'm home, and is wondering why I haven't greeted him yet.

"I should get him," I say.

"Before you go, can I have a word with you?"

Chloe steps up to the invisible boundary separating our properties. She drags the pink scrunchie from her ponytail, and – with a shake of her head – lets her hair fall loose, then unbuttons the top two buttons of her shirt to reveal a necklace of sweat.

I swallow and look away. "I'll get him and come back."

"Okay."

Hurrying around to the side of the garage, I adjust the tent of my pants, and open the garage door. Wallace almost flies into my arms. He licks my chin and his tail thumps faster than ever.

I walk back around to Chloe, who smiles when she sees Wallace.

"Hello, boy," she says, and scratches him under the chin and behind the ears. "*Hello*." She looks up at me. "This is who I wanted to talk to you about."

"Oh."

"It's nothing bad!" Chloe laughs. "I wanted to apologize for the way Vic's been behaving in regards to Wallace. I don't know what it is with Vic."

I do. He's a bastard.

"I'm sure he'll calm down."

"It's okay, Chloe."

"It's not. Vic has a temper and he should learn to control it. If he gives you any more grief about Wallace, let me know and I'll talk to him."

She doesn't realize how emasculating her offer is. I don't know how she controls him, he's that unreasonable. But I'm not privy to their relationship. It's not like Tarika, who I always hear hollering at the kids while her husband Chapal is virtually invisible. Nothing comes from Vic and Chloe Booth's house, although they mustn't see each other much with Chloe's shift work.

"Okay, thanks, Chloe."

Chloe smiles. "You're welcome, Casper."

It's her cue to leave, but she remains there, eyes locked on mine in a way that makes me feel naked.

Wallace writhes in my hands, breaking the spell.

"I should go," I say.

"Sure." She touches me on the arm. "Have a good evening, Casper."

"Thanks."

I feed Wallace, fill his water bowl, clean up his business, and throw a ball around for him a little bit until he's panting, and looking at me plaintively, as if to say, *You don't have to wear all this fur.* So I give that up and settle in the study with my sketchpad on my lap. After my efforts sketching Bianca today, I truly expect my imagination to be firing. Wallace, who sits on the couch, rests his chin onto his paws, sighs, then closes his eyes. I scowl back at my blank page.

Still nothing.

I check the time on my phone. It's getting on 6:00pm, which means Jane should be home soon. Expecting her makes it impossible to draw, knowing that at some point I'll be interrupted. It's hard – especially in the early stages – to resume a drawing. It's at the start that you have to capture the magic.

Putting down the sketchpad, I go into the kitchen and search the fridge. Neither of us have thought about dinner and it's too late to defrost anything, which means we'll probably have to order in.

I check the time. It's after six now. My mind ticks. I sit on the couch, turn the television on, and flick on the news. But I can't focus. Jane's *rarely* late. Six *is* late for her. If she's ever later, she texts me.

At 6:20pm I text her, asking her where she is. I sit through the sports report, but when there's no response I check that the message sent. I wait through the weather report, then check the reception on my phone – three out of five bars. Sometimes, the carrier jams up, regardless of what the reception's showing. I restart the phone. Still nothing as the current affairs show following the news begins. I consider sending her another text, then decide to call her, but as I'm about to select her name from the favorites, her response arrives:

> Car wouldn't start. The guys pushed it
> to garage. Getting lift home now.

How considerate of *the guys*. I squash down the bitterness. Perfectly logical explanation for her tardiness. It's another one of those things where previously, I wouldn't have thought twice. In fact, I would've been thankful for the guys, since what I know about cars could fit on the nub of my pencil.

But now I visualize one of the guys as being the owner of the condom. He's already moved in on Jane, already fucking her, and is now relieving me of my other duties, helping her out when I should be.

The fears tangle around me until I can't extricate myself. This has blown out of all proportion. All because of that stupid condom. For a moment, I relish obliviousness – it would be fine for her to do what the hell she wants as long as I don't know. But that's an ugly rationalization.

I'd rather know, for better or worse.

But I'd rather take her at her word.

I text Jane over the next fifteen minutes, and throw out suggestions for dinner I know she won't want – heavy stuff like steak and pasta. We settle on pizza. It's not that dinner's that important. It could wait until she gets home.

It's the thought of her chatting with whoever's driving her home – joking, laughing. I don't want her to have that repartee. I know it's stupid. I try to reason my way through the irrationality in my head. She probably has that repartee all day at work. But that *is* work. Her being driven home crosses boundaries.

Even that's stupid.

I sit on the couch in the dining room, by the front windows, and tap a foot on the carpet. Wallace jumps up onto the couch, and curls up on my lap. I scratch him behind his left ear. His eyes close as he enjoys the sensation. I go from scratching him to stroking his fur. He sighs contentedly.

A car approaches. After living in the street for as long as we have, I recognize the sounds of all the neighbors' cars. I twist – Wallace awakes and looks at me reproachfully – so I can pry open the blinds and peek out.

There's Vic, watering his lawn. Then a big blue Ford pulls into the drive. Jane's in the passenger seat, Kai in the driver's seat. He says something and they laugh. She reaches across to him. I don't see what her hand does. The movement suggests she's put her hand on him – hopefully just on his arm, the way you do when somebody's being funny.

Oh, you crack me up!

She gets out of the car. Kai reverses out of the drive.

Vic says something to Jane. She smiles politely. I scowl. Vic says something else. It must be a joke the way he grins. This time, Jane forces a laugh, the way you would when you're humoring somebody. Vic leans back to admire her figure as she walks to the front door. I seethe, and for a moment forget what I'm doing.

Jane's key hits the lock.

I hurtle across to the study, grab my sketchpad and stick it on my lap.

Wallace comes bolting in, and stands alert at the door looking at me, trying to work out if this is some game. Then he disappears as the front door opens. Moments later, he's back, heralding Jane's entrance. She drops her handbag inside the doorway.

"Hey," I say.

Jane nods at the blank page. "That picture not coming?"

I shake my head. "What's with the car?"

"Electrical system or something. It was lucky – another thirty seconds, and everybody would've left."

"You do have me, you know."

"You know what I mean. Henry, Barry, and Kai pushed the car to the garage. Don't know how long it'll take. Mechanic said hopefully Friday."

"How'd you get home?"

Jane pauses, like it's such a confrontational question. Maybe she saw me at the window, and is wondering why I'm asking about something I already know.

"Kai drove me," she says. "Did you order pizza?"

I open my mouth to respond, then don't.

"You forgot?"

"Sorry, I got caught up."

"With your blank page?"

"Yeah, I guess."

"Did you take the sheets out of the washing machine?"

I press my lips together to show speaking would incriminate me.

"You know, the world goes on outside your non-existent artwork there."

"Yeah. Yeah, I ..."

But she's already a blur out of the study.

Later, we sit on the couch, one of Jane's reality shows on television. A pizza box lies open on the coffee table. We both drink water – a habit from when we first began saving for IVF, and soda, juice, and alcohol, were deemed too big an expense. Wallace sits at our feet, awaiting scraps of ham from the pizza.

"You're going to have to take me to work tomorrow morning," Jane says.

"It'll have to be early so I can get back for the morning staff meeting. I've …" I stop. I was about to say, *I've missed both this week*. But Jane doesn't know that. "I've got to be on time because Stuart's so anal."

"If that means you have to drop me in at work at eight-fifteen or eight-thirty, that's okay. I have stuff to do."

"You really want to go in that early?"

"What choice is there?"

There's no direct train line to Jane's work and the morning buses are roundabout and filled with schoolkids. My Fiesta's a manual, and Jane can only drive automatic. She's right – there is no choice, and yet I can't help wondering if there's a reason she wants to get to work earlier. I can't stop the thought.

"You can take me in," she says, "then get me about five?"

"Okay … Shit, I'm meant to have drinks with Luke tomorrow after school."

"Since when?"

"I texted him today – you know, because Stephen said Luke wanted to catch up. I didn't expect him to respond." I reach for my phone. "I'll cancel."

Jane grabs my wrist. "It's fine. One of the guys can bring me home."

"Isn't it out of their way?"

"Kai's out this way." She drops the crust of her pizza slice into the box, picks up some stray ham that's fallen on the couch, and drops that in the box, too. She checks for any other pizza shreds, then goes to the kitchen sink, and washes her hands. I take the ham and hold it out for Wallace. He wolfs it down.

"Don't encourage him," Jane says.

"You talking to me or Wallace?" I ask.

She *harrumphs* and shakes her head. "How was Beth today?"

"She wasn't at school."

"No?" Jane comes and sits back on the couch.

"I'm worried. She was meant to confront Roger yesterday."

"You think something happened?"

I shrug.

"I wouldn't be surprised with him. I bet he's got a temper. You call Beth?"

"Yeah, rang out. Stuart said she had gastro."

"There you go then." Jane wriggles up against me.

"Stuart said it was Roger who called."

Jane looks up sharply. "That is weird. You'll see her tomorrow, so you can ask her then."

"Yeah."

Jane rests her head on my shoulder.

Nothing for a bit as we watch television. I recoil from all the lies I've told. I should've told the truth – I was concerned about Beth and called around to see if she was okay. But it's the reason for the urgency I had to talk to Beth that undermines me. I'm worried it'll come out, and then I won't know where we go from there, especially after this morning.

"How long will you be with Luke tomorrow?" Jane asks.

"A couple of hours, I guess."

"Don't drink too much."

"I won't." I think about her being driven home tomorrow, laughing in the car with Kai, or whoever. "How about we grab dinner there?"

She lifts her head. "At The Andion?"

I shrug.

"How many times are we going to go out to dinner this week? Monday, it was with Stephen and Renée. Friday it's with Sarah and her latest."

"This'll just be us."

"It'll just be us on Saturday."

I forgot about the anniversary dinner.

"Yeah, but that's like … an event," I say. "This can be something to do. Maybe you can get dropped off."

"We're meant to be saving for IVF."

"One dinner's not the end of the world."

"We keep saying that – do you notice?"

"Do we?"

"We're not putting enough away. We spend too much on frivolous stuff."

"Okay, I just thought as far as tomorrow went, it'd be convenient."

The bridge of Jane's nose wrinkles into two lines as she thinks about it. "Tomorrow, and that's it," she says. "Okay?"

"Okay."

"We have to be more frugal."

"Whatever you say."

"Are you humoring me?"

"No. I'm agreeing."

"I think it's amounting to the same thing."

"Never."

She pouts before resting her head back on my shoulder. We watch more reality TV. I hate it, although there's an addictiveness about it. You keep meaning to tear yourself away, but never end up doing it – the things that are bad for you are the hardest to give up.

"I'm sorry about today," I say.
Jane rubs my chest. "It's okay."
We fall quiet and watch television.

WEDNESDAY

12.

We get up forty-five minutes earlier than usual and yawn through our morning ritual. Only Wallace is unaffected. He joins us for breakfast, then goes out through his doggy door to chase some magpies from the lawn.

It's 8:00am when we lock up the house. Nobody else is out. It's too early for the neighborhood routine. It's too early for us. We've never done this run before so we want plenty of leeway. It's especially important for me. I can't miss another morning staff meeting. And I also want to talk to Beth – not so much about my own stuff, but about why she missed school yesterday. I hope she's okay.

We get wordlessly into the car, too tired for small talk. I start the engine and drop my sun visor. While it's another beautiful day with barely a cloud in the sky, I'm tired of the heat. You just never get used to it.

"I wish we could go back to sleep," Jane says with a yawn and leans onto my shoulder.

I pull off the nature strip and onto the road.

For a while we're quiet as I drive, still trying to rouse ourselves enough to interact. But it's nice. This is one thing I've always enjoyed with Jane: we don't have to always be talking. We can sit in silence and be comfortable with one another. Not a lot of couples enjoy that luxury.

"I want you to wear your charcoal suit on Sunday morning," she says finally.

"Sunday morning?"

"The picture."

"Oh, yeah, of course."

Our annual anniversary picture. I'd forgotten about it, even though we'd talked about the anniversary dinner last night. The whole day's an event for Jane – a reaffirmation of our marriage. It makes me feel good that she's still so caught up in it, that she speculates about what she'll wear and how she'll do her hair. I smile a tight, wry smile. In the rear-view mirror, it looks like I'm struggling to hold back tears.

I haven't even bought a gift yet either. I should do that today. I'm meant to have playground duty at lunch, but if I can swap it maybe I can duck out to the plaza and buy her something. I could ask Beth to come – get a woman's opinion. What is the seventh anniversary anyway? I have no idea.

"So what do you think?" Jane asks.

"About what?" I haven't registered a word she's said. We're on High Street now, passing an endless line of shopfronts and cafes.

"I asked you if I should wear that frilly red dress on Saturday night, or the tight black one. You weren't listening."

"Why do you ask me?"

"Because I'm interested in your opinion."

"And then you go make your own decision anyway."

"No I don't."

"You do."

"I'm asking your opinion now."

"I like the tight black one."

"Why?"

"Because it makes your butt look good."

"Really?"

"Yes, really."

Jane seems pleased by that. Then: "So my butt doesn't look good otherwise?"

"I didn't say that."

"But you said the black dress makes my butt look good. So how does it look when the black dress isn't making it look good?"

I pause. Mines, everywhere. "Your butt always looks good. The black dress accentuates it. The red dress is loose, so it doesn't. That's all I meant."

"But the red dress gives me cleavage."

"How about we just go naked? Then you'll have your cleavage and your butt."

"Don't be snide."

"I'm not being snide. You look good in whatever you wear. You decide."

"Is this how you handle your kids?"

"No."

"No?"

"No, the kids listen to me."

Jane laughs. She has always been able to take a joke at her own expense.

"Maybe I'll buy something new," she says.

"We're meant to be saving, aren't we?"

"I guess, but there are some great stores down here. And I'd like to be in something different, something you haven't seen me in before."

"Like?"

"Something different for this anniversary. Seventh anniversary is wool, or copper. Maybe I'll get something in wool."

"That'll be fun in this heat."

"Good point. Any suggestions?"

"Surprise me."

"Maybe I will."

Eventually, we reach Web Myriad. It's on the third floor of a three-story shopfront. Web Myriad itself looks great – it's entirely glass, and wouldn't be out of place in some affluent business district. But the first two floors are red brick with narrow windows. A neon sign on the first floor says Redux Travel. There's nothing identifying the second floor. It used to be an accountancy business.

"What's on the second floor now?" I ask.

"It's for lease."

"Wasn't it—"

"Adams Accounting. Rent went up and they couldn't afford to stay."

"So where are they now?"

"Found cheaper offices somewhere. Even Henry and the guys on the first floor are complaining about the rent."

"So it's vacant?"

"Henry says the landlord claims he's got lawyers who'll be moving in."

"Lawyers?"

"Yep."

I pull into a side street leading to the narrow parking lot that services many of the businesses in the area. At this time of the morning – the clock on my dash says 8:17 – it's almost empty. All but for Kai's big blue Ford.

"Whose car's that?" I ask, as if I didn't know.

"Kai's. He gave me the lift yesterday. There was a problem with one of the front ends he built, so he's been coming in earlier to work on it."

"Oh."

I think of Jane in the office with Kai for forty minutes before the official working day starts – not that that really matters. I don't know if Henry and Barry are there during the day or what goes on.

Jane undoes her seatbelt, leans across and kisses me on the lips. "I'll see you tonight," she says as she opens her door.

"Okay. Hey?" I dart across and force my mouth onto hers. She retreats initially, then leans into me. My tongue pushes her lips open and she meets me in the kiss. She tastes like coffee, which is a peculiar thing to notice given *why* I'm doing this, but my mind goes there anyway. My left hand cups her breast. I can feel the lace of her bra through the silk of her shirt.

"What was that for?" Jane says when we break apart.

"Just because."

"You need better timing," she says. She kisses me on the lips. "Love you."

"Love you," I say.

She gets out of the car, closes the door, then walks to the back door of Web Myriad. It leads into a small foyer. A doorway leads through to Redux, there's an elevator, and a stairwell that zigzags up to the other two floors.

Jane opens the glass door and goes in. As she moves to the first step of the stairs, I can still see her. She must be able to see me, too, because she waves.

Then she jogs up the stairs and disappears from my sight.

Driving away from Web Myriad, the sense that I've sacrificed Jane grows until I want to go back and get her.

But I don't.

13.

I sit in my car parked outside Sofia's.

Ruminating.

It's 8:44. Kids amble past. I identify Bianca, walking like she doesn't have a care in the world – or if she does, like those cares don't affect her. I think about Wallace. He sees Vic's stupid cat, he chases it out of yard, he moves on. But I can't. I should be at school, sitting in the stupid staff meeting. Instead, I'm fixated on this, and I don't know why.

A knock on my window startles me. It's Jean Jacket. I don't move. He knocks again. I wind down the window.

"You a cop?" he says.

"What?"

"You a cop?"

Under his jean jacket, he wears a T-shirt tucked into his jeans. Everything's too tight to be concealing a weapon.

"Because if you are and I ask you, you have to tell me."

His face is lined, aged prematurely, although there's still something handsome about him, something almost dignified. His hair reminds me of Roger's – scruffy in a way that's fashionable. Drug dealers and lawyers, they're the only ones who can manage it.

"So you a cop?" he asks again. His eyes are bright blue – I would've imagined they'd be bloodshot or have bags. He looks in better condition than me.

Despite the absurdity of the situation, my logical mind – the hyper-analysis I've been experiencing all week – kicks in. "You know, I don't think that's true," I say. "I don't think I'd have to tell you if you asked me."

"So you *are* a cop?"

"No!"

"Then why are you telling me that?"

"I'm just … saying."

"Just saying?"

"Yeah."

Jean Jacket snorts. "What are you then?"

"What do you mean, what am I?"

"Why are you sitting here?"

"I'm a school teacher."

"A school teacher?"

"Yeah."

"Why does a school teacher sit in his car?"

"I don't know."

"You don't know?"

I shrug.

"You sure you're not a cop?"

"No," I say, and also shake my head for emphasis.

"I've seen you sitting here a few times this week." Jean Jacket folds his arms across his chest. "Got a problem?"

I almost laugh. This is who's going to counsel me – a drug dealer.

"I'm … thinking, okay?" I say.

"Okay, okay." Jean Jacket looks around. "Can I get you something, school teacher?"

He's toying with me. My vulnerability is a plaything for him – if it's indeed vulnerability. The way I skulk around Jane, my need to consult Beth or Luke, maybe it's not vulnerability but cowardice. I don't like that possibility. I don't think I'm a coward – I don't remember doing anything specifically cowardly in my life, but now I'm scared that's exactly what I am.

"Why're you doing this?" I ask.

Leon appears in the doorway of Sofia's. I want to call out to him. There. Something cowardly. Maybe I'm only noticing those things now.

"What am I doing?" Jean Jacket asks.

Leon heads back into Sofia's.

"This," I say.

"What is this?"

I slide the window back up.

"Come on!" Jean Jacket says.

I start the car, reverse out of my parking spot – almost rear-ending an approaching car – and drive to school.

14.

I arrive at school as the bell's ringing and end up being the last one into my Literature class. Some of the kids admonish me in that cheeky way they think is funny, so I force a smile at them.

After class, I find Stuart waiting in the hallway, one foot drumming the floor. If banality has a beat, this would be it.

"I'm sorry, Stuart," I say. "It really couldn't be helped. My wife's car broke down."

"Really?"

"Yes." He doesn't have to know that it broke down yesterday. "I had to drive her to work and then drive back."

"Casper, you've missed three morning staff meetings in a row. Let me say, I'm dubious about your ongoing excuses."

"They're not excuses, they're reasons."

Stuart is unmoved, like he's trying to work out whether there really is a distinction. Maybe for people like him there's not. His glasses slide down his nose a little. Kids check us out as they hurry to their next classes. Stuart's such a bastard for accosting me like this in front of them. He should've waited until recess – although maybe this is a strategy.

"There's not a single problem with the rest of my work, is there?" I ask.

"No – other than for the noisy classroom."

I knew he'd bring that up, and I want to shove it back down his throat.

"And I was at the Tuesday after-school meeting."

"Casper. I am just concerned. About you."

No, he's concerned about the school. I'm one of the tiny screws that hold it together. He's trying to work out if I'm becoming faulty – not if I've *become* faulty, just if I'm on my way.

The hallways are empty now. All the kids are in their next classes, which means there's a classroom minus me. Stuart should be sending me on my way quick smart, but he's showing no urgency to resolve this.

"It's really an amazing string of coincidences that I haven't been able to attend the morning meetings."

"I see." He doesn't.

"It's never happened before, has it? And it won't happen again."

"You told me that yesterday."

"I promise."

He pushes his glasses back up his nose with his middle finger – like he's giving me the finger. But Stuart wouldn't do that – well, I don't think he would.

"I am taking you at your word," he says.

"You'll see."

"You better get moving," he says. "You're late for your next class."

I don't bother answering that.

The instant the bell rings to end second period, I stuff my things into my bag. I have two quests to fulfill during recess. One: I have to ask Shirley if she'll swap my playground duty at lunch today with hers tomorrow; two: I have to ask Beth if she'll accompany me at lunchtime to help pick out a gift for Jane. But when I step out of the classroom, Maya is waiting for me.

"Mr. Gray, can I speak to you?" she says.

I want to move on, but don't want to refuse a student's request – particularly Maya's, since she always tries so hard.

"Sure, Maya. What is it?"

"Can we go back inside the classroom?"

We do so. I lean back against the desk. Maya looks at her toes.

"What is it, Maya?"

"Would you …?" Her voice trails away as she takes a sketchpad out of her bag. It's small – only A4, with a worn cover and curling corners. She doesn't meet my eye when she passes it across.

I take the pad and open it to the first page, expecting gaudy teenager art, but I'm wrong.

The pictures must be from Maya's neighborhood. They're all seen through narrow windows. My impression of the first two is that they're different views from Maya's bedroom – an array of townhouses marching down a hill in one; a house under construction in the other, one builder on the roof, his head upturned as if he's caught her looking at him. Others are drawn from different windows, while the curtains – or the pane – offer an impeded view.

There's a surrealist quality I could never hope to mimic – not that surrealism is something I aspire to. I try to capture what's in front of me. But the strokes of her pencil, as well as her use of shade, are exquisite. These simple everyday settings bleed with a yearning melancholy, speaking to a life of somebody shut out from the world, and who can only live through her drawing.

"These are wonderful, Maya."

"Really?"

"More than really."

"I have others at home. In a bigger pad. I've drawn them in charcoal."

"I'd love to see them one day. How long have you been drawing?"

"Since I was old enough to hold a pencil. My parents thought it was important to develop a creative skill. I don't think they're very good. I don't really like drawing."

"You don't like it?"

I understand pushy parents – I see them often enough. But I would kill to have had parents who'd made me pursue drawing as religiously as Maya's parents have. She doesn't appreciate it. But I guess that's because it's been forced on her. Still, she has an obvious talent – it's because it's been forced on her that she hasn't embraced it.

"You know, Maya, anybody can draw competently given enough practice." *Even me.* "But you have a gift." I close the sketchpad and hold it out to her. "It's something you should pursue."

She takes the sketchpad. Her cheeks have flushed a bright red. She still can't meet my gaze.

"I'm sorry to rush out, Maya, but I really have to get going." I guide her to the door. "But that," I indicate the sketchpad in her hand, "isn't something you should be ashamed of."

"The other kids already think I'm a nerd."

"It doesn't matter what they think." We're outside the classroom now. I close the door. "It really only matters what you think, right?"

She nods.

"Keep drawing, okay?"

"Okay." Maya's smile is childlike.

"I'll see you."

"Bye, Mr. Gray."

Both Shirley and Beth are in the staff room with all the other teachers – including Stuart, who sits in a corner with a cup of coffee and the morning newspaper. His eyes are pointed at the newspaper, but I feel them on me.

Oddly, Beth doesn't look at me at all. She chats with Jerry Logan, the math teacher, who's almost as much of a windbag as Stuart, but keeps her nose buried in her exercise book, like she's trying to hint that she wants to be left alone.

I approach Shirley and hit her with the fact it's my wedding anniversary on Saturday and I want to use lunchtime to buy Jane a gift. Shirley's suckered by the emotion of the sentiment, which is when I hit her with swapping yard duties. She's more than happy to do so. For the next five minutes, she tells me how she and her husband were married for forty-four years before lung cancer got him. She dabs at her eyes with a handkerchief. It's now impossible to leave, and I spend the rest of recess with her as she tells me about how she and Harold lived in the same house from the day they were married and never once went to sleep angry.

"That's the key to a successful marriage, Casper," she says. "Never go to sleep angry. Thrash it out between the sheets if you have to."

I gape at Shirley, never associating her with sex, let alone angry, passionate sex. She laughs and pats my knee. The bell rings and the staff begrudgingly disperse. I extricate myself from Shirley like I've had my foot trapped under a boulder and had to gnaw it off at the ankle. I catch Beth in the hallway. It's been getting hotter throughout the morning, but she wears a pink silk blouse with long sleeves and her armpits are damp with sweat.

"Everything okay?" I say.

"Yeah," she says, but doesn't look at me. "Well ..." She shrugs. "To be honest, I'm a bit embarrassed about yesterday."

"I got the impression there was more happening than met the eye."

"Can we not talk about it?"

"Sure," I say. "Although I was going to ask you a favor."

We reach the art room. Beth stops at the door. Kids stream past us.

"It's my seventh wedding anniversary on Saturday. I've left getting a gift late. I was going to duck out at lunchtime. Would you come with me? I know what she likes, but I thought a woman's opinion couldn't hurt."

Beth sways – she wants to be gone, into the safety of her classroom, where she has control. If I'd asked last week, there wouldn't have been a problem. Yesterday, we invested in an elephant. Now she's worried I'm going to ask about it. But she's my friend, and I know she wants to help.

"Okay," she says. "Just …"

"I understand."

Beth smiles. "Thanks." She pats my hand.

My car's been cooking in the sun and it takes forever before the air-conditioning offers any relief, its whiny hum the only sound as we drive up to the plaza. Beth's unusually quiet, and constantly pulls down the cuffs of her blouse. I've never seen her so fidgety – or fidgety at all.

I want to unload on her, but now's definitely not the time, and as much as I want to ask her about her stuff I can't, so I tell her about the weekend Jane has planned – dinner Saturday evening, spend the night at the Sheraton, Sunday morning we put the exclamation mark on the anniversary with our traditional picture.

"That sounds lovely," she says, but her eyes brim. Telling her our plans has upset her.

"We're going to have dinner tonight at The Andion," I say. "I'm actually meeting an old friend there after school for a beer or two. Then Jane's going to come down for dinner. You and Roger should join us. Or that's something we could do. Dinner. As couples."

My attempt at a segue. She doesn't take it.

"Anyway, seems we're always either eating out or ordering takeaway. It was pizza last night. We went to a restaurant on Monday night. Out again tonight." I'm babbling, trying to catch Beth in my slipstream and take her away from whatever's on her mind. "Don't know what would happen if we did end up having a baby. I don't think either of us would know how to feed it."

Still nothing, and we're quiet until I pull into Westfield shopping plaza. Given it's early afternoon on a Wednesday, parking isn't too bad. I find a spot right under a tree by the entrance we need, and kill the engine. Beth's eyes are lowered. Her forehead glistens.

"We don't have to do this," I say.

"What about your gift?"

"I've got a couple of days. I can try do it after tomorrow's after-school meeting. Or Friday. I'll work something out."

"I don't know if I want to be with Roger anymore," Beth says.

Silence. On Monday, she wanted to get serious with him. Something's changed her mind quickly.

"Did he hurt you?" I ask.

Beth shakes her head. "Not in the way you're suggesting. And that doesn't have a lot to do with why I'm thinking like this. You get to a point where you want to move forward. I almost feel like I'm Roger's fail-safe, but he's on the hunt for somebody better – somebody who can be the trophy he needs."

The car's stifling without the air-conditioning. My T-shirt sticks to me, and my cargo pants are scratchy. Beth's not faring any better and her hair sticks to her face.

"Let's go inside," she says. "We need to get out of this car before we die of dehydration."

The shopping center is chilled, and the sweat cools on my skin. It'll be hard going back outside after this. Shoppers march obliviously past us. They're the usual crowd to me – mostly mothers with preschool kids; some guys and girls on their lunch breaks; and teenagers in navy blue uniforms from one of the nearby schools.

"You want to get something to eat?" I ask. "Or something to drink?"

"No. Let's go shopping for you."

"We don't have to."

"We should. Just because my relationship's a lost cause doesn't mean it should affect yours."

We go to Sunderland's, a place Jane shops regularly for jewelry. Rows and rows of rings, earrings and necklaces sparkle in the window. They all look okay to me and although I know Jane's taste, I don't really know what's suitable.

"What're you looking for?" Beth says as we go inside. Sunderland's is pristine, with glass counters and staff in suits. It's like being in a museum. The air-conditioning is even cooler in here.

"Anything."

"Anything?"

"It has to be good. Jane always gets me great gifts. I always feel inferior."

"What does she like? Rings? Necklaces? Earrings? Bracelets?"

Jane doesn't like wearing rings because she uses her hands so much for presentations at work, and flashy rings can be distracting. Necklaces are also not high priorities because they're often lost in the shirts she wears.

"Earrings or a bracelet," I say.

"What's your budget?"

"I don't know."

"Can you give me a range?"

"Five hundred or so, I guess."

Beth whistles. "Generous."

"Is it?"

"You don't think?"

"I don't know. Jane says the seventh anniversary is wool or copper."

"You want to buy her something in copper?"

"That doesn't sound very romantic."

"No."

"Wool, then – how about I buy her a sheep?"

Beth chuckles – the first joviality she's shown. "That's probably not going to do." She points out a bracelet. It's a fine gold chain with a small diamond set in its nub. "How about this?"

"Can I see this?" I ask the salesgirl.

The salesgirl could just as easily have applied for a job as a mannequin, her skin alabaster and features pointed. She has an air of casual aloofness, only warming when she deems shoppers worthy. Unlocking the counter, she takes out the box the bracelet is in, and holds it aloft. I reach for it and she draws it back, like she's afraid I'm going to pollute it.

"Can I see it?" I ask.

"Of course," she says, though her tone says something different. She doesn't want us to touch it. I can only imagine how we look – sweaty, dressed casually as we are. She's concluded we're window-shoppers.

I pick up the bracelet, but Beth takes it from me. "It's gorgeous," she says. She holds it above her right wrist, modeling it. Peeking out from under the cuff of her sleeve, running across her wrist, is a bruise. I wonder if it goes all the way around. Beth quickly drops her arm, letting her sleeve fall over her wrist.

"How much?" I ask.

"Six-hundred-and-forty-nine dollars," the salesgirl says.

"That's more than you wanted to spend," Beth says.

"Jane deserves it." I slide my wallet from my pocket, take out my credit card, and give it to the salesgirl like I'm doing no more than paying for groceries. "I'll take it."

"You will?" If her face could register shock, I'm sure it would now.

"Yes."

"Of course, sir."

The salesgirl runs my credit card through the scanner as Beth places the bracelet back in its box. I can see bruising on the top of Beth's left wrist, too. She's used make-up to try to cover it, but it's there.

"Love how you shop," Beth says.

"I like it, you like it, why wait?"

I punch in my pin. The salesgirl closes the box and puts it in a Sunderland's bag. She hands it to Beth, her eyes flitting to Beth's wrists. One finely plucked brow shoots up. She thinks I've done this to Beth and that the jewelry is a bribe.

"I'm sure your wife will love it," the salesgirl says as she hands me the receipt.

"I'm not his wife," Beth says.

"Oh, of course." The salesgirl's gaze strays to my wedding band.

Beth gives me an awkward embrace – well, it's fine on her behalf, as she grabs me side-on and nuzzles her cheek against my shoulder, but I go rigid. She feels soft and warm and totally inappropriate against me.

"We're having a tawdry affair," Beth says.

The salesgirl frowns, trying to work out whether it's the truth or whether Beth's making fun of her. Beth smiles back at her.

"Thanks," Beth says. "Let's go, honey. We can make love in the car!"

I take my Sunderland's bag and shove it in the side pocket of my cargo pants as Beth grabs me by the hand and leads me out.

We have about half an hour before lunch finishes, so we go to the food court and each grab a hot dog and Coke from Donut King. Then we sit down to eat, although I keep looking at Beth's wrists and hope she doesn't notice.

"What was that about?" I ask.

"That bitch already thought we were having an affair," Beth says. "How do people get the way they are?"

"Like what?"

"We all have our faults and stuff. But somebody like that, she's just fault."

"I'm sure she's got a crowd where she fits in, and we're faults to them."

"You're probably right."

We finish our hot dogs and I try to find something to say that won't upset Beth, but all I can think about is Jane and me, Beth and Roger, and how relationships are always offering surprises, regardless of how well you think you know your partner.

"You keep looking at my wrists," Beth says.

I don't say anything, and force myself to look at her.

"On Monday night Roger and I argued about getting serious – the worst we ever have. It didn't get much better on Tuesday morning. Then he went to work because he had a meeting. I think by the afternoon I'd decided to leave him. But his attitude changed. He promised to look at getting serious, although I think that's only because he realized he pushed me too far."

"Do you believe him?"

"He wants to talk more today. I don't know that I should give him the chance. But part of me wants to because, well, I do love him." Beth takes a deep breath, then asks, "You don't like Roger, do you?"

I start thinking of a diplomatic way to answer this.

"You can be truthful."

"You see something in him."

"I want to be like you and Jane. It's sweet You're shopping for an anniversary gift. You spent more on her than you intended. I'm sure she's got you something, too. Then you make an event of it. I want that. But I don't know if Roger will ever become that."

"You shouldn't have to sacrifice the person you are for your partner."

"Do you really believe that?"

"We all make compromises in relationships. Jane's a neat freak, so I can't leave my clothes lying around or dishes in the sink the way I did before we were married. But if she wanted to change something about me, or wanted things I didn't want, then we'd be useless together." *If we haven't become so.*

"I need time to think about this."

"What happened to your wrists, Beth?"

"We should get back to school."

"If you need to talk, I'm here for you – I hope you know that."

"Thanks."

On the drive back to school, Beth asks me about taking her art class yesterday. I tell her what I did, then remark that Maya showed me some of her drawings, which were extraordinary. Beth agrees that from what she's seen in class, Maya's got talent, and suggests Maya must have a crush on me to show me her work. I scoff. The conversation goes on like this – forced and superficial, until it bypasses whatever's gone on between Beth and Roger, and transforms into the typically inane work chatter.

Beth's told me as much as she will about Roger and her wrists. For now.

15.

After school, I have bus duty. I lean against the fence, sweating, thinking I'd love to go home, have a shower, and maybe change into some shorts. At least The Andion will be air-conditioned. The kids are oblivious to the heat – most still in full uniform, some even in blazers.

I'm there for half an hour, supervising the loading of four buses. Other kids walk home, or drift off in the direction of The Corner where they congregate to vape, or sometimes even smoke a cigarette, or – for those lucky enough – make out.

Then I hurry to the parking lot. I almost hope to see Beth, so I can offer her some encouragement, or reiterate my offer that she can call on me if she needs to. But she's well gone. I wonder how she'll go with Roger. It's sad that her act to affirm the relationship has turned out like this, but I guess that only highlights that the bonds that might seem impermeable are sometimes the most fragile bonds of all.

My car is roasting and the steering wheel too hot to hold. I start the engine and put the air-conditioning on full. Hot, stale air blows in my face.

Another couple of minutes and I'll have a beer in my hand.

The Andion's a squat brown building that's been around for decades, although sections of it have recently been refurbished. The bar itself is split in three: the bistro, which has a patio; a gaming room; and the bar, which opens up onto a cobblestoned beer garden. There's parking at the front and back.

The rear lot has trees planted intermittently to provide shade. I find one and park up under it. When I get out of the car, I see parked across the street a battered red van, although the passenger door – which must've been replaced – is blue.

Jean Jacket leans casually against the rear bumper, like he's posing for some car commercial advertising the luxury of owning a family van. As I make my way to the door of The Andion, my vantage point improves and I see Bianca striding away from him. Jean Jacket calls something unintelligible after her and grins. She casts a glance over her shoulder, totally unafraid, smiles, and hollers something – two words I'm sure I can lip-read.

You wish.

She jogs across the road, her skirt bouncing around her thighs. Jean Jacket sees me and shrugs, as if he's expecting me to sympathize, although I have no idea what just happened – whether she was passing and Jean Jacket was being smart, or whether she'd left him after some sort of interaction. Bianca might be socially precocious, but she's still a teenager.

Tomorrow at school, I'm going to have to talk to her.

There aren't many people in the bar, although that's not a surprise given it's a dump. While they put a lot of work into the gaming room and even more into the bistro, the bar itself has been unchanged for over twenty years. The carpet is threadbare and has absorbed so much spilled beer the smell's fermented into the air. The tables are small and rectangular – like we used to have in school when I was a kid – with two pushed together to form squares, around which plastic chairs have been crowded. The bar's in the center. On the other side of it is a betting outlet. The bulk of the bar's patrons are in there, cheering for their horses.

I go up to the bar and order a glass of beer. In the corner sit two women in short skirts and low-cut blouses, make-up so overdone it's garish. I think they're trying to recapture some element of their youth, but on closer study see they're young, maybe only in their twenties. One catches me looking and smiles, but there's nothing sexy or seductive about it. Here is somebody who life has pummeled the joy out of. I take my beer, spin away, and grab a table in the opposite corner.

As I'm checking the time on my phone – it's 4:16 – the door opens. I expect Luke, but it's Jean Jacket. He walks to the bar, and gives me a little nod, like we're old friends and have to acknowledge one another.

I sip at my beer – it tastes heavy and bitter compared to my usual Corona – and take out my phone, pretending to occupy myself, although I keep my eyes on Jean Jacket. The bartender hands him a glass that has Coke in it, but is probably a Scotch and Coke.

He starts for the two women in the corner, then instead comes over to me. "Hey," he says.

"Can I help you?" I ask. My phone, which I've been playing with, is still illuminated. It says the time is 4:18.

"Can I interest you in something?"

"Like what?"

"How about those two women over there? Want to fuck one of them?"

"I'm married."

"Both of them?"

"I'm *married*."

"So?"

I should ask him about Bianca. I need to go on the offensive. We're inside a bar. Nothing can happen. If he gets violent, security will arrive – well, at some point they would.

"What's your name?" he asks.

"Why do you want to know my name?"

"Being friendly, man." And his tone *is* friendly, although I sense an underlying belligerence. "So what's your name?"

"What's yours?"

"Mine's Bruce."

"Bruce?"

"Yeah."

"*Bruce?*"

"*Yeah.* What's wrong with Bruce?"

"Nothing …" I shrug. Bruce doesn't fit him. He'll stay Jean Jacket.

"So what's your name?"

I don't answer.

"So I tell you my name and you don't tell me yours?" He puts his hands on his hips.

"Casper."

"Casper?"

"Yeah."

"What sort of name is that?"

"It's the one I got."

"How about some downers, Casper?"

"No thanks."

"You look like you need to relax."

"I'm okay, thanks."

"Everybody needs something."

"Not me."

"No. Everybody. I'll work you out."

"Work me out?"

"What you need."

"No, really, *no thanks*."

The door opens and this time it *is* Luke. He looks around the bar, sees me, and comes over. He waits for an introduction to Jean Jacket, thinking he must be my friend.

"I was doing a little selling," Jean Jacket says. "You interested in anything?"

Luke wouldn't stand out in a crowd, and his plainness almost makes him unremarkable. *Almost*. He's not much bigger than me, but his shoulders are broader from the heavy lifting he has to do for work. Then there's the sense that there's something hard underneath it all, something that wants to unravel spectacularly and to hell with who gets in the way.

"Fuck off," Luke says, taking off the glasses he has to wear to drive.

"I'm ask—"

"Fuck. Off."

"No need to get angry, man."

Luke steps up to him. "I'm not getting angry. *Man*. I'm just telling you to go."

"Okay, cool." Jean Jacket holds up his hands to signal his peacefulness.

"Cool." Luke shakes his head.

Jean Jacket returns to the two ladies. This is typical Luke. When he, Stephen, and I used to go out, Luke never backed down from an argument, and he started his share, too. He got in so many fights I became an expert at wrangling him away from them.

"You want another drink?" he asks.

I've barely touched my beer. "I'm good."

"I'll be back in a minute." Luke heads to the bar.

Luke puts his beer down on the table, then throws his hand out. I shake it. His grip is tight. "How've you been?" he says.

"I'm okay," I say, sipping at my beer. "Working through some things."

"You okay?"

"Yeah, I think so."

"You, me, and Stephen should organize a night out. Catch up."

"Sure." We'll talk about organizing it – we always do. But nothing will ever come of it. It's probably not the way things should be, but our lives have gone in different directions with different responsibilities, so it's hard to get back on the same timetable.

"How long you got today?"

"A couple of hours. Jane's going to drop by later and we're going to have dinner here."

"Cool."

For a little while we reminisce about things we did together – nights out, arguments, and women. Our voices have the peculiar lament of people who know times like that will never come again – although that's never stopped Luke chasing them.

"I'm seeing somebody now," Luke says.

"Is it serious?" Luke never got involved because of the restrictions it put on his lifestyle.

"It might be."

"How long?"

"About six months."

"*Six*?" I say. "You kept that quiet."

"Why'd you need to know?"

"Not that I needed to, but we might've done something together – a dinner or something."

"I wanted to see how serious it is."

I note Jean Jacket and his two friends get up and leave. He doesn't look at me on the way out. I thought he might throw me a reproachful look, as if to say, *I'll get you*. But nothing.

"Who is she?" I ask. "What's her name? What's she do?"

"What are you? My mother?"

"I'm …"

"Curious, yeah?"

"Amazed."

"Her name's Chandra. She came in with friends at the club. We talked. It went from there."

"Just like that?"

"That's the way relationships are born. That's the way life *is*. Just. Like. That."

"So what makes this one special?" I ask.

"She sucks a good cock."

"That's classy."

"Just saying."

"That's the whole basis for your relationship?"

"She likes the way I go down on her, too."

"So that's it? The oral element?"

"Oral's not to be underrated."

"Yeah, but it's not the whole basis for a relationship."

"You know what the problem is in relationships? Partners *talk*. And that's fine. But *not* all the time. Not about everything. And not when you're not ready to. When you blurt it all out, somewhere along the line someone's bound to say the wrong thing, or take something the wrong way. You know what a lot of oral sex means? A lot less conversation. You want to know what's different about Chandra? She doesn't bust my balls. Not yet. I'm sure that'll change. How about Jane? How's she?"

"Yeah. Okay."

"You know, before you two were married, whenever you had a problem, you'd call me or text me and we'd end up sitting in some bar talking it out. Usually it was about some woman you were pining after."

"Isn't that exaggerating it a bit?"

"What about Andrea? Dumped you after a month, although you were convinced you had something with her. Or Leni, who wanted to take a break so she could study overseas? You seriously considered chasing after her."

"I didn't."

"Of course you did. You even looked up flights. Anyway, makes me think that's the surprise reason for your invite."

"I wanted to catch up."

"It's okay if it is. You should rely on friends that way. So what's up?"

"I found a condom in Jane's handbag." I say it before I have a chance to stop myself. Luke's right. That *is* why I invited him here.

Luke stops in the process of lifting his beer to his lips. "Did you ask her about it?"

"She says she bought a box for her friend and this one fell out."

"Do you know the friend?"

"Yeah. Sarah."

"Sarah?"

"She was one of Jane's bridesmaids. Very pretty. And loud. Gold hair. You know her."

"Yeah, yeah, I remember her. I think she made a move on me on your wedding night."

"Really?"

"Think so. I was pretty drunk."

"And you didn't reciprocate?"

"If there was less connection between us – like if I was some distant relative you barely saw – and Jane wasn't also my friend,

I would've done her. But for something to have happened that night, I would've had Jane on my back. Uh uh. There are bridesmaids who are out for fun and there are bridesmaids who want to be next in line. She wanted to be next in line. She still not married?"

"She's had boyfriends. Every one of them has been the one she's going to marry next, until it goes wrong."

"So it's possible it's her condom."

"Yeah."

"But it's still a pretty suspect story."

"Yeah."

"Jane ever go to work early or come home late?"

"She went early today because I had to drive her in and then make it back in time for school."

"Otherwise?"

"No. Well, yeah – she came home late the other night because her car broke down and she had to bring it to the garage."

"How late?"

"Not that late. Her co-worker brought her home."

Luke leans back in his chair. "So, really, she only took as much time as you'd expect she'd take to do all the things she told you she did."

"Yeah."

"She ever get texts or phone calls she tries to hide from you?"

"No."

"You checked her phone?"

"Nothing."

"You getting less sex than usual?"

"No."

"She smell of cologne or anything like that?"

"No."

"You're still worried, though, aren't you?"

"Do there have to be signs?"

"I guess there doesn't have to be. But there usually would be. You're telling me there's nothing."

"Not that I know of."

"My dad used to cheat on my mom all the time."

"Really?"

We've been friends for twenty years and Luke has never told me that.

"Yeah. Used to blame us — said it was the commitment that got to him. Then he'd beg my mom and she'd always take him back. Always. It was crazy." Luke shakes his head, then takes a drink. "That's why me and my brothers are the way we are."

"Ash is married."

"Ash bangs anything that moves while poor Cindy waits oblivious at home. Marcus is just a prick. Only Tom is remotely normal because he was so much younger and missed it all." Luke takes another drink. "Families." He shakes his head. "They specialize in fucking you up, and yet everybody wants one."

"That's encouraging."

"Look at your dad. Drank himself to a slow death after your mom died."

"Yeah, but that's … morbidly sweet in its way, that you could love somebody so much that you'd do that to yourself."

"Don't take this the wrong way, because your dad was a good guy, but it's also weak. Your mom died when you were fourteen or fifteen."

"A week from my fifteenth birthday."

"He had you to take care of; instead, he fell apart. What did you used to tell Stephen and me? That the house went from them arguing half the time to absolute quiet."

I don't think I ever told them how powerful that silence was, how it would smother me, and how every sound — a dripping faucet, a door opening, even my own voice – became alien, and at times I almost second-guessed whether they were real.

Luke scowls. "Your dad would be sitting there in his recliner, drinking. Only time I saw him sober after your mom's death was at your wedding, like he didn't want to ruin the night for you. I saw him in the toilet, you know."

"What?"

"I went in there about midnight. Your dad was sitting on a toilet in the cubicle, shaking."

"Shaking?"

"Shaking."

"It was probably from alcohol withdrawal since he wasn't drinking."

"That's what I thought. But then I saw his face." Luke pauses, lifts his glass to take a drink, but then sets it down. "He was upset. That's why he was shaking. He was upset."

That's difficult to accept. Dad was usually catatonic at best – he'd drink, only say what was required, do whatever he needed, and count the hours before he could go back to bed. There was never anything else.

"I was going to talk to him," Luke said, "but then it clicked: he was upset because your mom wasn't with him to share the night. Well, that's the way I read it."

"Why haven't you ever told me this before?"

"Don't know." Luke takes a drink. "What good would it have done? I wondered how he could love somebody so much to feel like that, when my dad could be such a cunt to cheat nonstop on my mom. Some people are meant to be together, some aren't. Some people knit, some grate."

"Growing up, I would've thought my parents grated."

"Yeah. But under the surface of what we see, under what's expressed, who knows? Every couple builds a dynamic. Being together's the easy bit."

"Really?" I can't keep the skepticism out of my voice.

"Think about it. Relationships aren't just about the time you spend together. They're about the time you *don't* spend together. You trust your partner will do the right thing by you, that when somebody flirts with them they won't take it too far; that if somebody propositions them, they'll shoot it down; that if they see somebody who's better looking and better built than you, they're going to control their lust. You trust that they'll do that – not that they need to tell you any of that's gone on, mind you. Anybody who says relationships need full disclosure is kidding themselves."

"That's pretty cynical."

"No, you *don't* need to know these things are happening because they just gnaw at you, and as long as they stay harmless, they *are* harmless. Look at what you're going through and it *could* be innocent. If it is, it would've been better you didn't know."

"And if it isn't?"

Luke leans back in his chair and runs a finger over the rim of his glass. "Do you work with anybody who's hot?"

"Yeah."

"You friends with her?"

"Yeah."

"What would you do if she propositioned you?"

"I'd decline." My answer comes out before I've even let the question sink in.

"Really?"

"Yeah. Really."

"You're sure?"

"Yes, I'm sure."

"If you," Luke thrusts a finger at me as he makes his point, "had long-term exposure to this person and they kept going for it, or even if they didn't keep going for it but the attraction kept growing, do you think you'd always be able to resist? You don't think you'd be worn down? You don't think maybe it wouldn't just happen?"

"I'd like to think it wouldn't happen if there was no reason for it to happen. I can understand if you have a shit relationship something might happen somewhere else – you know, because you're looking for what you're not getting."

"Is Jane missing something with you?"

"I don't think so."

"Then why would she look at someone else?"

I don't know. We've talked a big circle, but maybe shit does just happen. Do things really need to be bad before you consider somebody else? Can you consider somebody else just because they're also a good prospect? Like, if I had a million dollars and stumbled upon another million, would I not take it? Sometimes, you can want *more* of a good thing.

"Your alternatives are you either trust Jane," Luke says, "or you follow her. But you're not really being fair on her." He finishes his beer.

"I'm speculating."

"You just told me you'd knock back this other woman if she took her shot. So if you can trust in yourself to do the right thing, then you should trust Jane, shouldn't you?"

I don't answer because he's right. But still it gnaws at me.

"I'm getting another beer. Want one?"

"Sure."

Luke goes to the bar.

16.

Luke and I revert to reminiscing, and while I enjoy the nostalgia and it reminds me of a time I wasn't so fearful, I'm constantly checking the time. When Jane hasn't arrived by 6:00, I wonder if I should text her. By 6:30, I'm fidgeting with my phone.

"Do you really think she'd stop to have a quickie before meeting you for dinner?" Luke asks.

He doesn't understand. There's logic, but there's also doubt. Doubt can punch a hole in any logic. Jane and I had agreed "after work". That could mean any time.

"You need to work this out," Luke says. "One way or another."

"What do you think?" I ask.

"Anybody can cheat given the right circumstances. People are fallible, and some are stupid. But, fuck, you found a condom. And that's the only evidence you have. There's not a single other sign she's screwing around. That should be good enough for you."

I don't tell him about the two little bruises on her butt. There'll be logic for that, just as there's my doubt.

It's 6:47 when Jane comes in. I know because I check the time on my phone. She's dressed in knee-length skirt and sleeveless blouse, and her hair's been tied back in a girlish ponytail. There's something wrong about the way she looks, and it's not until she exchanges greetings with Luke and he mentions it that I realize.

"Hey, Jane," he says. "That the way you dress for work?" His looks sidelong at me.

"No, I went home to shower and change," she says. "You wouldn't believe how hot our office gets."

Luke finishes his beer. "I should get going anyway."

"Why don't you join us for dinner?"

"That would be great, but I have a date."

"Luke has a girlfriend," I say.

"Really?" Jane asks.

"Yep. I'm one of the fallen."

"We should all do dinner one night."

"Sure."

"Or you can drop in, you know. We hardly ever see you."

"Maybe I'll do that. I'll see you." Luke kisses Jane on the cheek. Then points at me. "And you, me, and Stephen – book it in."

"Sure."

He leaves.

There's an interconnecting door Jane and I use that goes through the gaming room on the way to the bistro. It's better air-conditioned in here. People sit at the slot machines, mindlessly shoving in their money. The machines ring and flash. I've never understood the fascination of playing a game you have so little control over.

"So how'd you get here?" I ask as we reach the small foyer that precedes the restaurant.

"Taxi," Jane says.

"How'd you get home?" I ask.

"Kai dropped me off."

We enter the restaurant and stop at the podium to wait for service. I can't help doing the mathematics. Jane takes about forty minutes to shower, do her hair, make-up, and get dressed – and that's when she's quick about it. It'd be a ten-minute drive here from our house. Maybe five minutes to wait for a taxi if she booked it in advance. That's an hour. She got here at 6:47. So she would've got home – if all my calculations are correct – about 5:47, which is normal.

Wailing fills my ears. It's a kid, probably no more than four, beetroot faced and screaming, tears pouring down his chubby cheeks, heels digging into the carpet as his mother tries to drag him along. She has another kid in her free arm, this one probably only two or so, with curls and pigtails, bearded in ice-cream – cute, despite her messiness, but that's probably the furthest thing from her mother's mind right now.

The mother rolls her eyes at us as she hauls the kids past. I arch my brows at Jane, as if to acknowledge the insanity, but she's still watching, longing on her face, until the trio disappear through a door into the toilets. Jane melts into me, runs a hand down my chest, then smiles, although there's no happiness there.

I kiss the top of her head. "We'll get there," I say.

She clenches my hand.

A waitress arrives. She's stunningly tall – taller than me – with a dark mane and a busty figure that threatens to burst her uniform of slacks and shirt at the seams. She seats us at a table in the corner and, when she leaves, I have to make a concerted effort not to watch her, occupying myself by picking up the menu.

"She was very pretty," Jane says.

"I didn't notice," I say.

"No?"

"I was surprised at how tall she is."

"Hmmm." Jane's smile is knowing as she picks up her own menu.

The Andion's bistro is functional more than anything else. You don't come here for a fancy night out but simply to be fed. There are booths against the back wall, rows of tables down one end to accommodate families, and smaller tables for more intimate groups. There's also a room with claw and arcade machines for the kids.

Jane and I look through our menus. I barely read what I'm seeing and decide on calamari even before I find it and check the price. Jane goes through the menu page by page, although she'll probably end up choosing from one of her regulars.

"Beth at school today?" she asks.

"Yeah," I say.

"What happened yesterday? Did she tell you?"

I know I shouldn't be censoring myself with Jane, but I've already omitted that I visited Beth yesterday. Now there's the bruises on her wrists. Beth tried to hide them. One day she might tell me about them. But right now it feels like a confidence I should keep.

"She said she had such a huge fight with Roger on Monday night, and on Tuesday morning she decided to leave him," I say. "But by then, he was promising her the things she wants."

"So where've they left it?"

"She says they're going to talk about it tonight."

"I think they're incompatible."

"Really?"

"From what I've seen, he's this materialistic, egotistical blowhard, and she's this spiritual, creative person who has no interest in his goals."

"Then why did they get together? Why have they stayed together?"

"People can stay in relationships a long time before they realize they're not right."

"Mine didn't work out that way."

"Never?"

I shake my head. "They all unraveled for one reason or another – they dumped me, or I didn't feel right with them … and then they dumped me."

"So what made me special?"

I think about that. "From early on, I was comfortable with you – it was always like we'd known each other for years."

"That's it?"

"You made me feel …" I search for the word, thinking there has to be something profound, but in the end, say, "*Right*. I hadn't felt that in a long time."

She leans across, and kisses me. "That's sweet."

"I try." And then, because I can't resist, "And there's one thing you did that I really loved."

Jane's face grows wry but curious. "What?"

"You never dumped me."

Jane laughs, genuinely amused, and she brushes my hand again – that little bit of reconnection that couples usually do so unthinkingly, but which now I measure.

"Maybe your radar's better for what you need," she says. "I had a couple of long-term relationships. People change. Not entirely. But they overlook little things about their partners to be with them and keep the peace."

"What do you overlook about me?"

"Nothing." Jane puts her hand on my knee. "We're *good*. I'm talking about Beth and Roger. I'm sure she overlooked that he's this career-driven bastard because she hoped he'd come around to her side. And he probably overlooked that she's a low-paid art teacher, thinking he'd mold her into a trophy wife. But people get comfortable."

"I'm not sure Beth's comfortable."

"I mean despite their circumstances. It's safer staying with what you know than looking for something new, because new is scary. Look at how you didn't move out of home until we got engaged. Your dad was a functioning but declining alcoholic, in a dysfunctional household, and you stayed with him."

"You think I was comfortable, too?"

"I'm not criticizing you. I think sometimes we go with what we know, even if it's not what's best for us. Sometimes the path we're meant to take is the scarier one." Jane taps the menu. "I think I'll get the risotto. Calamari?"

"How'd you guess?"

"You order the food, I'll get the drinks. Okay?"

"Okay."

We get up. Jane grabs my hand and kisses me again.

"I hope I didn't upset you bringing up your dad."

"No," I say. "Not at all."

I get in line at the counter, but keep my eyes on Jane as she goes to the bar. Luke's right. There's no evidence other than the condom – and that's been explained.

I need to move on.

Jane and I chat until our food's delivered. She laughs in all the right places, shows interest the way she always does in some things (like Maya's artwork) and tries to disguise zoning out over others. It's like it's always been.

Although I've been given a fork, I eat my calamari with my bare hands. Jane mows through her risotto.

"So what's happening with your picture?" she asks.

"My picture?" I don't make the connection.

"The blank page back at home."

"Oh. I'm waiting for inspiration."

"Why don't you draw Wallace?"

"I've drawn Wallace. I want a masterpiece."

"Wallace is a masterpiece."

"Yes, Wallace is. But I need something new, something to come from me."

Jane finishes her risotto, and takes my last few calamari.

"Hey, since when do you eat calamari?"

"I eat calamari." She pops one into her mouth.

"Not usually."

"They looked good. I have an idea."

"What?"

"You could draw me."

"Really?"

"I could pose for you."

"Naked?"

Jane laughs. "If you want."

The idea fires my imagination. It wouldn't be explicit. Maybe she could lie across the couch, her back partly to me, a sheet strategically covering her. That's always more alluring – what's held back from you, rather than what you see.

"Where's this come from?" I ask.

"What do you mean where's it come from?"

"In all the time we've been together, you've never offered to model for me."

"You need inspiration. Here I am."

"Oh, that's sweet."

Jane smiles. She's got a great smile. It's crooked and lights up her eyes. "It's obvious, I guess, isn't it? It's amazing we've never considered it before."

It is. But I haven't felt capable of drawing anything other than small, inanimate objects. Wallace is as ambitious as I've got. A whole person? I like the challenge. I don't know if it'll be my masterpiece, but it's a logical step from where I am.

"I actually want to go home and start this now," I say.

"Really?"

"If you're serious."

"I'm up to it if you are."

"Let's finish our …"

Beth and Roger stand at the podium. Beth's still in a long-sleeved blouse and a frilly little skirt. Roger's in slacks, shirt, and is still wearing a tie.

Jane follows my gaze and sees them. Then Beth sees me. Her surprise and reaction – a big wave – is overdone. She points us out to Roger. Roger doesn't smile. There's one small tilt of his head, like he's indifferent.

They come over, Beth bouncing and excited, Roger like he has to be dragged against gravity. I exchange a kiss on the cheek with Beth, then a loose handshake with Roger. Jane exchanges kisses on the cheek with each.

"Fancy seeing you two here," Beth says, although I told her we were coming here for dinner.

"Casper and I just finished dinner," Jane says. "How're you two doing?"

Now it begins – the sidestepping. Beth will know I share some of our discussions with Jane, but have no idea how much. Jane will have to know that Beth knows that. Roger will be oblivious, although there is yesterday – if he mentions that I came over, Jane will be pissed off that I left that out. Then it'll look like I have something to hide, although all I have to hide is that I felt I really needed to talk to Beth about that condom. I could tell Jane that, but that would be even more insulting given Jane had explained it. Then it's clear I don't trust her. The smallest omissions can cause the biggest problems.

"We're doing well." Beth opens her mouth but it's Roger who speaks. "We thought we'd have dinner out tonight. We don't do that enough. Do we, Beth?"

"No," Beth says.

"How about we join you?"

"They've finished, Roger," Beth says.

"We don't mean to be rude," Jane says, "but we were about to go."

"Oh, that's a shame," Roger says. "How about one last drink?"

Jane looks at me. I can't read what she's telling me. She doesn't like Roger. She doesn't really know Beth. So she has no tie to stay. I want to go, although now I'm concerned about Beth.

"Okay, one more drink," Jane says.

"I'll get it," I say, jumping to my feet. "Another wine?"

"Sure," Jane says.

"I'll come help you," Beth says. "Roger, Scotch?"

"Sure."

"Maybe you should grab some menus while we get the drinks," Beth says.

"Certainly," Roger says.

I exchange another look with Jane. She arches her brows. I shrug. Then I go to the bar to get the drinks.

Beth and I stand in line at the bar.

"I'm really sorry," she says. "I didn't mean for this to happen."

"It's okay."

I glance back at the table. A waiter – a young guy with a big white smile – clears Jane's and my dinner plates. Roger returns with two menus and sits down. He and Jane begin to talk. Jane laughs in a way I don't like – too delighted. Roger doesn't deserve such a response.

"It's not," Beth says. "I used you."

"What?"

"What'll you have, folks?" the bartender says.

We order – a red wine for Jane, a beer for Beth, a Scotch for Roger, and I have an iced water, since I'm pushing the limit and still need to drive. And draw. The bartender sets about getting our order.

"I wanted to get out and talk to Roger. You mentioned The Andion so it was the only place I could think of. I knew you'd be here but I shouldn't be intruding."

"It's okay."

"I panicked because I wanted to get out."

The bartender returns with our drinks. I hold out a twenty-dollar note, but it doesn't cover it. Beth reaches for her purse, but I grab another ten out of my pocket and pass it across to the bartender.

"Look, sorry, I shouldn't be bothering you this way," Beth says. "You and Jane finish your drinks and go."

"We can stay, if you want."

Roger says something. Jane lifts her head and laughs again. Roger pats her on the thigh, his hand there a moment longer than it should be – if it should be there at all. Jane brushes his hand aside abruptly. Roger continues speaking as Jane draws herself up.

I don't like the contact. It flares up the paranoia. Jane told me she gave Roger her card. Maybe he called her, they met, and something happened. Beth said Roger works late – maybe he's not working late some of those times. I hate the narrative unfolding in my head. Jane's never been late, although she does have the occasional girls' night. The insecurity grows. It's not just Roger, but the existence of possibilities.

"No," Beth says. "I really feel bad now. And I want to talk with Roger. That won't happen if you and Jane stay with us."

The bartender hands me my change. I stick it in my pocket without counting it. Then I grab my and Jane's drinks, while Beth grabs hers and Roger's.

"Have your drinks and go," Beth says. "I'll talk to you tomorrow."

"Sure?"

"Yeah."

"And …" I say as we start away, but then I pause.

"What?"

"Just, you know, last time you didn't show up to school."

I feel protective of her, and hate what Roger might do her – I'm already fearing he got physical with her in some way the last time. Beth admitted he gets *dominant*. Surely she wouldn't be with him if he beat her, but who knows? We all have our blind spots.

"I appreciate your concern," Beth says. "It'll be okay."

"If you're not at school tomorrow, I'm kicking down your door."

"Oh, really?"

Right now I would, because imagination doesn't need courage, but the thought of Roger hurting her does stir anger in me that I usually wouldn't express.

"I'll try," I say.

Beth leans into me like she might kiss me on the cheek, but then pulls back, perhaps thinking it'll be imprudent.

"I'll be okay," she says.

My fear that Roger will mention I dropped in to check on Beth is unnecessary since he can't stop talking about himself. He tells us about a civil suit he's leading against a drug manufacturer whose antidepressants have severe side effects in a number of users. He expresses no compassion – it's about the payout.

Then he segues onto Jane, saying he's still meaning to touch base with her about the possibility of a website dedicated to himself. When he questions Jane about what that would entail, he overdoes his curiosity as Jane talks about technical specs and quotes some prices. Occasionally, he reaches over and pats her hand.

I want to break my glass of iced water right over his head that he has the temerity to flirt with Jane right in front of me. Even Beth seems surprised, remarking several times that Roger should stop talking shop.

Given what Roger did the last time – at the Christmas party – maybe it isn't flirting, though. Well, not in his head. Maybe this is just who he is and how he communicates and he's oblivious to the effect it has on others.

Jane takes her last sip of wine. She's gone through it quickly. "We should really get going," she says, when Roger pauses long enough for her to get a word in.

"You sure you won't stay?" Roger says.

Jane gets up. "We both have early starts. Beth, Roger, it was great to see you. Maybe we can have dinner one night." The offer doesn't contain an iota of the sincerity it did when she suggested it to Luke.

Farewells are exchanged – Jane kisses Beth and Roger on the cheek, Roger giving her a sharp embrace; Beth kisses me on the cheek; Roger tries to break my hand this time with a tight handshake.

Then we can't leave quickly enough.

As I drive home, Jane is animated in the passenger seat, her seatbelt holding her together.

"What does she see in him?" she asks.

"I don't know."

"What did you talk about at the bar?"

"What?"

"You and Beth were talking at the bar. It seemed pretty deep. What were you talking about?"

"She said she'd come out to talk to Roger and apologized for intruding on us. I said it was okay and offered to stay – in case. She told me to have our drinks and go."

Jane runs a hand through her hair. Her eyes are fixed on me. My eyes are on the road.

"What do you mean 'in case'?" she asks.

"What?"

"You going deaf? You said you offered to stay in case. In case of what?"

"I don't trust him."

"What do you mean?"

"There's something … I don't know. It's like you said: he's cavalier …"

Jane waits for elaboration, turning to face me, her back against the passenger door.

I shrug. "Cruel, maybe."

"Did you see Beth's wrists?"

"Beth's wrists?"

"They're all bruised. I'm surprised you didn't notice them. She's done a good job of covering them with make-up, but you can still see the bruises."

I don't know why I don't admit I already know about the bruises. Maybe because it leads to another cover-up – that I chased Beth down at her house. I could've just told the truth, said I saw her wrists any time through school. That *was* the truth. But it's too late now.

"She was wearing a long-sleeved blouse," Jane says, "like she was hiding them."

"I didn't notice."

"You're hopeless." Jane slaps me on the arm.

"So you think he beat her?"

"I don't know. She wasn't moving like she was sore. It was just her wrists. Maybe she tried to get away and he grabbed her."

The allure of drawing Jane is gone – for tonight, anyway. Sitting with Roger has dampened the thrill. Then there's the thought of whatever he's done to poor Beth. I really think if she's not at school tomorrow I *will* go to her place and hammer the door down.

"Hey, I don't need a lift to work, by the way," Jane says.

"Why not?"

"Kai's going to pick me up."

"Why? I'll take you."

"I was thinking about it and what's the point? We have to get up earlier so you can drive me in half an hour before I start, then you have to go all the way back to school. Kai can get me on his way."

It's logical. But I don't like it. And I don't want to let it go.

"I thought you wanted me to take you," I say.

"And I did when it seemed to make sense. But after giving it a test run this morning, it doesn't."

"I should be taking you."

"What exactly is your problem here?"

"I'm your husband, I should be taking you if you need a lift."

"I really don't understand the issue here."

Because there was a condom in your handbag. I don't say it, although surely Jane's made the connection, unless she believes I accepted her explanation unconditionally. Of course, why wouldn't she? We're one happy family, me, her, and Wallace.

"Okay," I say.

"I thought this would be easier for both of us."

"Okay."

"We won't have to get up earlier."

"Okay."

"I thought I was helping you out, too."

"*Okay*, all right, fine. Wonder-Kai's getting you and dropping you off."

We pull into our street, and drive up to the house in silence. There's an unspoken expectation between us. We both want to unleash what's on our minds, although I recognize the irrationality of what I want to say. I don't know what Jane's exact words would be, but she'd want to drive her point home, even if it means repeating everything she's already said.

I turn into the drive, reverse onto the nature strip, and kill the engine. There's a flash of white and a thump at Jane's window. We both start. The thump again – it's Wallace, jumping at the car.

Jane opens the door and he hurtles onto her lap. She goes to pat him and he falls on his back so she can rub his belly.

"How did you get out?" Jane asks.

She lifts him like a baby and cradles him. He licks at her and she recoils. I put on the car's internal light and see that his nose is dirty.

"He's burrowed under the fence again," I say.

"Did you dig under the fence?" Jane coos.

"Great. Hope he hasn't done anything next door. As if Vic hasn't complained enough this week."

"You better check then." The flint is back in her tone.

"Fine," I say.

"Good," she says.

I get out of the car and choose not to respond to that.

17.

I begin at the hole Wallace dug on Sunday night, but that's still full, so I make my way down the fence, thinking it's funny how you can never tell what direction a day will take. Things hit a high point when Jane suggested she'd pose for me. It's Roger's fault. He put a downer on the night, although I guess even if Roger weren't around, I still would've got peeved at Jane revealing Kai's going to take her to work tomorrow.

About halfway down the fence, I feel a gap. I kick the dirt back into it, then stamp it down. Wallace will just dig it – or one of the other filled holes – back up. The dirt doesn't pack. I should take more permanent action. Jane's talked about starting a rose garden, so maybe that's something worth investigating.

Done, I go back in the house.

Jane's not downstairs. There's a light coming from the bedroom. Wallace is in the study, lying on the couch.

"No more with the holes, okay?" I tell him.

He sighs, puts his chin on his paws, and closes his eyes.

I rifle through Jane's handbag – for the hell of it – and find nothing. Then I check her phone where it's charging on the kitchen counter. That's clear, too. Satisfied, I trudge up the stairs, scowling at the trail of anniversary pictures, and our wedding picture. Those hopeful versions of us look toward a brighter future. Now all I can see is myself, worried about a condom.

Jane's in bed. "Sorry, I'm really tired," she says. "Early start. And I shouldn't have had that extra wine with Beth and Roger. Do you mind?"

"No," I say.

I undress, pausing as I yank off my cargo pants when I feel the bulge in the side pocket. It's the gift from Sunderland's. I check to see if Jane's looking, but she has her back to me. I take the gift out, and slip it into the top drawer of my bedside table.

Then I finish getting undressed and crawl into bed, my back to Jane.

THURSDAY

18.

The house is still when I wake. Jane breathes quietly next to me. A gust of wind blows outside. Spatter on the window – rain. What light comes in is gloomy. It's before dawn – how much, I don't know.

I could check the clock radio, but decide to lie there.

I think I stay awake, but must drift in and out of a light sleep until the clock radio goes off.

Jane rolls onto her side and slaps off the alarm. She sits up on the edge of the bed, and takes a deep breath. Her back arches. It's so smooth I want to run my finger down her spine to the crack of her butt peeking out above the top of her boxers. This is something I used to do unthinkingly. She would smile at me; sometimes we'd have sex – well, we used to; now it's more often than not a case of deferring to what the day expects of us.

She almost shoots from bed and into the bathroom. Her stretches are abrupt. She slides her boxers down her legs, steps out of them, and turns the faucets on in the shower. Steam fills the bathroom. She tests the water, casts a look over her shoulder, and catches my gaze. I close my eyes, although I don't know why. When I open them again, she's in the shower.

I push myself out of bed.

By the time I've finished my own shower, dressed, and gone into the kitchen, it's raining hard. I have to switch on the kitchen light it's so dark.

Wallace stands by the rear windows. He looks at me, lamenting what it's like outside. I fill his bowls, coax him to eat, and make breakfast.

The morning ritual is subdued. When Jane comes down, she picks up the coffee I've made for her and sips at it. I'm prepared to leave the dishes until I get home, like I always do, but realize that's a bad idea when Jane assumes her position by the sink and shoves the faucet on. She clatters through the washing.

"Did you find that hole last night?" she asks finally.

"Yeah. Filled it."

The doorbell rings. Wallace runs to the front door and barks at it. Jane finishes washing and shakes her hands dry over the sink. I watch, unsure how we'll part. She leans over the kitchen counter. We kiss without our lips ever touching the other's cheek.

"I'll see ya," I say.

"Bye."

Jane goes to the front door. "Sshhh, Wallace!" she says. "Quiet!"

She opens the door. I see a flash of Kai, still in black, hair still upstanding like he's had an electric shock. He grins at Jane, then greets her. I can't tell if Jane smiles at him, although I'm sure she must, and her response is effusive. She pushes open the security door, shoos Wallace back inside, closes the front door, and is gone.

Wallace runs up to the kitchen counter and looks at me. He's a creature of habit. He doesn't understand why the habit's changed.

I finish cleaning the dishes and go sit in the study.

I draw a line on the blank page in my sketchpad. Then another. Then another. Then another. I have a square. I dog-ear a corner. Draw a circle in the square. Then I rip out the sheet, scrunch it up, and throw it across the room.

Wallace pounces on it and tears it to shreds.

Good boy.

Pushing Wallace into the house, I slip out through the front. Locking the door, I turn to face the world through a curtain of rain.

Across the road, Josh and Karen scurry from their house, shielding their heads with their hands. Josh waves to me before they both slip into their car.

Tarika reverses out of her drive, Kirit and Pia in the back seat. I'm sure they wave, but it's too dark to know for sure. I wave anyway.

Chloe pulls up outside her house, and gets out of her car. She's dressed in her leotard, so must be back from yoga or Pilates or whatever it is she does. Unlike Josh and Karen, she might be oblivious to the rain, because she walks through it at a normal pace, not bothering to cover herself. Seeing me, she grins and waves.

I wave back, then step out into the rain. It hits me hard, splashes on my face, and drips down my collar. I should use my bag as a shield and run to my car. Instead I walk, and fumble with the keys. The door to Vic's garage slides open. His car reverses out, then screeches to a halt in the driveway. He pulls back up so he's adjacent to me. Rolls down his window.

"Hey, Gray, was your damned dog in my yard last night?" he says.

"I don't think so."

"I thought I saw him!"

Water runs through my hair, down my forehead, my cheeks and my neck. My jacket is soaked.

"I've warned you about him," Vic says.

"He's just a little dog."

"He's *your* little dog. Keep *your* little dog in *your* big backyard or we're gonna have a huge problem. I don't need him scaring my cat. You got it?"

Go fuck yourself.

"You got it?"

I open my door, and sink into my car. The rain's a drum roll vibrating all around me. Vic reverses onto the road so his car's parallel with mine. I can't see him with all the rain, but I can feel his eyes on me. Can almost imagine him shouting, *You got it?*

His car revs. Rear tires spin on the street and plume smoke.

He speeds off.

19.

At 8:42, I amble into the staff room – three minutes early for the staff meeting. The heating's on, so it's warm and toasty, although my clothes are damp. Stuart, seated on the other side of the staff room, gives me a thumbs up. I curl my lips – it's meant to be a smile but I don't know how it comes out. The other teachers sit or stand around me, chatting, the stench of their instant coffee pungent.

I scan the teachers, trying to find Beth, and just as I begin to grow anxious that she's not going to be here, she darts in, closing an umbrella and shaking it clear of water at the same time. She lays it against the wall by the door, then takes a seat next to me.

"Hey, how're you doing?" she asks, grabbing my wrist.

I'm not sure what to say to that.

"You okay?" she asks.

"Yeah."

"Sure?"

"I'm okay. You?"

"Good. Better than okay. *Great.*"

"Really?"

Beth nods. "I need to ask you another favor. Sorry – I've been such a burden on you this week."

"You're not a burden. And it makes me feel useful, I guess. What is it?"

Before she can tell me, Stuart calls us to attention. His big concern today is The Corner, and that kids have been "absconding" there. "Absconding" – that's how he puts it. He talks about how if that isn't worrying enough, he knows that teachers also go there to eat, but don't do anything about the kids they see, so it's up to us to not only be vigilant, but responsible.

The bell rings. I get up. This is the first morning meeting I've been to in a week, and it's hardly worth all the grief Stuart's put me through for missing the others.

"Can we talk during recess?" Beth says. "I have yard duty, although in this …" She gestures out the window.

"Sure," I say. "Is there anything for me to be worried about?"

"I'm leaving Roger."

"What?"

"We'll talk about it at recess." Beth laughs – a sound of genuine relief and delight. "It's okay. I'll tell you about it later."

"Okay."

"I need to get to class. But, Casper?"

"Yeah?"

"Thanks for being a friend."

She clasps my hand, then leaves the staff room.

In first period, I teach Humanities, but stumble through the lesson. Even the kids notice it, and they frown and whisper to one another – all but Maya, who sits in the front row and beams at me. It makes me all the more uncomfortable. The way she looks at me is the way you look at somebody who's infallible. If only she knew.

Next is Social Studies. Maya's in this class as well. But so are some of my regulars, like Justine, Dom, and Bianca.

I look at Bianca a lot. My manic thoughts fluctuate from Jane and all the horrid possibilities that have preoccupied me all week, sidestep Beth's declaration to leave Roger, and fix on Bianca, and whether she had interaction with Jean Jacket yesterday.

When the bell goes, I ask Bianca to stay back a moment. The other kids storm out. Justine and Dom go more slowly, but end up standing outside the door, peering through the window while Bianca shifts in front of me from one foot to the other, head bowed.

"What is it, Mr. Gray?" she asks.

"I don't know how to broach this exactly, Bianca," I say, "and it's not entirely my business because it wasn't during school hours or on school premises ..." It's the lamest start I could've made. I've disarmed any authority I might've had – that I *should've* had. "I saw you yesterday," I say.

Bianca looks up. Her eyes are dark. As are the shadows.

"Walking away from that guy with the jean jacket – that guy who's always at The Corner. You know the one?"

Bianca nods.

"I don't know the exact details, but he's not somebody you want to be dealing with."

Bianca says nothing. I've handled this terribly, confronting her with little information. I should've bluffed, told her I'd seen her with Jean Jacket, and awaited her explanation. That's how Stuart would've done it, although I'm unsure I should be aspiring to behave like Stuart.

"Well, Bianca?"

"I wasn't dealing with him."

"Is that the truth?"

Bianca's jaws clench. I've seen this reaction before – kids trying to work out whether to go with the truth or a lie.

"It is," she says.

I'm sure she's lying, but I don't know where to take this. "Bianca, I don't want to be the bad guy. I just want to know you're okay. We can talk here, or we could talk to Stuart – to Mr. Piper – who'll probably want to talk to your parents."

Bianca takes a deep breath. "He flirts with me, Mr. Gray. 'Nice smile,' he says. 'Killer legs.' Or, 'How about a date?' He's not serious. He's just teasing."

It's the truth – I'm sure of it; just as I'm sure it's only *some* of it.

"Mr. Piper doesn't want kids going to The Corner at all," I say. "I know it was after school, but he'll still think that's in his jurisdiction."

Bianca's head twists one way, body the other, then back again. She doesn't want to meet my eye. I should report what I saw. It's the responsible thing to do. But I don't want to be Stuart. I don't want to be anal. My relationship with the kids has existed in this easy rapport. If I assert myself like Stuart would, I lose that. But maybe this should be about being grown up. I've hardly handled Jane with maturity.

"It's okay, Mr. Gray. He's no different to the boys around here, like Anthony or Eric. I know they're always leering at me. I can handle them. And him."

"Stay away from him, please, Bianca. Give him a wide berth."

"I will, Mr. Gray. Can I go?"

I nod.

She leaves the classroom. Justine and Dom huddle around her. They disappear from my sight, but she's probably telling them everything I've said.

I hope I haven't made a mistake. I should've reported what happened – and still could, but it seems such an overreaction. Bianca can handle Jean Jacket with an aplomb I can't even imagine in myself. Maybe it's not her who needs the help.

It's still raining, so what kids are outside crowd into the locker room, in the toilets, or under anything that gives them cover. It means Beth's job performing yard duty is easy. When I find her, she's standing outside the canteen intersecting the two main buildings.

"Hey, I was wondering where you'd got to," she says.

"I had to talk to Bianca."

"Everything okay?"

"Uh huh. What's up? You're leaving Roger?"

"Yep."

"On Monday, you wanted to take the relationship to the next level. Now you're ending it?"

"Things will never get better than they are with Roger now. He wants what he wants. He can humor me otherwise, but that's all it is. And I'm sick of playing his games."

"His games?" I think of Beth in the reflection of the mirror, lying on the bed; of the buzzing I heard.

"Every relationship has games – how affectionate you are, what you put in, what you expect back, all the parameters that define it, and all the things you do to get what you want. Sometimes, couples mesh, like you and Jane seem to."

Seem to.

"That's when a relationship's selfless. But other times there's an unhealthy co-dependency. I like to think I'm selfless with Roger, but he's not with me. And he's not going to change. So that's it. This is why I want your help. I want to pack my stuff after work and go. Would you come with me in case Roger comes home?"

"You haven't told him, have you?"

"I don't want to engage in some protracted discussion with Roger. He said he wouldn't finish tonight until seven or so. So I can pack up after school and be out before he's home. But will you come in case? Sorry. That sounds ominous. I don't think he'll cause a scene if there's somebody else with me. And there's been enough scenes this week – I want a clean break and to move on."

"Where will you go?" I ask. "We have a spare room made up."

"That's kind. But I'm going to stay with my mom for a while. Then I'll look at getting my own place. So will you?"

"Sure," I say. "We have a staff meeting after school, though."

"Shit. Forgot about that. Well, we can go afterwards. We should still have plenty of time."

"Okay. I don't know how much help I'll be."

"You'll be a help just being there," Beth says.

She wants the chaperone, like I can be some knight. It's exciting, in its way, but I know my imagination and reality don't reconcile.

Hopefully, Roger won't come home.

Third period is Literature. I give the kids some reading to do, then text Jane:

> Beth's leaving Roger. Wants me to
> help her move her stuff out while he's
> at work.

I put the phone on my desk. It chimes not long after. I apologize to the kids and tell them to get back to their work. Switching my phone to silent, I check Jane's answer:

> Tell her she can use our spare room, if
> she wants.

I send back:

> Already suggested it. She's staying
> with her mom.

Jane answers not long after, the phone now vibrating noiselessly in my hands:

> Okay. Leave the offer open with her.

Jane's happy for me to help Beth and for her to even stay with us, but I can't cope with Kai giving Jane a lift.

I shove the phone in my pocket.

By lunchtime, the rain's stopped and it's grown overcast, which means the kids are out with abandon and I have the whole school to patrol again. After the uncertainty of the morning, everything's falling back into place. There's a sense to the world, or at least to *my* world, and how I'm meant to function in it.

I think I'm coming to peace with Jane; Beth's taking action about Roger – even if it's not the action she originally wanted, it's letting her move on; Stuart's off my back; I've dealt with Bianca and her interaction with Jean Jacket.

I can do anything.

Kids are crowded in the locker room. I hear the whisper of "teacher". I smell the rich fragrance from vapes, and an undercurrent of cigarette smoke as I go through the entry way. The kids hush. I can see some of the older kids standing conspicuously at the rear, hands behind their backs.

"Doubtful anything I say is going to stop you vaping or smoking," I say. "Just don't do it here."

Some of the kids cheer me as I leave because I *am* like a pal. That makes me think I've done the wrong thing. I should be sending the *right* message to them – that's what school's for: to establish standards. But maybe there's something to not being arbitrary, to letting the kids know that not every adult needs to be some draconian authority figure. Well, that's how I rationalize it.

I head out the back where there are kids milling around. They filter past in their own individual slipstreams. I hear snippets of conversation. Some greet me. I smile and nod. Then I pause, enjoying their presence. Sometimes – inevitably *always* in the classroom – they'll swell to a cacophony. But outside, where they're happy, where they're unencumbered, the noise is different. It's free and alive. It's something you lose as you grow older, as everyday life cages you in.

A drop hits me on the ear. Then another. It's an indecisive spatter, as if the rain can't decide whether to make a comeback or not. It's enough for the kids, who retreat to cover. I look into the gray sky. It's amazing weather after the week of heat, although the humidity remains thick and uncomfortably sticky.

It occurs to me I look odd standing here, so I resume my yard duty, heading back the way I came. I round one of the main buildings, see the entrance to the locker room ahead, then decide to go have a look behind the lockers. Sometimes, when the kids have been reprimanded for smoking in the locker room, they'll go out and smoke behind it.

The concrete finish of the courtyards doesn't follow the locker rooms all the way around. Instead, it's all grass. My feet get wet. I consider not bothering, but hear sounds – something muffled. The rain grows a little harder.

I round the locker room and see two students grappling, kissing. The guy has his hands in the girl's skirt, one hand into her underwear and onto her buttock.

My first thought is that it's David and Deidre, who've become the item of the week, and who I've already seen in the locker room twice this week – the second time when I was with Stuart. But then the girl lifts her head – so the guy can kiss her neck – and she sees me.

Justine.

She gasps, pushes the guy away, and smooths out her skirt. The guy – none other than Dom – is confused initially. Then he sees me. He smiles shyly, runs a hand through his hair. Justine bows her head, her face ripe with embarrassment.

"Mr. Gray …" Dom says, but for once there's nothing else.

"It's starting to rain," I say. "You two better get under cover and not get caught out here again."

"Thanks, Mr. Gray." Dom rockets past me.

"Thanks." Justine can barely be heard as she follows Dom.

Justine and Dom – that wasn't a pairing I saw coming. I would've thought Dom and Bianca were likelier, although I never actually expected *any* pairing from that trio.

The rain starts to pound.

After the staff meeting, Beth and I hurry into the parking lot. She bounces as she walks. I'm amazed that the man she wanted to get serious with has been such a weight on her. Now that she's freeing herself from him, the change is extraordinary. What would've happened had her solicitation forced Roger to advance the relationship? How long would they have lived that lie? And would they have even known it was a lie?

"I'll meet you at my place," she says when I walk her to her car.

"Okay."

I walk over to my car and get in. My heart's sped up. It's not excitement. I'm nervous about seeing Roger. But Beth needs me.

My phone buzzes. It's Jane:

Helping Beth?

I write back:

On my way.

I put my phone down in the change compartment, start my car, and drive out of the parking lot.

20.

Beth unlocks the front door to her house. I half expect Roger to be there, lurking at the bottom of the hall. Nothing but silence. I follow Beth in. She heads straight to the bedroom. I stand in the doorway and lean on the jamb. The house is pregnant with threat.

Antique stuff fills the bedroom. The king-size bed has ornate bedposts, a yellow scarf wrapped around the right one. A big mirror with baroque gold trim hangs on the wall and in the corner sits a hulking armoire with intricate patterns inscribed across the doors. Whose taste is this? Beth's? Roger's? Or both? I decide it must be Roger's – ostentatious.

Beth steps into the walk-in robe in the corner of the room and emerges with a bag. She opens drawers and stuffs clothes into the bag until it's bulging. Then she disappears back into the walk-in. I hear her at work, but don't know what she's doing.

"Casper?"

I join her in the walk-in robe. She's filling a suitcase with dresses and other outfits that hang from a clothes rail. Underneath them are several pairs of shoes. From another rack hang Roger's suits, an array of uniformity. He has more shoes than Beth.

It takes Beth a while to fill the suitcase, even if she just folds and drops everything in. When she's done, she closes it but the seams of the zip don't meet. She sits on top, but to no avail. I sit on top of it with her. She laughs. We could be kids sneaking a smoke, or about to make out in secret, like Dom and Justine.

She yanks the zip on one end and I pull from the other end. I get my side going first, dragging it over seams that don't want to knit, and meet Beth past halfway. She clasps my hand and smiles at me.

"Can you take this and my other bag out to my car?" she says.

"Sure."

I heave the suitcase up, carry it from the walk-in robe, and grab her other bag on the way out. My progress is slow. The suitcase keeps threatening to topple me over, and I'm worried the zipper will split. It's even harder going down the stairs. The rain's not letting up.

About halfway down I skid on the step and fall back. The suitcase slips from my grasp and bounces down the stairs. I cringe, expecting the case to burst. But it hits the bottom and is still. I hoist the bag over my shoulder, hurry down, and pick up the suitcase. It's scratched and the corners are scuffed, but it's otherwise fine.

A car slows in front of the house. I look up sharply. But it's not Roger. The car drives on.

I get to Beth's car, open the front door, and find the lever for the boot. I pull it open. Then, two-handed, haul the suitcase into the boot, followed by the bag.

Done.

I return to the house. Beth's filling two other bags with clothes and toiletries, and a box containing some books, her hair dryer, and a little ceramic elephant. I keep standing in the doorway but really want to get out of here. I'm sure at any moment Roger will return.

"I sorta dropped your suitcase down the stairs," I say.

"Clothes don't break," Beth says.

"The suitcase got a bit banged up."

"That's fine. It's his."

I incessantly check the time on my phone. At one point, Jane texts and asks how we're going. I tell her we're almost done. But it hardly seems that way. Beth often disappears into some part of the house and returns with something else to pack. Some of these things don't seem important. One time she brings back a spatula. Another time, a box of incense sticks. I wonder if she wants us to get caught so we can have a confrontation with Roger. And then, sure enough …

Beth perks her head up. "Is that a car?" She frowns at me. "Can you check?"

I can't hear anything, but retreat from the doorway. Stop just a few steps down the hallway. Listen. No. I can't hear a car – can't hear an engine, or a front door opening and closing. And I can see the back of my car in the drive from here – Roger would have to park behind me. Beth must be imagining it. I pivot, make my way back to the bedroom doorway.

And stop.

Beth's placing something on one of the bedroom pillows – the sight of the object shocks me initially, because it's so hard to reconcile. But then I'm sure: it's a lavender dildo. Or a vibrator. Not that I have experience distinguishing either. But I see her depress something on the base and hear it whir.

Then, as Beth turns, I step back, and by the time she makes her way out of the bedroom, I'm sure she must think I'm on my way back from the front door.

"See anything?" she asks.

I shake my head.

"Hang on – just one more thing …"

She ducks through an archway into the living room, and comes back with a box full of knickknacks, a worn oven mitt the crowning glory.

She nods with satisfaction. "I think that's it," she says.

I look at the two bags and the box. Like the suitcase and bag before them, they're overflowing. "You sure?"

"Yep," Beth says.

I pick up the two bags. She holds onto the box.

"I feel like I'm robbing my own place," she says as we head for the front door.

"You going to leave a note?"

"I think the absence of my clothes and other stuff will tell him what's happened."

As well as the vibrator, I think.

We exit the house. Beth takes two keys from her key ring and throws them into the hallway; they skitter across the hardwood floor. She grabs the front door.

"Wait!" I say.

She halts in the process of slamming the door.

"You're sure you got everything?"

"I've got everything I need."

"You *are* sure?"

"Maybe after all the dust settles I can get the rest, but right now, I've got all I need. Life's not about *things* anyway."

She slams the door.

I help Beth pack the rest of her stuff in her car. Some of it is stuffed in the boot, some on the back seat, and some in the passenger seat. The car itself has now become the most untidily packed container. It's the strangest, most surreal sum of a life, although I don't say that to Beth.

When we're done, she throws her arms around me. She fits differently into my body, her face up on my shoulder, not on my collarbone. Her breasts are larger against me. This feels inappropriate, like it's more than a hug a friend would give. But maybe I'm imagining it, or just paranoid, because of what I've been going through.

"Thank you," she says.

And then it's uncomfortable silence because this embrace feels like something more than a quick comforting hug. I feel not only protective of her, and worry for her, but there's also a closeness that now becomes evident – something that has trickled beyond our friendship. Maybe she feels it, too. This might just be how easily things get started.

Her phone rings. She breaks the hug, pulls her phone out of her pocket, and rolls her eyes. "Roger," she says. She declines the call and shoves the phone back in her pocket. "That was then. This is now." She smiles at me. "Thanks, Casper. Not just for today. But for everything."

"Any time."

"If you ever need anything, feel free to call me, okay?"

"Sure."

She clasps my hand. "I mean it."

"Thanks."

She kisses me on the cheek, then gets in her car. I close the door.

"See you at school tomorrow, huh?" she asks.

"Sure."

I get into my car.

On the drive home I pass a florist. Flowers would be good, given the mess with Jane last night, and how understanding she's been about Beth. I watch the florist disappear in the rear-view mirror. No, I should do this.

I make a U-turn, and drive back to the florist to buy a bouquet of red roses. They sit on the passenger seat on the drive home, their fragrance filling my dingy little car, and convincing me that things are going to be okay.

21.

It's about 7:00pm when I pull onto my nature strip. The neighborhood's quiet. Everybody might've packed up and gone.

Grabbing my roses, I walk up to the house, and reach for the security door. Wallace barks with anticipation from inside. I open the front door to Wallace jumping at me. I scoop him up in one arm and scratch his chest while he tries to lick me. His little paws are cold against my skin.

He starts squirming, wriggling free from my grip, and the moment he lands on the floor he's springing away to dash to the entrance of the dining room. Spinning – his ears perked, his little tail bouncing – he looks at me expectantly. He's telling me where Jane is. Or telling Jane I'm here. He barks once. Then his jaw hangs open, making it look like he's grinning.

I drop my bag in the study, walk into the dining room and stop.

Jane lies on the couch naked, watching TV. My bathrobe lies on the armrest. On the coffee table are two plates. One has a half-eaten tuna sandwich. On the other plate is a ham, cheese, and lettuce sandwich. Resting by it is my sketchpad. One of the kitchen chairs awaits in front of the coffee table.

Wallace hurtles up onto the couch, sits by Jane's belly, and looks at me, his tongue out.

Jane's face softens at the sight of the flowers, and she begins to get up, but then stops herself. "Well?" she says.

I put the flowers in a vase, place them on the coffee table, then proceed to pose Jane, getting her to lie on her right side, her right elbow planted on the couch, the side of her face resting on her palm. I move her left arm so that her hand covers her crotch and reposition her left leg so it's cocked over her right leg, accentuating the arch of her hip.

Wallace, meanwhile, remains seated where he was. That's okay. I can draw around him. Or maybe even draw him.

"Good?" she asks.

I don't know if it is. I'm sure there needs to be much more thought put into this – the aesthetics of the angles, the lighting in the room, and even my own position, but I want to get underway.

Grabbing a beer from the fridge, I open it, leave it on the corner of the coffee table, then sit on the kitchen chair. I pick up my sketchpad, flip it open, and try to digest every detail of Jane.

I've seen her every day for the last eight years, I've lusted after her, I've loved her, I've supported and cared for her, I've fought with her, and, at times, I've even been bored by her, but now I want to deify her.

I put pencil to paper.

"Thanks for the flowers," Jane says as I draw.

"You're welcome. I'm sorry."

"About?"

"Last night."

"It's okay."

I smile.

"What happened with Beth?" Jane asks.

I tell her about getting Beth's things from her house, about the nervousness of expecting Roger to come home at any minute.

"Beth looked like she didn't care in the slightest," I tell Jane.

"What did you expect?"

"I would've thought she'd mourn the relationship – regardless of what's happened to it. She was like, I don't know, gleeful."

"What do you think happened between them?"

"When?"

"Whenever she got the marks on her wrists."

"I don't know," I say, although I think about visiting her, of the way she got up gingerly, of the whirring sound, and the vibrator she placed on the pillow. It's all so irreconcilable.

"She might've wanted to get serious with him," Jane goes on, "thought he was the one, then he did whatever to bruise her wrists like that, and she realized he wasn't. You should give her credit."

I pause only long enough to take the smallest sip from my beer. Wallace, who's been sleeping with his chin on his paws, rolls onto his side.

"A lot of people will kid themselves and keep going back to something that isn't right," Jane says. "They'll tell themselves it's okay or it'll change. Like battered wives who go back to abusive husbands. Beth's realized this relationship is no longer for her."

"So, if I did something to you that you didn't like, would you leave me and be happy about it?"

"I think we know pretty much everything there is to know about one another."

"What about this?"

"What?"

"You. Lying naked on a couch. Posing."

Jane looks like she wants to shoot me down and continue championing her point, but she has nothing to say.

"I never would've expected this from you," I say.

"Okay. But we're married."

"How's that different?"

"I guess I feel safe with you, so I can push those boundaries."

"I don't know if that's any different."

"Couples explore boundaries. Especially after they've been together a while."

My pencil stops. My face remains bent toward my sketchpad, but my eyes lift up toward Jane.

"So, we're … what? Stale? Experimenting?"

"I didn't mean it like that," Jane says. "We *know* each other. But it's still nice to surprise one another. Don't you say it to me all the time? 'Surprise me'. Here you go – you were surprised. But I bet Roger broke some boundary. He seems that sort of person."

I can't argue with that.

"You should eat your sandwich."

I sip my beer. Keep sketching.

"How long will this take?"

I shrug.

"Don't you have any idea?"

"You're only the second naked woman I've drawn."

Jane looks at me sharply. "What?"

"Oh, sorry – I've said too much."

She laughs. I smirk, and pick up my beer. We've fallen back into the rhythm of our relationship with that steadiness and familiarity that we've forged over time, and everything seems right again – until a thumping at the front door interrupts us. Wallace immediately sails from the couch and runs out, barking. Jane and I lock eyes. The thumping continues. Jane sits up.

"What the …?" She slips on my bathrobe.

I get up and go out into the hallway. Wallace barks at the front door. I pull the curtains aside from the windows enough to peek out. It's Roger. He has the security door open and is about to hammer the front door again. But then he sees me.

I pick up Wallace. He wriggles in my arms. His tail hammers my chest. Then I realize it's not his tail but my heartbeat. I unlock the door, but the moment I open it an inch, Roger shoves through.

"Where is she?" He storms into the house, peers into the study, then looks up the stairwell. "Where is she? Beth!"

"Wait a minute—"

Roger strides into the dining room. I chase after him. Jane's sitting on the couch in my bathrobe. When Roger barges in, she jumps up. For a moment, her leg's exposed right up to her hip and I think – or maybe I imagine – there's a glimpse of pubic hair. Then the robe swallows up her legs. But I'm sure Roger has seen her because he looks longer than he should.

"Tell me where she is!"

Roger sways back and forth, taking everything in. Wallace keeps barking. He writhes so hard in my hands that I have trouble holding him.

"She's not here!" Jane says.

"I've seen the way you look at her!" Roger says.

"What?" I say.

"You want her, don't you, you bastard? You talked her into leaving me!"

"Maybe she left because of the way you treated her!" Jane says.

"What the fuck are you on about?"

"We saw her wrists! What did you do to her?"

Roger pauses just long enough to show he's surprised, but then he blusters on. "Whatever happened between us was consensual. Now tell me where she is!"

Jane grabs her phone from the kitchen counter. "Get out or I'm calling the cops," she says.

Roger storms up to me. Wallace snarls and barks. Roger points a finger at me. Wallace tries to snap it off – and would've, but I jerk him back. I have to give Wallace credit – Roger's size means nothing to him.

"I know what you did."

I shake my head. "What did I do?"

Roger keeps pointing.

"Go! Okay?" Jane says. She hits three keys on her phone. I can hear it. *Beep-beep-beep* – emergency.

Roger leaves the dining room. I follow him to the front door.

"You're a cunt, mate, you know that?" he says to me. "A cunt."

He stomps out, smashes the security door open. I close the front door, then think twice. I open it, lock the security door, and close and lock the front door.

Wallace struggles in my arms. I lower him. He jumps before I reach the floor and hits the ground running. He barks at the front door, runs some circles, then barks some more.

"Wallace," I say, but there's no conviction in my voice.

He runs up the hallway, through the dining room and, moments later, I hear the doggy door thump. As I re-enter the dining room, I see him running back and forth across the backyard, then around the side of the house, barking. He's on patrol, as always, checking that the threat's gone.

Good luck to him.

I sit on the couch. Jane, still in my robe, sits next to me. She draws her knees up to her chest. I have the smallest tremor in my arms and can't settle it. I hope Jane doesn't feel it. I pick up my beer and take a big swig. Wallace has stopped barking outside, but he's still whizzing around.

"I didn't expect that," Jane says.

I'm about to agree that I didn't either, but then realize that Roger's such a self-absorbed boor, his response actually isn't that surprising.

"I'd have thought Roger would shrug off a break-up like he didn't care."

I finish my beer, but fear there'll be more thumping at my door. Jane rubs my arm. She *knows* how scared I am. Fuck. It's she – and Wallace – who chased Roger out.

"So you have a thing for Beth?"

I spin my head to Jane.

"Roger said you wanted her."

I don't know what to say. But Jane breaks out that crooked grin. She rubs my arm again, rests her head on my shoulder.

"I'm kidding," she says. "I know he was mouthing off."

"We're friends obviously at school."

"I know."

"But that's it."

"Casper, you don't have to defend yourself."

"And I didn't do anything to them. I really didn't."

"I know."

"She talked to me on Monday, about wanting to get serious with Roger."

"You told me."

"That was it."

Jane takes the empty beer bottle from my hand and puts it on the table. Then she straddles me. Her nose tickles my cheek. Her eyelashes flutter across my forehead. She bookends my face in her hands, and kisses me. The tip of her tongue traces my lower lip.

"It's okay," she says.

I hope she doesn't know how Roger's made me feel. But of course she knows – after all our time together, she knows my secrets. She knows my meekness. She knows who I am. I wish I could be somebody else for her. I don't even know how I've become this.

"It's okay," she whispers.

I lower my face, almost ashamed to look at her. She kisses me slowly, her tongue parting my lips. I still don't want to look up, but she continues to kiss me. Her hands frame my face. She wants to reassure me – it's what you'd expect from any partner, but in this moment, trembling and afraid, it's humiliating. The self-loathing burns through me. I want to take command. Want to be assertive. Want to be strong. I slide my hands down her thighs, under her buttocks and hoist myself from the couch. Jane shrieks. Her legs lock around my thighs, her arms around my neck.

"What're you doing?" she says.

I thrust my mouth onto hers until she's recoiling. I bite her lower lip, and tug at it between my teeth. She raises her head. I kiss her jaw, her neck. The robe slips down her right shoulder. I run kisses down her collarbone, bite her right shoulder. She pulls away from me, although not in fear or defensiveness, but to bare herself to me – to offer her own vulnerability.

Desperation fuels me – desperation and fear that I'm losing her without even knowing it, that I'm unraveling in the chaos unfolding around me, so I hold her tighter than I should, kiss her harder than I should, want her with an overriding passion, if not lust, like I can brand my claim on her, or override any doubts she might have through the sheer power of my desire.

I plant her on the kitchen counter where I plant her coffee every morning and pull the belt of the bathrobe hard so it unfurls from the belt loops. The bathrobe opens like curtains, unveiling her breasts. I throw the belt aside.

"Hey—"

I kiss her and her protest explodes into a gasp of breath. She throws her head back and I kiss her neck, drawing the robe down her arms. Leaning back against the counter, her breasts stand pointed, her areolae swollen, her nipples stiff. Her fingernails dig into my back.

I take her left breast in my mouth, and tug at her nipple between my teeth until she hisses. I release it, swirl my tongue around the nipple. My hand cups her other breast. Squeezes. I kiss her cleavage, her belly, outline kisses around her small pubic triangle. She slides back onto the counter and wraps my head in her hands. I grab her thighs. She lifts her right leg onto my shoulder. My tongue penetrates her. She gasps. Her back arches. Her crotch thrusts into me. She pushes my head down. I drive my tongue onto her clit. Her moan fills the kitchen; her right leg presses into my back.

I drive my tongue back and forth on her clit – her gasps accompanying my rhythm – as I unbuckle and unzip my jeans and push them and my underwear down my knees. This is not me. Even at my most passionate, I'm still measured, yet my neediness now is desperate.

My cock unfurls in front of me. I'm so hard I worry I'll pop straight away. Rising onto my tiptoes, I guide – if fumbling is commensurate with guiding – myself into Jane. I hold myself still, my hands gripping her hips, still worried about exploding prematurely. Then I build my rhythm, although there are times I stutter and slip out of her. The counter's a bit too high for me.

I pick her up. The bathrobe unwinds behind her like a cape. Her legs tighten around my hips and she draws up to kiss me. I spin on the spot and lower her onto the carpet, using my shoulders to push her legs back high and wide. My knees skid across the carpet as I struggle for purchase.

Again, I thrust into her, but now it's slow, and I almost slip out. She moans in my ear, and one hand clasps the back of my head. I continue at the same pace, although it has less to do with technique and more to do with getting comfortable in the position. My thrusts grow harder, faster. The carpet burns my knees. I feel my forehead strain, sweat running down my temples.

My eyes fix on her, the way her breasts bounce, the way her body shimmies. Her moans elongate into a wail.

My teeth grind and eyes clench as I explode. My next thrusts slam into her, then I slow, each thrust growing progressively tamer. I collapse on top of her. Kiss her. She exhales into my mouth, tasting of her tuna sandwich, and kisses me. I slide off her and let her curl into me. I close my eyes, trying to catch my breath. A presence surfaces behind my head. I open my eyes to see Wallace, his head tilted, his tail shaking, as if he's trying to work out whether we're okay. Jane lifts her head, smiles at him, then laughs.

She kisses me again, rests her head back on my shoulder, and puts her left hand on my chest.

I drape the robe over us as Jane cuddles into me, her fingers twirling in my chest hair, her breath warm on my neck. Outside it's dark, although it probably isn't much past 8:30pm.

"Where did that come from?" Jane asks.

I don't say anything, and think about the way I capitulate to Vic, to Jean Jacket, to the kids at school, and now to Roger. I hate it. *Hate* it. But I'm growing to hate myself more.

"You okay?" Jane asks.

"I don't like …"

Jane scrambles up onto me, folds her arms across my chest, and dabs my chin with her index finger. "What?" Her mouth teases a wry grin. "What're you thinking?"

"Sometimes, I don't like …"

"What?"

I look away.

"Talk to me."

"Sometimes, I don't like the way I handle things … Like tonight."

Jane ruffles my chest hair, the way she might ruffle the fur of Wallace's head when he's been a good boy. "It's okay."

I'm unconvinced. She kisses my chin.

"I wasn't always like this," I say. "I …"

"What?"

I don't know when to trace it back to – Mom's death, and living in the silence of the aftermath, cowering in my room, drawing because there was nothing else anymore? Was that it? The transition was so gradual it occurred unmarked and I never knew I'd changed until long, long after, when I recognized my new normal as something differently entirely.

"It *is* okay," Jane says.

She kisses me on the lips. I hold her tight and appreciate her efforts, but I can't convince myself she's right.

FRIDAY

22.

The alarm buzzes. Jane slaps a hand onto it. Sits up in bed. She yawns and stretches, back arching. I flip onto my side and run a finger down her spine to the crack of her buttocks. She smiles at me. Yawns again.

"I'm so tired," she says, rising, then teetering.

"You okay?" I say.

"Yeah."

She stumbles into the bathroom, flips on the shower, forgets her stretches, and enters the cubicle, standing there with her face upturned as water sprays her. I contemplate following her.

Rapid little footsteps distract me. Wallace jumps onto the bed and licks my face. I pat his head. He rolls onto his back. I scratch his belly. Our transactions are so simple yet rewarding. His eyes shut and his mouth curls into that ecstatic grin.

"Come on," I say.

When I get down to the kitchen, I see through our rear windows it's gray outside. It'll probably be another day of sticky humidity and rain. I also see Vic's cat Silver strolling across the backyard.

"Wallace, look!" I say, and point to the window.

Wallace beams at me.

"Look!" I point again.

He stares at me, unsure what I want.

I scoop him up and carry him to the rear windows, pointing like he's a child I'm trying to show something to at the zoo.

"Look! Look!"

He finally sees Silver and squirms in my hands. I lower him and he hits the ground running, bolting for the back door. He blurs into the backyard, feet barely touching the ground. I can still hear the doggy door rocking.

Silver's head spins. He shoots off, hitting the fence midway up and scaling it. He balances on the top, hisses at Wallace, leaps from the fence and disappears.

Wallace runs around the yard barking, then performs his check of the entire property to make sure Silver is gone. He sniffs at the Guptas' fence, then at the fence that separates us from Vic's house. When he sniffs at holes I've filled, I'm worried he might dig his way through so he can search for Silver. But, as if satisfied, he comes back toward the back door. I'm sure I don't imagine that his chest is puffed out.

Moments later, he's inside. He stands before me, head tilted.

Job's all done, boss.

I fill his bowls and give him a treat, too.

The morning unwinds like every other morning. I shower, dress, make breakfast. Jane comes down about fifteen minutes later and picks up her coffee. She looks amazing: her slacks tight around her hips, her buttoned blazer like it might burst. Or at least I imagine it could. She's pulled her hair back into a topknot ponytail.

I decide it's actually not like every other morning, not least of all because I have an erection again. I move around to Jane, and run one hand down her hip.

"What're you doing?" she asks.

I press my crotch against her so she can feel my intentions through my jeans.

"Oh."

I kiss her neck. My other hand slides in between the buttons of her shirt.

"I can't," she says.

"Why?"

"Work."

"So?" I run my hand down from her hip to her crotch.

"I've just showered and dressed."

"*So?*"

I kiss her. She's hot against me. I want to tear her clothes off, although I've never done such a thing. We've undressed quickly and clumsily, but you never read about clumsiness in romance.

"There's no time," she says.

"I'll only be, like, two minutes."

She laughs. "There's no time for me to shower and get ready again."

"Stop being such a wimp."

"Wimp?" Her brows arch.

"Yeah."

She kisses me, cups my crotch, then yanks my zip down. "Who are you calling a wimp?"

Before I can answer, the doorbell rings.

"It's Kai," Jane says.

I check my phone. Kai's early – seven minutes early. I tell Jane.

"It's a lift," she says.

"Tell him to go and I can take you to work."

"You'll be late. Especially if we keep going." Jane pecks me on the lips. "I should go." She cups my crotch. "But to be continued."

The doorbell rings again. Jane picks up her case.

"Don't forget Sarah and dinner tonight," Jane says as she backs toward the hallway.

"Oh, the joy."

Jane darts back and kisses me. "Come get me at work about six?"

"Okay."

She kisses me one last time as the doorbell rings again.

"Love you. Bye."

"Bye," I say.

She heads for the front door.

Sitting down on the couch, I pick up my sketchpad, and open it to my portrait of Jane. She's an outline and some features that hint at something tawdry. If the kids from school saw this picture they'd think it lewd enough to comment on. But I haven't yet captured any of the nuances which'll breathe life into the picture – *if* I can breathe life into it.

I imagine the strokes of my pencil, see the result as something Elizabethan, like Jane's some tortured heroine. I'm unsure why *that* image comes to mind. I don't have any particular interest in that style, although Jane does read the occasional Gothic romance novel.

But it's the first time I see the complete picture in my head. Usually, I discover it as I'm drawing. Now I can't avert my eyes. I should've kept her here, should've ravaged her, as cliché as that sounds. Well, maybe after this stupid dinner with Sarah and her latest.

I close the sketchpad.

Tonight awaits.

It's murky outside, and none of the other neighbors are around. I pull out my phone and check the time: 8:42. I'm running late. Everybody's already underway.

I hurry to my car.

23.

It's 8:54 by the time I stride into the staff room. I dread Stuart's reaction, but the usual morning hubbub greets me. Jerry Logan raves about the fishing he'll do this weekend. Max Loughlin talks about the game he's going to see tonight. Ed Welling studies the financial section in the paper as Olivia Harding gushes about the art show she's attending on Sunday. Beth listens to Stan Doyle who sits, shoulders slumped, whining about the disaster that is his life. Other teachers are engaged in their little cliques. The chorus of chatter is warm – workmates sharing their lives with one another. It seems so different a dynamic from usual for this time of the morning. That's when I realize the obvious: Stuart's nowhere to be seen.

Beth notices me standing in the doorway. She excuses herself from Stan – whose shoulders slump further – and ushers me out into the hallway. Kids scurry past. I see Maya. She fixes her eyes on me from the moment she approaches to the moment she passes and it becomes physically impossible for her to keep looking at me.

"Hey, I'm sorry about last night," Beth says.

"Last night?"

"Roger came around to your place, didn't he?"

"How did you know?"

"He came to my mother's."

"And?"

"We argued."

"That's it?"

"There's a bit more to it. The argument got pretty heated. But the upshot is now I'm *sure* I deserve better."

"Yeah?"

"Yeah. I'm going to take some time for myself."

"Good."

She leans in like she's going to kiss me on the cheek. Every set of eyes in the hallway fixes on us. Beth stops. Rumors will be running through the school by recess.

"Let's go back inside," Beth says.

"Good idea."

"And Casper?"

"Yeah?"

"Your zip's down," Beth whispers.

Embarrassed, I pull it up, and follow Beth back into the staff room.

Beth sits back down with Stan, prompting him to pick up where he left off, lamenting how he found a first edition of *David Copperfield* in a second-hand bookstore for a ridiculously low price given it was a first edition, but his wife refuses to let him "splurge". Poor Stan. I don't think I've seen him happy for as long as I've known him.

As what little time we have before the first bell whittles away, talk turns to Stuart. People speculate where he is. Shirley fears he might've been in an accident. Olivia says she thought she might've seen him in Principal Hetrick's office. Jerry says he was there earlier and, as far as he saw, Principal Hetrick was alone. Arnold Jeffs, the geography teacher, says he could be down with a cold because there's one going around. Bob Sorenson, the legal teacher, suggests we all enjoy the peace while we have it.

But we don't get to do that as the bell rings.

Time to go to work.

First period English is uneventful. I scan the usual suspects: Dom and Justine sit close together, holding hands under the table. Bianca is absent. Deidre Kent and David Jenkins sit on opposite ends of the room – they express no interest in one another, so I guess they must've broken up. Anthony Tselikas sits straight, grinning like he knows something I don't. Maya also sits upright, but she is rapt with my every word. Eric Duff scribbles on his books.

Second period, I have a spare and sit in the staff room, marking papers. Stan sits on the opposite side of the table, reading *The Great Gatsby*. I'm sure he's read it a dozen times since I've known him. At the end of the table sits Olivia, studying a Greek phrase book.

It's then I catch my first sighting of Stuart. He whizzes past the door several times. On one occasion, he's accompanied by a man in a suit and an older, smartly dressed woman.

"I wonder what that's about," Stan says.

"Looks like the board of education," Olivia says.

During recess, the staff room is rife with speculation that Stuart has somehow been inappropriate and that he's under investigation. Some of us laugh about this. Shirley points out that it's the quiet ones you have to worry about. Jerry then talks about how neighbors are always the last ones to know they're living next door to a serial killer.

Third period is Humanities. We talk about culture and the way it's developed over the last two hundred years. But as the class wears on, I get the feeling that some of the kids – Dom,

Justine, David, and Deidre – are looking at me. Of course they are, they have to, I'm the teacher; but now their expressions are speculative. I check Maya, but her attention is fixed on her folder.

Toward the end of the class, Stuart peeks through the door's window, expressionless. Then he steps away, but I can still see him out there in the hallway, leaning against the wall, like he's waiting for me.

When the bell rings, the kids spill into the hallway. Stuart comes in and stands in the doorway.

"Stuart, we missed you this morning," I say.

"Let's not make a scene, Casper."

"A scene?"

"Principal Hetrick would like to talk to you."

"I have yard duty," I say.

"Max will cover for you."

"What's this about?"

"I think that's best left for her to discuss with you."

I stop in the process of stuffing homework into my bag. "Have I done something wrong?"

"You can discuss that with Principal Hetrick. Now, Casper."

I close my bag, nod, and shuffle out the door.

Principal Hetrick is stoic and unblinking – we could be playing a poker hand, with her refusing to offer any indication of what she's holding. In the corner, arms folded across his chest, is Stuart. His glasses have slipped down his nose, and his beady eyes glare at me. But he has none of the gravity of Principal Hetrick. She is carved from a time a principal's authority was totalitarian.

"What can you tell us about this?" she asks.

She has a manila folder on her desk. Without opening it more than a sliver, she eases out a sheet of lined paper and holds it up for me to see. It's my sketch of Bianca.

"That's one of my students," I say.

"You drew it?" Stuart asks.

"Yeah. In the art class I took on Tuesday when Beth was sick."

"Do you have a relationship with this student?" Principal Hetrick asks.

"Relationship?"

"Yes."

"Are you asking if I have a physical relationship with her?"

"Yes."

"No. God, no. She's a kid."

"Why did you draw the picture of her?" Stuart asks.

"I gave the kids the task of drawing something. I was seated at Beth's desk. Just at that moment, I thought Bianca had a really good pose for a portrait."

"So you admired her?" Principal Hetrick says.

"I'm just saying that … *aesthetically* – the way her head was bowed, the way her hair fell over her face – that she looked good to draw. From the point of view of an artist, that is. Not, you know …"

"What?"

"Not from the point of view of somebody with any sexual interest in her."

"You must know drawing her is inappropriate."

"I didn't mean anything by it."

"Your intent is irrelevant."

"I draw. I mean, at home, I draw. Beth – Miss Buckley – can tell you. I didn't think, okay? It was just a good picture to draw at the time. Why? What's happened?"

"Bianca was sexually assaulted."

"Bianca was raped?"

"Assaulted."

"Sexually assaulted," Stuart says.

I want to ask what that means exactly, but decide it would be inappropriate. "Is she okay?" I ask.

"She's in hospital. *Shock*."

"At the moment, she's not speaking ..." Stuart says.

He leaves it hanging, the bastard, as if to suggest that it's inevitable she will speak, and when she does ...

"And I'm a suspect because of *that*?" I point at my picture.

"We're just trying to place where everybody was."

"When did this happen?"

"This morning. Possibly around eight-thirty while Bianca was on her way to school," Principal Hetrick says. "Where were you?"

"At that time, at home."

"Can anybody corroborate your story?"

"I really don't like where this is going," I say. "I drew a picture. *Just* because."

"You're meant to befriend the students, Casper," Stuart says. "Not over-friend them."

"I don't even know what that means. I have a good relationship with my kids. There's nothing untoward. I really resent the accusation—"

"There's no accusation leveled at you, Mr. Gray," Principal Hetrick says.

"Then I resent the unspoken accusation. *Just* because I drew a picture."

"Have you drawn a picture of any other students?" Principal Hetrick asks. "Perhaps of a male student?"

"I drew a picture because I had to take Beth's art class. That's it."

"So that's the *only* reason?"

"Yes."

"Because you filled in and took this art class."

"Yes."

"And because at the time it seemed a good picture to draw."

"Yes."

"Then perhaps you'd care to explain this."

Principal Hetrick slips another lined sheet of paper out of the manila folder, this one all wrinkled. She smooths it out on her desk, revealing it has a giant cartoon cock on it. It's the one I drew on Monday morning.

"Where did you get that?" I ask.

"After we discovered the first picture," Stuart says, "I checked the bins of your classrooms. I discovered that also."

Discovered. Like it was a secret I'd hidden.

"That's a …" I don't know what to say.

"Yes?" Stuart asks.

"Are you in the habit of drawing pornography?" Principal Hetrick asks.

"I was trying to draw on Monday morning. I was frustrated because I was blocked. It just came out." I rub my forehead. Worst phrasing.

"You drew this in an English class?" Principal Hetrick says.

"Yes."

"Although you claim you only drew in the art class because you filled in."

"We all doodle at times while the kids are working in class. That's just one of those stupid scribbles we all do."

"I have never scribbled a penis," Stuart says.

There's not a lot I can say to that.

"Let's get back to this morning," Principal Hetrick says. "Where were you between 8:15 and about 8:45?"

"Home."

"Alone?"

"No, my wife would've been with me."

"For all that time?"

"For most of that time. She had to go to work."

"So how long was your wife actually with you?"

I want to lie, and I'm sure Jane would alibi me, but that Kai picked her up concretes the facts. Of course, he might be willing to lie, but that's when things unravel. There's no point lying anyway. I haven't done anything.

"Probably about ten minutes," I say.

"That's not most of the time, is it?" Principal Hetrick asks.

"No."

"Then?"

"I sat at home until it was time to come to school."

"What time did you get to school?" Stuart asks.

"Ten-to, five-to. You can ask the others. I was there in the staff room."

"So you were late for the staff meeting? *Again*?"

"There was no staff meeting."

"But if there had been, you would've been late."

"I guess."

"Can anybody account for the time between when your wife went to work and when you showed up in the staff room?" Principal Hetrick asks.

"I don't know. Probably not. But let me get this straight: after my wife leaves for work, I sexually assault Bianca, then show up for work as if nothing happened? I have like all of twenty-five minutes. And that's not even counting time needed for driving, parking, getting in and out of the car, and that stuff."

"Improbable, maybe," Stuart says, "but not impossible."

"Mr. Gray," Principal Hetrick says, "we have spent the morning talking to detectives. They will proceed with their investigations.

They may eventually want to talk to you. We would therefore like to establish that you have nothing to hide."

"I had nothing to do with this."

"Can you think of anybody else who may have assaulted Miss Orsino?" Principal Hetrick asks.

The answer's obvious, but I worry how the information will portray me.

"Well?"

"There's a guy who hangs around The Corner—"

"Corner? What corner?"

"It's a line of shops at the corner of Stark and Werner," Stuart says. "The kids call it The Corner."

"I only know his first name is Bruce. He wears a jean jacket all the time. He's a drug dealer or something. I can't be sure, but I think Bianca had some sort of interaction with him on Wednesday."

"Some sort of interaction?" Principal Hetrick says.

"I think so."

"And you didn't report this?" Stuart asks.

"All I saw was her walking away from him. I didn't know if she was leaving him or just passing. I didn't see any direct communication."

"Still—"

"I *did* talk to her yesterday about it. She said he was being flirtatious, she handled it and that was that."

"She handled it?" Principal Hetrick asks. "You were satisfied that a *teenage* girl handled the dalliances of a possible drug dealer?"

"I saw the same thing on Monday morning before school," I say, remembering. "He called out something to her and Justine Gardiner; they laughed him off and kept walking."

Neither Principal Hetrick nor Stuart speak. Or move.

"I can't report every incidental interaction."

Principal Hetrick and Stuart exchange a glance. They're trying to work out if I'm concocting an alibi or whether I'm telling them the truth.

"You go ask anyone who runs a business on The Corner and they'll tell you about this guy. They've even called the cops on him. The cops will know him."

"Mr. Gray," Principal Hetrick says. "*Casper.* Is there anything else you'd like to tell us?"

Right then, I know she'd cover this up to avoid a scandal. Then there'd be a forced resignation in a month or two when nobody would connect it to whatever's happened. *Oh, Mr. Gray decided he'd had enough of teaching.* I want to confess to something I haven't done to shock her.

"There is nothing *to* tell," I say.

"Mr. Gray, we will have the truth in this."

"There's no truth to have outside what I'm telling you."

"Mr. Piper lauds your teaching," Principal Hetrick says. "He says the kids respond to you. Regardless," she jabs first my portrait of Bianca with her index finger, then the cartoon cock, "you seriously need to examine every course of action you intend to take *before* you take it. I wonder if you understand the responsibility you wield in this position. You are not a teenager yourself. You are entrusted with the next generation of society."

I'm unsure what to say. Jumbled thoughts tumble through my mind.

Principal Hetrick takes my two pictures and puts them back in the manila folder. She closes the folder and crosses her hands over it.

"I think that will be all," she says.

I get up, start for the door.

"One more thing," Stuart says.

I turn.

"You're meant to have bus duty after school, aren't you?"

"Yeah."

"Perhaps it's best you skip that. I'll find a replacement."

"Good idea," Principal Hetrick says. "You may go, Mr. Gray."

I leave the office.

The moment I'm out of Principal Hetrick's office, I tear my phone from my pocket and call Jane.

It rings through to her voicemail.

I try twice more, but get no answer.

When I exit the school building and head into the courtyard, I'm sure all the kids are looking at me, wondering about me, and concocting worst-case scenarios about me.

Humanities makes sense now – the strange behavior of Dom, Justine, David, and Deidre. Bianca gets assaulted, they find out. Maybe Justine's curious why Bianca's late in the morning and rings her up. Justine gets her mother. Her mother cries to Justine. I don't know. But they begin with a germ of information that mutates. Rumors in schools are killers.

I want to run. Get out of school for the rest of the day. But that would be like an admission of guilt. That's something which could stick on me even after they find whoever's guilty – *if* they find them.

Although I'm not on yard duty, I walk around the school, trying to look as unconcerned as possible. I try Jane several more times, but to no avail. She could be in a meeting.

I get to the back of the school and stop. Kids play on the basketball court. There's nobody on the soccer ground – it'd still be too wet. But I remember seeing Bianca, Justine, and Dom sitting in the goals on Monday. I thought they'd been passing around a cigarette. In retrospect, nobody shares a cigarette that way, do they? Most of these kids vape nowadays anyway. Maybe it was a joint. Perhaps they scored it from Jean Jacket.

I'm sure now he must be responsible. He extorted sex from Bianca. Being a naïve teenager, she thought she could handle him. But things got out of hand. It makes sense – or at least makes more sense than this belief that I'm responsible.

"Hey!" It's Beth. She comes up behind me. "What's going on?"

I start walking again. I don't want to be in a fixed position where kids can overhear me. Beth hurries to keep up.

I tell her everything that went on with Stuart and Principal Hetrick. I even tell her about the big cartoon cock, putting it in the context of finding a condom in Jane's bag so I had it in my mind that – at the time – I was worried she was having an affair. I go on to detail Bianca's interactions with Jean Jacket. Everything spills out because, as I talk, it becomes real to me that something I haven't done could finish me.

"It's okay," Beth says. She puts a hand on my back and rubs it up and down. "They'll find who's responsible. You'll be okay."

We've come around to one end of the school, where it adjoins the parking lot. I stop. Beth waits for me. My shoulders are so tight that my arms are coiled and ready to spring. I clamp my hands in front of me. I don't want Beth to see me shaking. She puts a hand on mine. I'm reminded of my response to Roger's intrusion last night and hate myself for my weakness, for my fear – twice, accused and convicted of something I didn't do.

"It's all right," she says, and I think she's telling me that it's not only okay for me to be scared, but also to show it. "You've had a tough week – this stuff with Jane, me unloading on you, Roger last night, now this. You should've told me about you and Jane."

"You had enough of your own stuff going on."

The bell rings. Kids zip past. If Beth were Jane, I'd hug her now and plant my head on her shoulder. But it's Beth. And this is school. And even though the kids are getting to class, there are still too many of them around to be indiscreet. I'm sure by the end of the day there'll be all sorts of rumors about me. God knows how they'll fester over the weekend.

"You want to call me and talk, you do it, okay?" Beth asks.

I don't answer, thinking of dinner tonight with Sarah, the anniversary dinner tomorrow night, the Sheraton overnight, and the picture on Sunday morning. I want to escape from the world and all its obligations.

"Okay?"

"Thanks, Beth."

On the way back to class I take my phone out and twice call Jane. Again, it rings through to voicemail.

I put the phone away and get to class.

Fourth period is an elective Creative Writing class. These are kids I see only for this very class, but their eyes are hard. Whatever suspicion eddied around me during third period has grown into a flood. Kids know I'm at the center of whatever's going on. I wait for one of them to question what I've done.

When the bell rings to signal the end of class, I jump out of my chair, but then have to force myself not to flee, because that really would make me look guilty. The kids file out. They're too quiet. Every one of them looks at me. I've already been convicted in a court of opinion. I consider ringing Jane now, but there wouldn't be time to unload everything. I'll have to wait.

In the final period, I have Social Studies with the kids I see most often through the week. I expect them to hate me. Bianca was one of their own and now the belief is that I've done something to her.

I get up and open my mouth. I want to tell them that whatever stories are circulating are just that: stories. Of course, they're kids. They'll put circumstantial evidence together to fit the most spectacular scenario, and anything I say would just seem like I'm trying to cover what I've done.

It proves almost impossible to run the class. The kids are distracted. I assign them reading to do and several of the quizzes from their exercise book, but they chat in hushed whispers. I don't push the work, and monitor that their quiet discussions remain just that – quiet. Throughout, I keep expecting the door to crash open and for the detectives to charge in and arrest me in front of everybody.

My phone rings. It's Jane. I grab it, ready to charge out so I can take the call. Kids look at me. This isn't the time or place. I decline the call and send her a text: *In class. Talk later.* She responds: *Okay.* I put the phone away. Kids condemn me with their eyes.

What if Bianca *blames* me? I don't know why she would, but this sort of stuff occurs. Wrongful accusations are made. She might want to cover up for somebody else – perhaps a boyfriend none of us know about. My mind races with worst-case scenarios. No, wait. I'm past that. I'm an English teacher, but all I can think is that these are worster-case scenarios.

When the bell rings, I again have to stop myself rushing out of the room before the kids. I let them filter out while I pack my bag. Maya casts me one last forlorn look.

Then I head out the door myself.

I stride down the hallway, planning to jump in my car and go home. But I stop. I can't do that. There's another suspicious behavior. So I detour to Principal Hetrick's office. She's at her desk – she's always at her desk – going through some paperwork. I knock on her door.

"Come in."

I open the door and poke my head through the doorway.

"The police …" I begin.

"Yes?"

"I'm unsure what I should do. Should I go home or should I wait around in case they want to talk to me?"

"You can go home."

I hold my breath. Is she tacitly telling me I'm okay?

"We have your address if they need it."

I nod and close the door.

24.

When I get home, I sit in the car, parked in the driveway. Wallace barks from inside the garage. There's nobody else out.

The whole week evaporates, condensing into a shadowy paranoia that I divorce myself from, that I hate myself for creating. My head always works overtime. Maybe that's the part of me responsible for whatever creativity I nurture, that wants to transform a blank page into something wonderful and breathtaking, only to ever find something pedestrian.

I drag my phone from my pocket, but this has gone beyond a phone call. Maybe I can swing past Web Myriad a bit earlier when I pick Jane up for dinner tonight. I shudder thinking how she'll deal with this. But she'll be strong. She is whenever she needs to be – or needs us to be. She always has been.

I get out of the car because Wallace's barking is insistent. There's a break in the clouds directly above me. The sun blinds me. I shield my eyes. It's been cooler these past two days, but tomorrow's meant to be hot again. I dread it, especially because of all the anniversary stuff we'll be doing.

I open the garage and Wallace leaps at me. I catch him and hoist him up to my chest, pivoting back and forth on my heels. Wallace licks at my neck and his cold nose nuzzles at my cheek. I scratch him between the ears and tell him he's a good boy, swaying, trying to work out what to do next.

I'm there for a couple of minutes. If anybody were to walk past the house, they might think I was trying to rock a baby to sleep. It's not until Wallace starts squirming that I move again.

I put him down, follow him into the garage, and grab the sledgehammer.

The wall is as stubborn as I am anxious. I heave the sledgehammer again and again until the stones chip and the reverberations rattle into sledgehammer's head, jangle down the handle, and jar into my body. Wallace zooms around the yard barking, like he's worried I'm going to hurt myself. But I keep at it until my shoulders are sore and I'm drenched in sweat. I've made no headway, but I feel better for my efforts.

I take out my phone. It's 4:05 – I've only been going at it for about fifteen minutes. God knows how I'll ever manage to take this wall down.

Putting the sledgehammer back in the garage, I go into the house and have a quick shower, then change. When I check my phone, I find I have two texts. The first is from Beth, telling me she's sorry she missed me after school and asking if I'm okay. The second is from Luke, asking how things panned out with Jane.

I tell Beth *I'm okay* and Luke *Okay*. They're unsatisfactory answers, I know. Beth will understand. Luke will think I'm short-changing him, the way both Stephen and I have short-changed our friendship with him since we each got married. I should explain things better and promise myself that I will when things have calmed down.

Right now, I want to get moving. I need to be out of here.

When I get in the car and swing out of the drive, I get another text from Beth telling me she's around if I want to talk. I send her a *Thanks*. Luke doesn't get back to me.

The drive to Web Myriad is a crawl. It's 4:33. People are finishing early and eager to get home or go out.

I think about this unspoken allegation festering at school now. If it hasn't been settled by Monday, teaching will be unbearable. There'll be innuendo and suspicions will filter back to parents. In all likelihood, parents will complain about me teaching their children, particularly if those children are daughters.

At some point, I'm sure the police will want to talk to me. What will the neighbors think if police show up in a marked car? It's bad enough what's going on at school. I don't need it at home, too. Neighbors *do* gossip.

A beer would be good right now. Maybe several. It's a pity I have to drive.

Tonight, I want to let go.

25.

It's 4:44 when I park outside Web Myriad – way too early, but I don't care. I want to talk to Jane. Hopefully, I can pull her out of work or whatever meeting she's in, or see her before it starts. If I can't, I'll wait in the foyer.

I get out of the car and enter the building from the back. There's a lift but I bypass it, jogging up the zigzagging stairwell the way Jane does – her "aerobic workout", she once told me. When I reach the third floor, I open the door. There's the small foyer, then the Web Myriad offices. Their name is emblazoned across a glass partition and the door.

Jane's boss, Henry, comes immediately into view. I always think of him as rumpled, and not just because of his wrinkled shirt and loose tie, but because it seems life's packaged him in a way where he can't straighten himself out. He's slumped in front of a PowerPoint presentation while talking to two pudgy thirty-something men in suits. I stop before I reach the door, but he sees me. He frowns. Then it clicks to him who I am. He beckons me, so I open the door and pop my head in.

"Casper?" he asks, unsure if he's got my name right.

"Yeah."

"Jane's already gone. She wasn't feeling too well."

"She wasn't feeling well?"

"No. Bug maybe. There's a nasty summer one going around."

"Oh," I say. "Thanks."

I close the door, start down the stairwell, and ring Jane. I stop in front of the exit to the second floor because I think I hear ringing. I put my ear to the door. It *is* ringing – Jane's ringtone.

I open the door.

Hot, dense air blasts me so hard I almost fall back a step. My breath becomes thick in my chest. It's dark – gloomy, so it takes a moment to make out details. I remember Jane telling me the business here went bust, so the glass partition to the office is clean. Sunlight diffuses through the drawn venetian blinds in thin fiery slits, and bounces off the glistening form of Jane – naked but for her heels – bent over a desk, her butt thrust in the air. Kai fucks her. That's how simple the sight is: he fucks her, his right hand dug into her hair, the way a rider would twist his hand into the mane of a bronco trying to buck him, his left hand poised over her left buttock, which he slaps every now and again, like he's spurring her on.

He's scrawny – scrawnier than me, so it's not like Jane's opted for some male hunk. I'm sure I can see his sternum. He has a sparse tuft of hair on his chest that's almost pathetic. But he's a powerhouse of motion. Jane's whole body shimmies every time he drives into her. Her buttocks quiver, her breasts bounce, her hair – tied so tight this morning – tumbles free. A vein sticks out on her forehead. Her face is mottled. A guttural wail rises in her throat.

I have never made her look like that.

I have never made her sound like that.

Kai must be huge. Or maybe he is fucking her anally – from this angle, I can't tell.

I see her handbag inside the door, lying on its side – everything spilled out, the way all this began. Her phone's still ringing, vibrating on the carpet like an overturned turtle trying to right itself. Alongside it is a little white bag from Joe's Chemist.

I go to hang up my phone. My hand paws at it. Jane's scream pierces the office until it reverberates in my head and can't find a way out. My hand hits the phone and hangs it up. But my eyes are fixed on Kai. He pulls out of Jane. His cock gleams in the sheath of its lime glow-in-the-dark condom. He's no bigger than me. Maybe thinner, too.

He jerks Jane by the arm. She spins, falls to her knees before him as if she's supplicating herself. Kai drags her head back by her hair with one hand. With his other, he tears the condom from his cock, and flicks it over his shoulder – it whizzes haphazardly to the floor, like an errant firework – and masturbates himself to ejaculation.

The first spurt hits Jane's cheek. I don't know where the next goes. But the next hits her lips. She takes him in her mouth. Holds him, her face buried in his pubic hair, which is trimmed into a stupidly neat triangle. Then runs her mouth up and down his shaft. The cum lathers on her lips. Kai grins down at her, the way I would approve of Wallace after he's performed a trick, but there's also something else with Kai, some hint of condescension or superiority or something.

My feet move. I still have the door to the stairwell open. Now I trip back over the threshold and fall onto my butt. The door surges toward the jamb. Pauses abruptly. Gently closes.

Quiet.

It wasn't Jane. Just some other raven-haired woman. Kai probably has a ton of girlfriends. Girls fall for accents and fuckwits. And Henry said Jane was gone. She's probably already at the bar waiting for me, or on the way back home. Forget the fact that her phone was ringing and vibrating on the floor, that I saw her, or recognized the bounce of her butt.

I should go in there and confront them … although I don't know what the etiquette is. I suppose that as the husband of the woman getting fucked it's to face down the fucker, to confront him violently. But there's nothing there. No imperative to do so. Just shock – numbing me until it coalesces in my feet and shoots up my throat.

Rising, I vomit over the balustrade of the stairwell.

The vomit plows through the air like a meteor shower and splatters on the ground floor.

There. Done. Now there's nothing.

Nothing but the humiliation.

I bolt down the stairs.

I sit in my car, still parked in the lot behind Jane's office building.

The same thoughts flit through my mind as before. There's no way I could've seen what I did. The explanation must be simpler. I've had a bad day. I've imagined this. A breakdown. That's it. This fear has weighed on my mind all week. Now I've hallucinated it. Surely that's possible.

Starting the car, I pull out of the lot.

On the drive home, I consider another possibility. Maybe he was raping her. Her strained face suggests she was being forced. Maybe I didn't realize it. Although if that were the case, she seemed more than willing at the end when he came all over her face and she took him in her mouth.

I clench my eyes to shut out the world, but only lock in the horror of her face buried in his pubic hair.

I open my eyes. There's pain on either side of my neck. The numbness in my mind evaporates. The improbabilities are accepted for what they are: attempts to rationalize what I've seen. That leaves what I saw: Kai fucking Jane.

Jane fucking Kai.

26.

I pull into my drive and reverse onto the nature strip. Sit there. Stare at the garage door through the windshield. I hear Jane's wailing in my ears. My chest tightens until my breath feels like it's not getting past my throat.

All the typical questions explode in my mind: *Why? How long? How did it happen? Is Kai the first time this has happened? Have there been others? Are there others?* The questions keep coming – the same ones, new ones, and variations of the same ones. But they're not important – at least not right now. Nothing is important but what I do from here.

The typical responses present themselves to accompany the typical questions: *toss all Jane's stuff out. Pack my stuff and leave. Beat up Kai.* But despite all the options, there's a vacuum in my decision-making ability. I've overloaded and just can't think about what comes next.

I get out of the car. There's nobody else out in the neighborhood – thankfully.

Rounding the garage, I see Wallace sitting by the front door, whimpering. He gets up. Limps toward me, holding his right paw up.

I pick him up. He whines and nuzzles me with his dirty nose, like he wants me to do something. As carefully as I can, I check his leg and paw to see if they're cut. They're not. But the lower half of his leg looks crooked, although I'm unsure if that's how a dog's leg is shaped. I try to compare it with his other leg, but he howls so I stop jostling him.

"What did you do?" I ask him.

Wallace continues to whine.

I carry him back to the car and place him in the passenger seat. He shakes, and lifts his head, his deep brown eyes soulful. I tousle the fur between his ears and tell him to stay, rush around to the other side of the car, get back in, and start the engine. My phone vibrates. It's a text from Jane saying she's finishing early and to come down now.

I pull off the nature strip.

Wallace's vet is nearby. It's a big clinic that usually has four vets on staff, as well as several nurses. Given it's nearing six on a Friday, I don't expect to find Wallace's regular vet, Dr. Lidia Dudek, still available, but she is.

Dr. Dudek is maybe five years older than me and has a narrow face with an aquiline nose that makes her seem austere, but when she smiles I see the kid who must've loved animals so much she decided to become a vet. She wears casual clothes, as if she's just knocked off and is preparing for a night out with her husband – the way things should be on a Friday evening when you don't find your partner fucking somebody else. She shows me into the examination room; I rest Wallace on the table.

She has me call to him until he limps toward me, then checks his leg, feeling it and moving it gently – even when Wallace growls at her – as she tries to determine what's wrong. She asks me how this happened. I tell her I don't know, that I came home from work to find him like that.

She speculates that he has a mid-shaft fracture of the radius and ulna, saying some blunt force trauma must've been responsible – possibly a car. She decides to take X-rays – if Wallace will sit still for them. Wallace is docile now. I think he understands we're trying to help him.

She shows me back out into the waiting room, then goes to organize Wallace's X-rays.

Jane messages and rings several times.

I don't respond.

I sit down, my hands shaking, and hope Wallace will be okay. Of course, he should be. It's probably a break. But there could be complications – maybe breaks are worse in dogs with their spindly legs. I hate the thought of him in pain.

Is this what it feels like worrying about a kid? Lucky Jane and I didn't have any. *Don't* have any. I don't know which tense is applicable.

Jane rings again. I let it ring out. This time she leaves a voicemail. I check it.

"Hey," she says. "Where are you? Why aren't you answering your phone?"

I delete the message, hang up, and consider texting her. *At vet – Wallace has been hurt,* I could write. She'd come here then, even if I told her not to. I don't want that. I don't know what I want. But I don't want that.

Dr. Dudek returns and tells me she was right: Wallace has a fracture. She discusses options – there are plates, like they'd insert for a person. But she tells me it's an expensive procedure – upwards of four thousand dollars. I think of the money Jane and I have been slowly saving for IVF. This takes a big bite out of it. It's a conversation Jane and I should have.

"Insert the plates," I say.

"Are you sure?"

"Insert them."

Dr. Dudek goes on to tell me that Wallace will have to fast at least ten to twelve hours. I tell her Wallace probably hasn't eaten since breakfast, but obviously I can't be sure as he's a dog and might've found something to nibble on. Dr. Dudek suggests the best thing to do would be to feed Wallace a little something now, keep him in overnight, and operate in the morning. She says she doesn't work on Saturdays, but will come in for Wallace.

I hate the thought of leaving Wallace here alone. He's wary about the clinic, since it usually means examinations and vaccinations. Fortunately, he's never had anything else really wrong with him. But he's not comfortable here, although I don't know how comfortable home will be either.

"Come on," Dr. Dudek says. "You can feed him something and settle him in."

I get another text from Jane: *Where are you?*

I nod to Dr. Dudek.

Out the back, they have a room with glass pens where they keep the animals. I place Wallace in one. He blinks at me, trying to work out what's going on. Dr. Dudek brings me a can of dog food. She opens it and hands me the can and a plastic spoon. I scoop out a chunk of meat. Wallace eats it from the spoon. We get through the can quickly like that.

Dr. Dudek laughs. "He's eating fine," she says. "That's a good sign."

I pat Wallace and stroke his head. He's not shaking anymore, which makes me feel better. In fact, he looks tired, like he wants to drift off. But each time his eyes close, he rouses himself, checking I'm still here. I really don't want to leave him. My phone vibrates incessantly in my pocket.

Wallace finally falls asleep. Dr. Dudek pats me on the shoulder and escorts me through the clinic and toward the door.

"This is probably the best time to go," she says. "I'll give you a call tomorrow to let you know how things went."

"Thanks, Dr. Dudek. I realize you were probably finished for the night."

"You caught me minutes from leaving."

"I'm sorry for inconveniencing—"

"It's okay. My plans can wait. Are you all right?"

"Yeah, I'm …" I don't know what to say.

"He'll be okay."

I nod. She opens the door. I leave.

I sit in my car, in the clinic's parking lot. The dashboard clock says it's 7:05pm. I thought it would've been later. Usually, there's a wait to see a vet. It's lucky – for me, *and* Wallace – that I grabbed Dr. Dudek when she was free and off-duty.

I pull out my phone. Jane's alternated between texts and voicemail.

"Hey, where are you? I'm going to the restaurant," her first voicemail says.

Then it's a text from the restaurant: *Here with Sarah and Alex.*

Another voicemail: "I'm getting really worried. Please call me immediately."

Then a text: *What's going on?*

And another: *Please call me!*

A final voicemail: "What's happened to you?"

And a final text: *I'm coming home.*

I start the car.

27.

I pull into my drive, reverse onto the nature strip, and get out of the car just as Chloe's emerging from her house, dressed in her nurse's uniform.

"Hello, Casper!" she says. "How're you?"

My wife's cheating on me, I'm being accused of rape at school, and my dog has a broken leg.

"I'm great," I say.

Chloe stops before she gets into her car. "You sure?"

It's nice she can show concern. I guess that's the nurse in her. Or maybe it's just her being human. It's easy to forget given she's married to such a moron in Vic. If Chloe and I were better friends, I might spill everything to her. But we're not. We're neighbors – we exchange pleasantries, dally in an occasional conversation that never delves too deeply into our personal space, and then go about our separate lives.

I nod.

Chloe is still frozen, about to sink into the driver's seat. I must look bad for her not to move.

"Sorry," I say. "Just distracted."

"Okay." Chloe purses her lips. She knows I'm lying. But she can't push it. Work awaits her. And when people ask if you're okay, do they really want to know? "If you need anything, you know where I live," she says.

"Thanks."

"I mean that, Casper – okay?"

"Sure."

She gets into her car, although her eyes remain on me.

I don't know what comes next, what I'm meant to be doing.

Front door.

That's it. I begin to move.

Grabbing a beer, I sit on the couch in the dining room, and take my sketchpad from the coffee table. This morning I was contemplating how to finish my sketch of Jane. Now I see Kai's hands on my wife, see his hips smacking against her buttocks, see his cock against her face. This is the unseeable, the picture that's now become the standard.

I hear a car – Jane's VW. I forgot she was picking it up today and didn't even think about how she'd get home. Within moments, her keys jingle and the front door swings open. I don't move, don't breathe. Jane's footsteps thump down the hallway. There's the briefest pause as I hear her drop her handbag in my study. Then she's at the archway of the dining room, hands on hips, shoulders cocked forward. The little white bag from Joe's Chemist dangles from her left hand. Maybe it's more glow-in-the-dark condoms.

"Where the hell were you?" she says. "Do you know how worried—?"

"Wallace broke his leg."

Her head cranes forward. "What?"

"I had to take him to the vet."

"Is he okay?" Jane puts her bag on the kitchen counter. "Where is he?"

"The vet's keeping him overnight. They're going to perform surgery tomorrow morning to insert plates."

"How did he break his leg?"

"I found him waiting on the front doorstep like that when I came home." *From seeing you fucking Kai.*

"On the front doorstep?"

I take a swig of beer.

"Then he was out?"

It hadn't even occurred to me. Of course he was out. His nose was dirty. He must've burrowed back under the fence.

"Maybe he got hit by a car," Jane says.

No. Now I realize how improbable that is. A little dog like Wallace, if he tangled with a car there'd be evidence. He never goes on the road anyway. He had an encounter all right. But it was with Vic – Vic, who threatened to dropkick him.

"Why didn't you call?" Jane says.

"I got caught up."

"You *should've* called."

I take another swig of beer.

"Or at least messaged."

I keep drinking.

"You called earlier. Tons of times."

That's right. I did. Which is what led to the peep show.

"What was that about?"

I'm not quite sure I can find the words.

"Was that when he got hit?"

I drink again.

"Well?"

"I don't remember."

"Is he going to be okay?"

I don't say anything.

"Well?"

"I guess."

"You're acting weird."

I snort. A few hours ago, I wanted to lean on her because of everything happening at school. I *needed* her to assure me. Now I can't imagine where we go from here. If I lean on her, I'm leaning on a lie. Lies don't hold up, and I don't expect them to hold me up.

"Are you okay?"

Everybody keeps asking me that. My fingers trace my sketch, smudging the outlines. She puts one hand on top of mine and shadows me.

"This is hardly the time to be thinking about your drawing," Jane says. "Are you all right?"

Genuine concern. It seems such an weird thing, an unreal thing. *Concern*.

"Hey," Jane grabs my wrist and gives it a little shake, "talk to me."

"This morning I couldn't stop thinking about how I could finish it," I say, because that's true, and it's like a bookend on the day. "Like maybe I could draw a little bow around your neck."

"A bow?"

"Or your hair up in braids."

"I don't think so."

"Or maybe I should draw you with Kai's cock in your mouth."

Jane's hand jolts mine still. She gapes at me. Her mouth opens like it did when she fellated Kai's cum-covered cock. I expect a barrage of excuses now. Her lower lip quivers. Her mouth's still open, her chest still. But she must see something in me – see that this isn't a suspicion or insecurity or paranoia but irrefutable knowledge.

She gets up. Walks from the couch. Stops. I glower at her. She spins away. Leans on the kitchen counter. Bows her head. Then rushes from the dining room. I hear her pick up her bag from the study.

The front door opens and closes.

Her car cunts out of the drive.

28.

My mind is still. I must've had a breakdown. My mind shouldn't be this still. It should be raging with everything that's going on. I should be angry. Upset. Manic. *Confused.* All of that. But I'm not. I just don't know what this state I'm in is, although there's some element of dread, some expectation that this is about to explode and I won't be prepared to process it.

I put my beer on the coffee table. I've drunk about half. It's not going down well. Some days they go down. Some days they don't. But go down it will.

Maybe that's what my dad thought when he began drinking. That should frighten me. Like father, like son, like this is a genetic trait I might inherit – alcoholism.

I clench my teeth, scrunch my eyes. I should be crying or something.

But nothing comes out.

I think about Jane. Maybe she's gone to Kai now. Maybe he'll console her. Fuck her. They'll have sex. He'll treat her in ways I never have, like I saw them this afternoon. And she'll enjoy it. Lap it up. Meanwhile, I'll sit here, and wait for the police to question me about Bianca while I worry about Wallace.

Poor little Wallace.

I get up.

29.

I ring and ring the bell to Vic's house.

His footsteps thump down the hallway. The door swings open. Vic stands there barefoot, in jeans, a T-shirt, and a Coopers in hand. He's unshaven, face chiseled into a permanent state of disapproval. Moans echo down the hallway. The dining room is directly adjacent. I can see half the TV – a black guy is having sex with a blonde doggy style. The camerawork is shaky. So this is what Vic does with his spare time – he watches amateur porn.

"What?" he asks.

I shake my attention from the television. "Wallace got hurt today."

"So?"

"Did you do something to him?"

"I told you if he came in here again I'd dropkick him out."

"So you kicked him?"

"I taught him a lesson."

"You broke his leg."

"That's his bad luck."

"His bad luck?"

Vic takes a long drink, like he's trying to tell me he's in no hurry to respond. "Fuck off, Casper. You want to avoid this happening again, you make sure that little shit stays in *your* yard."

Vic slams the door closed.

I knock on the door again. Nothing. I knock, then slam the door with an open palm. Vic's intention must be to ignore me, but I hammer relentlessly. Finally, footsteps thud down the hallway. The door swings open. The moans are gone. The image on the television is frozen – the blonde's now on top of the black guy, head thrown back, ponytail caught mid-bounce.

"Vic, I need to talk—"

Vic grabs me by the scruff of my T-shirt, yanks me toward him, then hurls me – effortlessly, like I'm weightless – from the doorstep. I fly through the air, hit the ground on my hip, roll, and sprawl onto my back. Vic advances, leaning over me, and thrusts one finger at me.

"I've warned you about your dog!" he says. "Time and time again! I've warned you about that fucking mutt!"

My hip's sore and palms burn. I rub one of them into my left eye. It's not Vic. It's everything. I'm aware others are out now – my hammering on Vic's door has drawn them. Behind me, Josh and Karen have just pulled into their drive, and are frozen halfway out of their car. Tarika Gupta shields her kids, Kirit and Pia, on her front doorstep. Vic surveys them indifferently, almost like he's challenging them to defy him, each of them averting their gaze. Then he glares at me.

"You gonna cry?" he asks.

I shake my head – not so much at him, but at the day.

"You got anything more to say about it?"

I sit up and rub my hands together.

"I didn't think so. Now get the fuck off my property before I dropkick *you* out."

He towers over me, arm outstretched, finger pointed at my place, like a parent admonishing a child and telling them to get home.

Hauling myself to my feet, I slink away and do just that.

30.

Once inside, I yank my phone out of my pocket, unlock it, jab my finger toward the keypad, and stop. Who do I call in a situation like this? Emergency? No. Of course not. I would have to call the police station closest to me – there's one over in Greenbrook.

I don't know what the penalty is for breaking a dog's leg, but there *must* be a penalty. It's animal cruelty. Not to mention Vic assaulted me. Of course, he'd get out of it somehow, if not use it as a moral triumph that I ran to the authorities. I put my phone on the kitchen counter.

Right now, it's not just about Vic. While there's humiliation in being bullied in front of the whole neighborhood, it's nothing compared to the humiliation of seeing your wife behave like a porn starlet at the hands of some scrawny ingrate.

I grab another beer, wrap my hands around it to absorb the cold on my burning palms, and sit cross-legged on the couch.

I can't fathom what Kai offers that must be so appealing to Jane. If she'd been cheating with Roger, I could almost understand that. He's … well, he's kind of handsome, and as boorish as he is I can see how he'd be considered charismatic, and he's definitely successful. Kai looks like a reject from some pseudo Gothic band.

Taking a long drink, I finally absorb that the house is too quiet. No, it's more than that. It can contain Jane and Wallace and still be quiet.

It's too empty.

I pace around the dining room, trying to think of something to kill the time as I kill my beer. I'm not sure what I want to kill time *until*. There are nights Jane's gone out with her girlfriends (although now I question those), and I've killed time until she's come home. But now I don't know.

What lies on the other side of this?

I go into the kitchen, open the fridge, and grab another beer. The half-beer I left behind before I went to see Vic still sits on the coffee table. I sip from it. It's lukewarm. I down it in a couple of gulps, gagging repeatedly.

I put it and the fresh beer down on the coffee table, sink onto the couch, and hold out my hands.

They're steady.

I open the fresh beer.

I try to find something on TV to occupy my mind – there's a choice between football and movies. Nothing grabs me. My mind's Teflon.

I pick up the sketchpad, trace my fingers over my picture of Jane. I should rip it. Or scribble on it. Or something.

Something.

I finish what's left of the beer in the fridge – another five. I drink because it seems the right thing to do, until the stillness in my mind spasms into some semblance of activity.

Luke said things happen *just like that*.

But how can everything change just like that?

And how does it always seem to change for the worse?

There are good news stories – people who win lotto, things like that. But that always seems to be somebody else. Bad news is always you.

Jane, Wallace, Vic, the neighborhood, and Bianca: tomorrow they'll all be there. But my connection to them has changed, and I don't know what that means for me.

I use the toilet, then go up the stairs, trying not to look at the anniversary pictures, but of course I do. At what point did the facade become a facade? When did Jane start fucking Kai? They've worked together for five years. Could they have been going that long?

Once I reach my bedroom, I stop like I've hit an invisible barrier. The empty bed confronts me, a stark denouement to the day's events. This could become my life – an empty bed, a house too big, and alone at the end of the day.

Stripping where I stand, I throw my pants, T-shirt, and socks into the bedroom, but remain in the doorway. Maybe I should sleep in the spare room, although that'll probably only continue to emphasize how wrong everything is.

I force myself into the bedroom, each step growing increasingly heavier, inebriation fueling my courage. Crawling onto the bed from the base, I pull myself up onto my pillow, and slide under the covers. My head spins and bile rises in my throat. I haven't had enough beers to be sick, but I've had a lot in a short space of time – and on an empty stomach, too. I kick the covers clear. The clock radio says it's 10:47.

Again, the emptiness of the house hits me. There should be breathing sounding beside me. There should be Jane's warmth. Jane's presence. I should be able to run my fingertips down her back when she curls away from me. I wrack my memory for the last time I slept alone, but I can only guess it was pre-Jane.

Maybe this is it. Maybe this is the beginning of post-Jane.

I roll away from her side of the bed and close my eyes.

The beers were a bad idea. I didn't need my mind to loosen.

Images plague my mind: Kai fucking Jane; Kai blowing on her face; Bianca, in art class; Bianca strolling away from Jean Jacket; Wallace, whining on the front doorstep; Wallace, forlorn at the vet; Vic towering over me, taunting me.

I realize now what I'm killing time for – the reckoning.

I'll have to talk to Jane, although I don't know if I can ever look at her now without seeing Kai's cum on her face. Who knows where we'll go? Thoughts of hating her and wanting her out of my life are reflex, although maybe they're not so far from the truth either.

But what will she do when police question me about Bianca? When I get labeled a pervert? How do I face the street now when everybody probably thinks me a coward? How do I escape my life when my life has become nothing but cowardice, diffidence, and insecurity?

At least Wallace will be there. Wallace, as always, without judgment.

I close my eyes and drift off.

SATURDAY

31.

My eyes snap open. The room's dim – there's the glow from the clock radio's digital numbers, as well as the light seeping through the window. Something *feels* wrong. My internal clock suggests it's maybe 3:00 or 4:00am.

My shoulders shake. A chill settles on my skin – the sort where you feel like you'll never know warmth again.

Sitting up, I glance at the clock radio: 1:12am.

I pull the covers up around my shoulders, wrap my arms around myself and rock. There's a ringing in my ears and a restlessness in my midriff, like an overtired muscle that can't relax.

Something acidic rises in my throat. Then I gag.

I jump from the bed. It feels like I land on a trampoline. My first step has me stumbling into the bedside table and I knock the clock radio onto the carpet. I don't stop to recover it and bolt to the bathroom.

Bile burns in my throat, tasting of beer – it's the only thing in my stomach. It erupts just before I reach the toilet: vomit splatters across the floor. The bathroom stinks of it. Just as well this is … was … is Jane's bathroom. I drop to my knees and vomit again. Partially digested beer hits toilet water. My hands come down on the cold bathroom tiles. Again, I vomit, but then nothing. Something sharp jags in my throat.

I flop back against the wall, draw my knees to my chest, and rest my chin on my forearms. It feels like I could vomit again any moment, although there's nothing left to come up. I'm still shivering and the bathroom sways in front of me.

I close my eyes.

I don't mean to sleep, but I drift off for a bit. The bathroom floor chills the soles of my feet and my buttocks. My drying vomit reeks so badly that my sinuses cringe.

This is marriage.

That's what goes through my mind. Like when I had the food poisoning a few weeks ago. Relationships are pretty when you first get into them. Everything's pristine because you offer only the best part of yourself. But as you go on, those unattractive everyday things – like Jane standing over me as I vomit uncontrollably into a toilet – dull the luster. Maybe that's why an affair is so appealing, because it's unsullied.

Eventually – I'm not sure how long it is – I get up. The floor's still unsteady and I stumble back into the bedroom. Because the clock radio's been knocked over, I can't tell what time it is.

Falling onto the bed, I curl into a fetal ball, and pull the covers over me.

I put one arm on the empty half of the bed and close my eyes.

32.

I'm sure I don't go back to sleep, but the next thing I know daylight's streaming through the window.

Yawning, I sit up in bed, and tow the clock radio up by its power cord like I'm hauling in a battling fish. The time's 7:03am.

On any other weekend, I'd lie back down. Jane and I might cuddle. Or have sex. Or just enjoy being lazy. But those options aren't available right now and I don't want the stillness. I don't want my mind open and receptive to everything. I need to keep occupied. The stench of vomit also drifts in from the bathroom. That's going to have to be cleaned up.

I get out of bed, walk to the window and look out. Not a cloud in the sky. The pool in Vic's backyard draws my eye. It'd be a beautiful day to lounge poolside with a beer in hand. Or go to the beach. Or do anything other than confront the day that's going to be my world.

Wrestling on my robe, I leave the bedroom and am halfway down the stairwell with the intention of feeding Wallace when I remember he's not here. As soon as it hits 9:00, I'll ring the vet and see what's happening. I wonder how he went overnight.

I wonder how Jane went.

I go back to the bedroom, grab some shorts and a T-shirt, then go to my bathroom to shower.

After showering, I go downstairs, stand in the dining room, momentarily at a loss as to what comes next. The paper bag Jane put on the kitchen counter last night is still there. I ignore it. Or try to. I turn away from the kitchen. I'm not hungry.

I sit on the couch, unsure what to do. My usual Saturday morning routine is to walk Wallace, try and draw, read the newspaper, watch a bit of TV, and maybe surf the net. But those things don't appeal to me. I should clean Jane's bathroom of my vomit. But that's not something I want to face yet either.

So I sit there.

I have to break the day into signposts to survive. The next one is 9:00am, when I can ring the vet to check on Wallace.

After that, I don't know.

I lie on the couch and clench my phone in my hands, willing Jane to contact me. I don't know what she'd say – maybe she'd want to talk, want to explain why. Maybe she'd tell me she wants a divorce because she's leaving me for Kai.

Anything would be better than nothing.

At 9:00, I grab my phone and call the vet. My eyes fall on Jane's paper bag. The phone continues to ring. An automated message answers, reciting the times of the clinic. I hang up, thinking I'll give it a minute before I call again, but decide to hell with it, grab my keys, and drive over there.

The veterinary nurse, Rebecca, has a smattering of freckles and a big toothy smile that must assure every pet owner who comes in here. She's surprised to see me and tells me they're prepping Wallace for surgery. I ask to see him, so she takes me out the back where Wallace lies on a cot.

His tail spirals and he lifts his head when he sees me. There's a moment where I'm sure he's going to try to get up. I hurry across and pat his side, making sure that he doesn't. He licks my hand, probably in gratitude.

Dr. Dudek comes in. "Casper," she says, "what're you doing here?"

"I thought I'd see him before he went in."

Dr. Dudek rubs my arm. "He'll be okay. We'll call you in the afternoon."

"I could wait."

"You could, but I'm sure you've got things to do."

I can't tell her my world's collapsed.

"Go home, do whatever you've got to do," she says. "We'll call you. Okay?"

"Okay, thanks."

Dr. Dudek rubs Wallace under the chin. "Ready, champ?"

Wallace's spiraling tail slows.

"Okay," Dr. Dudek says, "here goes."

She wheels Wallace out. He watches me until he's out the door.

I don't want to go home to an empty house and since I should have breakfast, I drive to The Corner. Lots of people are out because it's a Saturday morning, so there's no parking. I end up in The Andion's lot, and even debate going in for a beer, although it's only 9:45. No. Definitely not the path to take. I go with my original intention, cross the road, and order a latte and a chocolate donut from Sofia's.

Caroline smiles as she fixes me the latte. Usually, I'd find a table and one of the waitresses would bring out my order, but while Sofia's has a decent morning crowd, there's nobody in the queue behind me, so Caroline does me the courtesy of fixing my order on the spot.

"You're out and about early for a Saturday morning," she says.

I hold up my hands as if to say, *What're you going to do?*

"How's Jane?" she asks.

"Our dog broke his leg," I say, almost robotically.

"What? That's horrible. How did that happen?"

"I'm not sure. I came home and it was broken. The vet's going to operate. Put plates in."

"They do that for dogs?"

"I guess."

"I hope he's okay."

"Yeah."

She finishes fixing the latte, and slides it across the counter. Grabbing some tongs, she picks up a donut and puts it on a plate.

"Where's Leon?" I ask before she can return to Jane.

"He plays golf on Saturday mornings."

I give her the money for the latte and donut.

"You know how it is." She gets my change.

"I know how it is?"

"When you're married. You each have those things you do."

Or people you do.

"Yeah," I say.

"Keeps you sane."

"Keeps you something, all right."

She gives me my change, we trade goodbyes, and I grab my latte and donut. I slip into the corner of the cafe, to the table Beth and I shared on Monday, sit down, stir my latte, and take a bite from my donut. It's too sweet and I have to force myself to chew and swallow. It isn't a very good breakfast choice. Neither's the latte. I barely drink coffee. This is something Jane would have for breakfast.

I take out my phone and rest it on the table.

What I should do is find out where Kai lives and kick the crap out of him. That'd be the typical husband reaction. Somehow, he corrupted Jane. He seduced her. She's innocent in this. Although that's pure hopefulness. It takes two to fuck. And regardless of how it started – even if yesterday was the one and only time they did it – she got involved.

I put my phone in my pocket, get up and go.

My latte remains untouched, my donut with a single bite missing.

It's really warming up outside. I sweat as I cross the road and stride into The Andion's parking lot. I should buy some beer to take home, but don't want to lose control. I won't fall into the same trap my dad did. Normalcy. That's what I need. I should go about my day. The onus isn't on me. It's on Jane. She cheated on me. She left. I'm in the house. If she plans to stay away, at some point she'll need clothes and things.

Of course, if she takes that route – if she comes to collect her things and that's the end of it – then fuck her.

Fuck her anyway.

I stop when I enter The Andion's parking lot. Jean Jacket leans on the driver's door of my car. He's still in his jean jacket, despite the heat. I walk on, get my keys out.

"Hey, buddy," he says. "Shit news about that school girl, huh?"

"Yeah."

"Cops talked to me about her. You put them onto me?"

"What?"

"The other day, when we saw each other … You tell the cops I was harassing her?"

My hand tightens around my keys. "Look, I don't know why you do this to me, but I can't do it right now."

"Do this? Do what?"

"This. *This*." I gesture at him, at me, then back and forth again.

"What? *What?*" He mirrors my gesture.

"This thing we have … between you and I."

"You and me."

"*This*. Dammit."

"Man, you're really uptight."

I unlock the door to my car.

Jean Jacket reaches into his pocket and pulls out what I initially think is a rolled-up cigarette – but of course it's not. He thrusts it in my face.

"Joint?"

"No thanks." I grab the door handle.

"It'll take the edge off."

I open my door. "Leave me alone."

"It's something to relax."

"No."

He yanks something out of his other pocket with his free hand – it's a small transparent bag containing capsules. "Uppers?"

"*What?*"

"Get you up."

"Get *me* up?"

"Happy. You seem a little bleak."

I begin to slide into the driver's seat, but he grabs my shoulder, pinning me against the car. I throw my hands up, although I'm unsure why – whether in surrender, or whether in self-defense. Even my own brain hasn't synchronized to the reflex. But there must be something about me – eyes wide, flaring nostrils, jaw tensed as my mouth draws into a thin line – because Jean Jacket's hand draws back.

He smiles and nods – maybe in approval. "You should stand up for yourself more."

"Thanks. I'll take that under advisement."

I slide into my car and yank the door shut. The heat in the car is stifling. I roll down the window. Jean Jacket leans against the door, his face poking in the open window the way a friend might when they're about to see you off.

"Come on, you must want something," he says. "Everybody wants something."

"I don't want anything."

He reaches into his pocket and plucks out all these baggies, each of them containing something different. "Something to relax?"

"No."

"Something to hallucinate?"

"No."

"Something to get you full of energy?"

"No."

"Something to make you forget?"

I pause, but it's only for a millisecond – long enough for me to think about how nice it would be if I could *un-know* all this. Jean Jacket notices because even though I tell him no, he's right on me.

"So you want to forget?" He grins. His teeth are perfect, and the seediness leaves his face. He holds up a bag of white pills. "How about these? One of these and you won't know anything."

"Nothing. Thank you."

Jean Jacket thrusts another baggy into my face, one that contains triangular blue pills. "Viagra?" he asks.

"What the fuck am I going to do with Viagra?"

Jean Jacket is unblinking and the smile fades until he's earnest – somebody sharing a confidence. "Have some sex. Sex never hurt anyone."

I start the car. "Wanna bet?"

33.

As I approach home, I see Chloe getting out of her car. She's in her nurse's uniform, so she must've just finished a shift. I consider driving past, but she looks over her shoulder and sees me.

I slow the car, but she shows no sign of going into her house. Naturally. So I pull into my drive, slowly reverse onto my nature strip, brace myself, and get out.

"Hi, Casper," she says.

Her hair's tied in its usual topknot ponytail, and her shoulders are upright. She looks bright and perky so, for a moment, I'm sure I've read that situation wrong – she hasn't just come home, but is preparing to leave for work.

"I heard about what happened with Vic," she says. "I'm sorry."

"It's …" *It's not okay. It's deplorable.* That's what I should tell her. "I have to get going."

"Wait, Casper. Wait."

I stop, but don't face her.

"I'm going to have Vic apologize to you."

"No!" I spin back. "God no."

Chloe recoils, surprised at my vehemence.

"I appreciate the thought, but the last thing I need is you fighting my battles."

Chloe unbuttons the top buttons of her shirt. "I understand; I'm sorry. It shouldn't be a battle, and I understand a lot of this is Vic's fault – his temper. All this over a little dog."

I hold up my hands, as if to say, *Well, he's your husband.* "I should go."

Chloe cocks her head, pointing an ear toward my garage. "He with Jane?"

"What? Who? *Vic?*"

"Wallace. He barks when you get home. It's quiet. He's not home?"

"Didn't Vic tell you why we argued?"

"About Wallace coming into our yard."

I *hmph*. "It was a little more than that."

"What?"

"Maybe you should talk to him about that."

"I will – when he gets home. He went into work today." She looks up at the sky, and unbuttons a third button on her shirt. I'm sure I catch a glimpse of something maroon and lacy. "It's going to be a beautiful day. It'd be a shame to be indoors. Maybe I'll sit out by the pool for a little bit."

"That sounds …"

She unbuttons a fourth button – one button too far for modesty (if the third wasn't already), although the lapels of her shirt remained sealed. "You should come over for a swim one day."

"What?"

"You, Jane, me, Vic – maybe we can all sort this out. I don't like this friction. I want us to be good neighbors."

"Good neighbors?"

"*Great* neighbors – the sort who do things together. I've told Jane that when we've gone to the movies."

I open my mouth because that's what you do when you want to respond to somebody, but I have nothing to say.

"If nothing else, you should feel free to come over – enjoy our pool."

"Enjoy your pool?" My voice is hoarse.

"It can get hot. And if you see me splashing around, feel free to join me."

Again, that same offer. "I ... should get going." I thrust a thumb back to my front door.

"Sure. Have a good day, Casper."

"Thanks."

We start up the respective paths to our respective front doors.

"Oh, Casper!"

I turn. Chloe smiles at me.

"Don't forget my offer," she says.

She twirls coquettishly while I stumble for the appropriate response, and disappears into her house.

I make myself a tea, gulp down a glass of orange juice, and force myself to eat two slices of toast. Jane's paper bag still sits on the kitchen counter. It's stupid, but the way the paper's crinkled, it looks like a craggy face watching me. I shy away from it as I contemplate Chloe's offer.

Signs are never something I've been good at reading, but I'm sure Chloe hit on me – twice. The first time she tried to redeem her offer of a swim by claiming to be neighborly and including Vic and Jane in the invitation. Was that an advance also? I don't know. I think of the amateur porn Vic was watching when I went over last night. Maybe they have an open relationship. Maybe they're swingers. Maybe they're into group things? Who knows what goes on behind their closed doors – behind *any* closed doors? I can't straighten things out in my head. And as far as Chloe goes, I've never understood how she can be married to Vic – or how anybody could – but who knows how and why couples become couples?

For a moment – or perhaps two or three moments – I entertain the notion of dropping around to her place. It's false bravado, but I can dream. It'd be just me and Chloe. We'd chat poolside, flirt, and who knows where that could go? It would be payback against Jane, and a *screw you* to Vic.

I plug my phone into charge and sit it on the kitchen counter, then wash my dishes. Done. All that remains now is the ugly job of cleaning Jane's bathroom.

I grab a bucket, fill it with hot water and detergent, and carry it and the mop upstairs. The landing smells of vomit. It's worse in the bedroom, and in the bathroom it's so thick that I gag and have to lift the collar of my T-shirt over my nose, like a makeshift gas mask.

Opening the window, I wave my hands, ushering the stench out. I clean the toilet, wiping the seat down, and flush repeatedly. Then I mop the floor until it's glistening, rinse and clean the mop, and dump the water down the laundry sink. Once I'm done, I feel like a beer, although it's still early and I know I shouldn't.

I go back up to the second floor. The smell's still there, so I open the windows in our spare rooms, in the landing, in the bathroom, and finally in the bedroom. The curtains flutter as a breeze wafts through the bedroom.

I stop.

Chloe emerges from the back door of her house. She wears a pair of sunglasses, a sunhat, and a frilly little red silk robe, her legs bare. She carries a couple of small bottles in one hand – I'm sure one's water. The other might be suntan lotion. In the other hand she holds a magazine.

She walks around the pool. The hem of her robe bounces around her hips – it looks like she's not wearing anything underneath. She drops her stuff on one of the banana lounges, then slips off her robe to reveal a tiny red G-string bikini bottom. Her skin is latte all over – no tan lines, so maybe she does this regularly, although neither Jane nor I have ever seen her. Her breasts are pointed, the nipples swollen.

I run my hand down the front of my shorts. Chloe's sultriness overwhelms me, and this voyeurism is tantalizing, although I've never experienced this before. I shouldn't be horny, but now all I can think of is how much I would love to fuck Chloe – to fuck somebody who's not my partner the way Jane did.

Chloe bends toward her banana lounge to clear the things she dropped there, putting the two bottles on one side, the magazine on the other. Her buttocks arch into taut curves. The G-string may as well not be there.

I run my hand inside my shorts. The top button of my shorts opens. I slide my hand across the length of my cock.

Chloe sits on the banana lounge, grabs her small bottle, and squirts it at her chest. White lotion splatters her skin. I'm reminded of Kai blowing on Jane's face. I push the image from my mind. Chloe massages the lotion over her breasts and down her belly until her torso's shining like the bathroom tiles I've just mopped.

I unzip my shorts, let them fall around my ankles, and push my underwear down. My erection stretches forward. I run my hand up and down it and think about how it would feel to have Chloe's lips wrapped around me, how she would compare to Jane. She would be better. At least in this fantasy, on this day, she would. I close my eyes and think about how it'd happen. I'd march around to her backyard. She'd tell me she wants to make it up to me for what Vic did. She'd drop to her knees, and take me in her mouth. I masturbate faster.

I open my eyes. She has her left leg held aloft and is massaging lotion into it. Then she does the right leg, finishing by running her hands up the inside of her thighs, her thumbs outlining the triangle of her bikini bottom. She lies back. Her breasts splay. I imagine how they'd bounce if I were on top of her, fucking her, the way her legs – shorter than Jane's, but with the sharp curves of a gym junky – would wrap around my hips, her arms locked around my neck, the sound of her gasping in my ear.

Her head swivels. Although she's wearing her sunglasses, I'm sure her eyes are on my window. I stumble back, shorts wrapped around my ankles, get tangled in the curtains and pull them down as I hit the bedside table and fall onto the bed.

I sit there, the curtain tangled around me like a web. Surely she saw me. There'll be a knock on the door, and Chloe will lambaste me for spying on her. Who knows how far it'll go once Vic gets involved?

Hauling myself up, I lift the curtain. My erection is like a compass pointing to the window. I tiptoe back.

Chloe's now lying on her belly trying to rub lotion on her buttocks and back as best as she can. Perhaps she saw me, and this is her way of covering up. Surely it's not part of her tanning cycle. She'd just started on her front. Of course, if she knew she was being watched, she'd go inside – unless it's her intent to be watched.

I restore the curtain, then stroke my erection.

Perhaps this *is* all for my benefit. Vic's out for the day. Maybe she put the thought of the pool into my head, then decided to provide this exhibition. Do people's minds work that way? Or is this my imagination? Would I have thought this before I found that condom?

The phone rings from downstairs.

I freeze. My hand remains wrapped around my erection, my eyes fixed on Chloe's butt.

The phone continues to ring.

I want to ignore it, but there's too much going on *to* ignore it.

I drag up my underwear and shorts, zip and button up, and rush downstairs.

34.

As I run downstairs, I consider who could be ringing: Beth, checking up on me; Stuart, with some developments on what's happening with Bianca; the police, wanting to question me about Bianca (although I don't know if that's how they work); the vet, updating me about Wallace; and – I find I'm hoping for this most of all – Jane, because she wants to talk.

I slide into the dining room, cross the floor to the counter, and grab my phone. I don't recognize the number.

"Hello?"

"Mr. or Mrs. Gray, please?" It's a man's voice, very crisp.

I amble into the kitchen and grab a beer from the fridge without even thinking about it. "Mr. Gray speaking."

"Good morning, Mr. Gray. This is Oscar Finchley from Finchley Photography. I am confirming an appointment for 10:30am tomorrow for your anniversary portrait."

I hang up.

Oscar Finchley calls back immediately. I answer before a quarter of the ring is out of the phone.

"Mr. Gray?" he says. "I'm sorry, we seem to have been cut off. So 10:30am tomorrow?"

It's absurd – beyond absurd. But I think of all the anniversary pictures that have preceded this one, the line of photographs commemorating each year spent together, me in those pointed suits, starched shirts, and asphyxiating ties Jane hand chose for me. What happens when nothing comes next? Is it like an incomplete bridge over some incomprehensible chasm? Do we drive off it and plummet forever?

"Call my wife!" I say, and hang up again.

Breath ragged, heat fuming in my temples, I want to run back to my bedroom window and see what Chloe's up to. I want her to fellate me and I want to fuck her. I want to bend her over her banana lounge, fuck her anally, then spray her face in cum. I want to do to her all the things Kai did to Jane. It's karmic. And therapeutic. I want to know what a woman gets out of that. What Jane – who's hardly ever been adventurous beyond a few positions – gets out of it. And *why* she gets whatever she does out of it.

Is it passion that transcends physicality? That borders on aggression? There's the cliché of becoming one in lovemaking. But what I saw yesterday was subjugation. I'm not sure what lies there. The destruction of inhibition? Then what's left? Sex? Nothing?

My erection is gone now.

I bound upstairs, into the bedroom, open my top drawer, and take out Jane's anniversary gift. Opening the box, I snatch the bracelet, then throw the box as I stride to the bathroom. The box bounces on the carpet. I don't know where it lands.

Inside the bathroom, I drop the bracelet into the toilet, then flush.

I leave the bathroom without looking back.

35.

I attack the backyard wall with the sledgehammer, my swings wild but unrelenting.

My shoulders get sore first. Then my biceps. Then tearing pains in my chest. Then my throat burns from my heaving breath. Sweat stings my eyes. Fingers and palms blister. Lower back tightens until claws dig into my buttocks. My T-shirt sticks to me. My calves bulge. The soles of my feet grow sore – it feels like the skin under the ball of my right foot has sheared right off. The constant clash of the sledgehammer against the rock wall is like gunshots.

But I go on until the first cracks appear in the mortar. A stone falls. I kick at the wall with my sandaled feet, oblivious to the pain that erupts in my heel. Then I smash the top of the wall with the sledgehammer again. Another stone tumbles free almost shyly.

I collapse onto the grass, exhausted. The sledgehammer falls from my grip. I bury my head in one hand.

My chest heaves. My eyes tighten. My left eye squeezes out a single tear. I grimace, fall onto my side and curl up. The tears will come now. They'll wash me away. But there's nothing more. Maybe I'm dehydrated, although I don't know if crying works like that.

I should sit up. I should go inside. I should shower.

I should do anything but continue to lie here.

But I lie here all the same.

I stare up into the sky. This is when Wallace should nuzzle me. When I should go inside and Jane should be there. When we should talk about what we're going to do tonight – maybe catch a movie or go out somewhere to eat.

We could do anything.

My clothes dry quickly but I must smell from the sweat. Muscles and blisters ache. I'll feel it tomorrow but that's okay. I wonder if Chloe heard all this going on. Maybe she'll come and check on me. Maybe not. Maybe from now on I'll be alone and that's the way it'll be – just me and Wallace.

The wall looks like somebody's taken a bite out of the top. It should satisfy me, but its destruction seems irrelevant now. Why do I want to be like everybody else who's torn the wall down? There's nothing wrong with being different. I stand up. The wall's fine – except for the damage I've done, as pathetic as it is.

I twirl the sledgehammer. I've put it through so much for nothing. At least it's been faithful to me – *he's* been faithful to me. I've decided: the sledgehammer is a male. He's a good sledgehammer. I should take him to school. Teach with him. Do yard duty with him. Supervise kids during busy duty with him. That'd go over well.

"What're you doing?"

I recognize the voice before I turn – Luke.

"I rang the bell," he says.

"Don't always hear it from here."

"Your neighbor – hot little blonde nurse with a ponytail going to work – said she thought you were out the back because she heard banging."

"What're you doing here?"

"Jane told me to drop by. I've got a couple of hours before work. So I thought I'd drop by."

"Really? In all the time we've lived here, in all the years you *haven't* dropped by, you thought you'd drop by?"

"I was a little worried by your response yesterday when I texted you. Everything okay?"

I shrug.

"Where's Jane?"

I hold up my hands.

"What's going on?"

I brush the grass from my shorts. "I need a drink," I say.

Luke drives us to The Andion. Neither of us say anything, like we're embargoing serious conversation until we get there.

We grab a couple of beers, sit at a table by the window, and settle in. The air-conditioning in the bistro is cool and the beer cold. Luke has a porterhouse steak while I force myself to have a veal schnitzel, which tastes surprisingly good – I must be running on empty, so maybe my body appreciates the meal even if I don't.

It could be any other Saturday afternoon.

But it isn't.

"You know where this Kai lives?" Luke asks, after I finish telling him about Jane. The knuckles bulge on the hand that holds his steak knife.

"No."

"Can you find out?"

"I guess."

"Find out."

"So you can beat the shit out of him?"

"You're too fucking soft."

"What?"

"When we were kids, me, you, and Stephen were fearless. Stephen grew up to be this safe, solid, boring guy, but you became hypersensitive to everything."

I don't say anything. It's the truth.

"What was it? Your mom? Your dad? What a loser you were with girlfriends before Jane?"

"I wasn't a loser."

"*You* were a loser – you were too … fairytale sweet."

"And what were you? Model perfect—"

"I've got my own issues. We all do. It's how you deal with them in the here, in the now, that matters."

"That's very Zen."

"It's reality. We're *here* now. Okay? And being here, everybody faces a time in their lives where they have to take a stand."

"I've gone through all this in my head. Where's it get me to beat up Kai?"

"It gets you satisfaction. You're telling me this cunt sprayed Jane? He put his mark on her. Have you thought about that?"

"I don't want to think about it."

"You should. He didn't just fuck your wife, he branded her. Do you think that's an intimate gesture?"

"I don't know what it is."

"That's like a *You're my slut* gesture."

"That's what it is?"

"That's what it is."

"Have you done it?" I ask, although I really don't want the visual in my head.

"Yeah, but that's like in … *sex*. When anything goes."

"Have you done it to this girl You're seeing? What was her name? Sandra?"

"*Chandra*."

"You done it to Chandra?"

"She's *my* girlfriend."

"Why'd you do it to her?"

"Because it's a fucking turn-on."

"For you or for her?"

"She hasn't complained."

"What do you get out of it?"

"I get out of it that she'd do that for me, and that when we're fucking, she's basically my slut."

"I'm amazed you haven't been married, you know?"

"I'm not saying that in a derogatory way, okay? Sex is about no inhibitions. No defenses. Nothing. So if your partner's fine with it, anything goes. When we're having sex, she's my slut. I'm her … well, whatever the equivalent is. Manslut, maybe. I'd do anything for her."

"You know, let's put this conversation away."

"It's the ultimate vulnerability – giving yourself where there's no defenses. The ultimate trust. No restrictions. Nothing."

"Well, that's what I saw."

"There you go," Luke says with aplomb. "With *him*. Not you. *Him*."

"Look, I just want to work out where I go from here."

"There's nowhere *to* go from here."

"How can there be nowhere to go?"

"Where *do* you go from here?"

I take a drink from my beer and look at what's left of my veal schnitzel.

"Three things can happen from here," Luke says. "One: she leaves you for this cunt. Two: she leaves both of you. Three: she comes back and wants to move on. Let's say it's the third option. Do you want to move on with her?"

I'm about to answer, but Luke cuts me off.

"Hang on. Think about this: she wouldn't still be able to work where she does – well, she better not want to. Whenever she's not with you, you're going to wonder where she is. If she's late home, you'll wonder *why* she's late. If she gets messages or phone calls or emails from anybody you don't know, you'll wonder who they're from. There's a fuckload of things like that to consider. Don't give me some bullshit answer that if you choose to move on, you'll have to rebuild the trust and all that crap. Okay, that's what's meant to happen. Can *you* do it? I couldn't. We could be together another fifty years, she could be beyond reproach, and I'd still never trust her the same."

Luke puts down his knife and fork and thrusts out his right arm. Just under the elbow is a jagged, round scar about the size of a beer cap. When we were fifteen, Stephen, Luke, and I were riding our bikes when Luke crashed on a gravel path. He tore this gash out of his elbow. They had to stitch it up, but it got infected and it took forever to heal.

"Remember this?" he asks.

"Yeah."

"I never have any problems with it. Most of the time I forget it. Time will fade it more and more. But it *is* there. It'll *always* be there. And every time I look at it I remember what happened and all the shit I went through to fix it. Jane's going to be your walking fucking reminder. Kiss her and see this cunt's cum over her lips. See his cock in her mouth—"

"Okay, okay—"

"No, not okay *okay*. This is what you'll have to deal with. If you can move past all this shit with her, then either you're fucking moronic or you got some heart of gold and love her with love she doesn't deserve. Or maybe they're the same thing. Me? You two get back together, I won't be able to forgive her because there's some shit you just don't do. People say shit, they do shit, but some things can't be undone. Some things can't be unsaid."

"Nothing's been said."

"Things will be said. She'll blame you in some way – maybe you weren't finding her attractive enough. Maybe you weren't paying enough attention to her. *You* drove her to it. It'll be your fault. I heard my dad use this shit with my mom. Do me a favor when Jane starts that shit? Tell her to grow the fuck up. Cunt. Sorry. But she is. She shits me that she's done this."

"I couldn't tell."

Luke mimics a laugh. "You know, whatever happens, you need somebody to talk to, you need a place to crash, *anything*, *any time*, you can call me. Remember that."

"Thanks."

"I fucking mean it. People make offers they never see through. I'm telling you, okay?"

"I nod."

Luke lifts his glass in half a toast.

I finish my beer. It's starting to go down well.

After we leave The Andion, I give in and buy a case of Coronas. Then Luke drives me home. Outside my place, he reiterates his offer to call on him any time.

"I'll drop you a text tomorrow, okay?" he says.

"I'll be fine."

"Humor me."

I thank him, grab my case of beer from the back, rest it on my lap and open the door.

"You know," Luke says, "watch the drinking, too."

"What?"

"It's okay; have a few. Take yourself apart. It's what you're meant to do in shit situations. But you have to put yourself back together."

"I'm not my dad."

"It's a warning applicable to anybody at a time like this."

"Okay. Thanks."

"One last thing," Luke says.

"Yeah?"

"You stink, mate."

I chuckle, get out of the car, and slam the door shut.

36.

I cram all twenty-four Coronas from the case into the fridge. If Jane were here, I'd put six in the fridge, maybe another six in the small fridge we have in the garage, and let the others sit around until needed. Usually, a case would last me a couple of months. But for now, there's something satisfying about seeing them all lined up.

Since I've had a couple at The Andion, I have the taste to keep drinking, and consider popping one. It's 2:34. If I keep drinking from hereon, I'll be out of it by 6:00. Maybe that's not such a bad thing. Maybe it is, in fact, the best thing. But it scares me also. So far, I've maintained this eerie control. What sits on the other side of it?

I take another shower, leaving my sweaty clothes scattered across the floor, then go downstairs, feeling fresh and relieved, like the day is new and full of possibilities. Right then, I'm sure I can get through this, that I'll be okay.

I check the time again on my phone: 3:01. I should've heard from the vet about Wallace by now. Surely nothing's gone wrong? Although they would've rung me if something had – unless they're afraid to tell me the worst. Of course, vets don't work like that. They're professionals.

I call the vet – Rebecca, the nurse, answers immediately.

"Hi," I say. "It's Casper Gray. My dog Wallace was having surgery this morning to have plates inserted for a broken leg."

"That's right, Mr. Gray."

"I was wondering how it went."

"It went great."

I wait for elaboration.

"And?" I have to prompt.

"I'm sorry, Mr. Gray – your wife was in here earlier. Dr. Dudek spoke to her. Haven't you spoken to her?"

"No."

"I'm sorry. We assumed she was coming home."

"No. I haven't spoken to her. She went out."

"Oh, okay."

"So, Wallace …?"

"Dr. Dudek thinks he'll make a full recovery. She said the break was clean and the bones aligned perfectly. Wallace is sleeping in recovery. You should be able to get him tomorrow."

"Thanks. Is it okay if I come in and see him?"

"You can. But he'll be sleeping off the anesthetic."

"Did my wife see him?"

"Yes. She and her friend saw him."

"Thanks."

I hang up.

◙

I grab a beer, and sit on the couch.

◙

Friend. Jane brought a friend to see Wallace. Did she bring Kai? Is he that close that he's lending emotional support? I'm an idiot. I should've asked who the friend was. It mightn't have been Kai. Maybe it was Sarah.

I take my beer and jump in the car.

I finish my beer on the way to the vet. By now, the afternoon's so hot that I feel it burn in the air. I'm sweating again. I'll need another shower. And I'm busting to piss.

When I reach the vet, I stand briefly under the door, the air-conditioning firing cool air right into my face. In the waiting room there's a couple of people with dogs, somebody with a Ragdoll cat, and somebody with a parakeet. The eyes of the animals have that soulful inquisitiveness that only animals and children have, like they're trying to work out why they're hurt, how it's going to be fixed, and who are all these humans they have to navigate?

Rebecca, sitting at reception, smiles when she sees me. "So you came to see Wallace after all?"

"Yeah."

"He's asleep."

"Can I see him?"

"Come this way."

Rebecca leads me out the back. Wallace is sleeping on a cot. A drip leads from his heavily bandaged right leg. I hate the sight of the drip. I know it's probably providing pain relief and fluids, but it makes me think of where needles go when dogs are put down.

I scratch Wallace behind the ear and watch his chest heave regularly. Poor little thing is going to struggle over the coming weeks. I'll have to take his basket out of the laundry. God knows how I'm going to arrange for him to be watched while I work. Jane's parents don't work. They could babysit. But who knows their availability, given the circumstances.

"Poor boy," Rebecca says. "Did you find out how it happened?"

"No."

I kneel by Wallace. His eyes are closed slits and the tip of his tongue pokes out from his mouth. I blink. Now there's a couple of tears. I wipe them away.

Rebecca pats me on the shoulder. "It's okay, Mr. Gray. He'll be okay. In six weeks, he'll be as good as new. You're going to have to take extra special care of him when you get him home."

"Like?"

"Dr. Dudek explained everything to your wife."

"Could you … you know, for my sake?"

Rebecca stares at me, failing to make sense of that.

"I'd like to be prepared."

"You'll have to restrict his movement. Keep him locked in the laundry – or, better yet, get one of those kid playpens and keep him in that."

"It's not like he's going to be running on it, is he?"

"No. But he'll probably start experimenting on it within the next day – you know, putting his foot down, seeing how much it hurts, so you have to restrict his opportunities. The playpen is best. Only take him out to do his business."

"What else?"

"You'll have to bring him in every couple of days so Dr. Dudek can check for inflammation and infection, and so we can change the dressing. He's in for a tough time, but he should make a full recovery. Dogs are resilient like that. They're not like us. They don't have the same hang-ups. They adapt, they move on."

I get up. "Who was my wife in here with?"

Rebecca blinks, unprepared for my change of tack. "Sorry?"

"My wife. Who did she come in with?"

"Some woman. She was very pretty. Very made up. Looked like she was going clubbing!"

Sarah. My whole body loosens. So Jane didn't run straight to Kai, although she could've gone to Kai's, then to Sarah's, or even spent the night with Kai, then gone to Sarah's in the morning, but I prefer to think she went straight to Sarah's and Sarah's the only person Jane's dealt with.

"Is everything all right, Mr. Gray?"

I wipe my eyes with a wrist. "Yeah. I …"

I'm going to make up an excuse: *I don't like seeing Wallace like this*. And part of that's the truth. But Rebecca doesn't have to know.

"Thanks," I say.

I leave the recovery room.

37.

When I get home, I jump in the shower in Jane's bathroom, urinate in there, wash my hair and myself, then stand under the water until it grows tepid. I get out, change into yet another set of fresh clothes and leave the old ones strewn across the floor like they're victims at a crime scene.

I go downstairs and stand in the dining room, again unsure of what to do. There's that hateful sense of waiting. I'm tempted to text Jane, and ask her to talk, although I don't know what I'd say. It's then that I decide I need her to come to me before I can formulate any response of my own.

I get my sketchpad from the kitchen counter, sit on the couch, and open the sketchpad to a new page.

A lot of great artists suffered. Maybe this is what I needed – at least as far as my drawing's concerned. I take a deep breath, and wait for inspiration to move me. And, if this were a movie, it would. There'd be a masterpiece. That's what would come out of all this. I'd enter some fugue and draw something breathtaking. Maybe Jane would see it and the picture would signify my pain and she'd understand.

The blank page remains blank.

I grab a beer, sit back down, but nothing. I go through the sketchpad, look at the pictures of inanimate objects and the portraits of Wallace. This is the way it was before all this began and this is the way it is after. Maybe all I have in me are simple pictures. I don't look at the sketch of Jane, or think about what could've been.

Finishing my beer, I grab another. My mind relaxes, but not in the right way. I fixate back on the house's emptiness. Kai's responsible. I think of Luke's simple violent solution. Vic would do it. Luke definitely would. Wouldn't most men?

I don't know where my rage is.

Kai.

He's responsible.

Kai ...?

And then I wrack my memory, trying to remember his surname. He introduced himself that day he returned Jane's handbag.

Kai ...? Bardot? No. Vardy? Uh uh.

Bardy. That's it!

Kai fucking Bardy.

I have no plan in mind. It's curiosity more than anything. But I use my phone to pull up the White Pages and look up Kai Bardy. In all likelihood, I won't find a listing, and that'll be the end of it. But I do. And not far from me – but, of course, Jane did say he lived out this way.

I lie on the couch, sip at my beer, and think about the things I could do to Kai, think about where I could shove the sledgehammer, think about what I could smash, and, most of all, think about where it would get me. No. This isn't helpful. That's Luke talking.

I pick up my sketchpad again, and now my mind's working, it's really working. But it has nothing to do with drawing. How can one man take another's wife? How can he break up their home? How can he be so oblivious?

Finishing my beer, I grab another, and sketch an arc across the blank page. It's wrong. I tear out the page, scrunch it up, and toss it on the floor. I start a new sketch, a single line that serves as a cornerstone. Now I have it. Nope. Nothing else comes. Another crushed page joins the first one on the floor.

Over the next several hours, I begin sketches, although perhaps *begin* is a misnomer. I draw lines, break the virginity of the page, sure some masterpiece will unravel from my imagination now that I have a cue. But only emptiness follows, emptiness and the page ripped from the sketchpad, the page crumpled up, and tossed to the floor.

Inevitably, I run out of paper. Some forty scrunched-up sheets litter the floor, mocking me, while my empty beers stand stoically in a ring, like pallbearers, around the dying roses in the vase on the coffee table – the roses I bought Jane the other night.

I flick back through the sketchpad, ending with the unfinished portrait of Jane – Jane, when I was sure she loved me, loved me exclusively and devotedly, and we shared an evening that I thought crystallized our union into something beyond reproach.

I close the sketchpad.

Time to visit Kai.

38.

I jump in the car. Start the engine. Look at the dashboard clock: 4:51pm.

As usual when I try to draw, time's slipped by.

Or maybe it's not the drawing and this new space I live in. Maybe the rules of physics and logic don't work here, which would explain why I'm sitting here, thinking about confronting my wife's lover.

I shut off the engine and sit there.

I get out of the car, get the sledgehammer from the garage, put him in the back seat, and restart the engine.

I kill the engine. Get out. Grab a beer from the house, open it, and jump back in the car. I put the beer in the cup holder and start the engine.

39.

As I drive, I rehearse scenarios in my mind. In some I beat up Kai. In others I rant at him, like he's a naughty kid who needs a talking to. I know none of it will work out close to the way I imagine. Real life never does. But I want to see him. I want him to look in the eye the husband of the woman he's fucking.

Of course, he already did that earlier in the week when he returned Jane's bag. I'd forgotten about that. They'd probably been fucking then. My right hand tightens around the wheel. It'd probably been a joke to them. I swill a third of the beer. Jane had been showering. She'd come to the balustrade of the landing in her robe.

I couldn't believe it when I saw you at the door, Jane might've said to him the next day.

You looked good in your robe, your leg sticking out.

I was thinking of you.

Yeah? What were you thinking of?

Fucking you. Fucking you hard.

I take another drink and weave through traffic. Honk people going slow. Cars are too close. If I'm pulled over, that'll be it. I'll be over the limit. I will also have to explain the sledgehammer in the back seat. I try to come up with a reason for it, but with no luck.

My phone buzzes. I dig it out of my pocket. It's Beth:

Hey you. You okay?

I look up just in time to see the traffic's stopped. I slam on the brakes. The tires shriek, the car jolts. I'm thrown into the steering wheel. The breath's squashed from my lungs. I sit up. Inhale. There's a pain in my chest, but it'll pass.

I grab the seatbelt and put it on, then take a drink to steady myself.

And to keep me going.

There're a lot of little winding streets and I get lost several times. I'm about to pull over and check the GPS on my phone when I reach the top of a hill and see the turn-off to Kai's street.

Taking the corner, I brace myself.

The first thing I spot is Kai's big blue Ford. It's so ostentatious in a sprawling lot that must serve as parking for everybody who lives in this block. The flats themselves are unspectacular – an array of dirty, tan-bricked flats that might've been vomited out in design, and which can't be much to rent monthly.

Parking by the curb, I finish what's left of my beer – which has gone warm and makes me gag – and get out.

I walk across the block's parking lot. There's a dull roar in my ears. I don't know what it is. My breath's catching. I feel my heart too hard and so fast it might be accelerating to an implosion. But it feels good. It's the driving tempo of whatever I'm feeling. Anger, indignation, outrage – I don't know if any of them are accurate.

But at least it's something.

The security door on Kai's flat is scratched and the flyscreen's ripped. When I pull the door, it squeals and comes too quickly. The piston that should control its pace is busted. The top hinge of the door is also loose so the door hangs askew in the jamb.

I knock on the door. I want to thump. I want to kick it down. But I don't want to give Kai cause to *not* answer, or to hide.

The door opens. Kai stands there in a shirt that might've once been white, cut-off jeans hanging halfway down his hips (exposing the rim of blue boxers), and bare feet. The door jerks in his hand, like he wants to slam it shut. He stops himself, and holds my gaze, although I can see in his eyes he's forcing himself to. There's a shake in the arm that holds the door.

I don't know what I plan to do. I go to hoist the sledgehammer over my shoulder – just a threatening little gesture, but it's now I realize I've left the sledgehammer in the back seat of the car. I wonder how it would look if I excuse myself to get him. Of course, I can't do that. New plan of attack. I could punch Kai – an uppercut into his guts. Or I could kick him in the kneecap. Or in the balls. That would be more fitting. But facing him, I don't know why I'm here.

I shove him in the chest. He bounces back inside. I enter after him into a well of heat that's unbearable.

A little hallway shoots through an archway into the dining room. The curtains are drawn. What looks to be a seventy-inch LCD TV stands on a cabinet. There's some music clip on I don't recognize. In one corner, a small fan blows uselessly across the room.

The dining room itself is a mess: there's a little coffee table with magazines and newspapers all over it, their pages fluttering under the fan's duress; clothes (some of which look unwashed) lie on a tattered couch; and I count three glasses – one on an end table by the couch, one by the foot of the recliner, and one on the

TV cabinet – which seem to have been forgotten. Several laptops and a desktop computer tangled in a web of cables crowd a small table in one corner.

"She's not …" Kai starts.

I spin, and now the rage escalates. His voice. His fucking voice. This is the voice that somehow seduced Jane (I rebuke the thought that maybe she seduced him), and it's such a whiny, pretentious voice I don't know how it appeals to anybody.

He stands in the archway. Bows his head.

I go into the adjoining kitchenette and rifle through the cupboards. There isn't much food; all I see are cans – canned tuna, canned beans, canned corn. I open the fridge. It's small, pitiful, and doesn't have much in it either, although there are three beers on the bottom shelf. The brand's Asahi, a Japanese beer.

This could be a commercial now. I could grab a beer, smile, and pitch to camera, *Your wife cheated on you? Try an Asahi – straight from the adulterer's fridge. You know you're drinking the best when you're drinking Asahi.* It's such a random, aberrant thought – one that a mind in shock must regurgitate when no other reason remains.

I grab one of the beers, leave the fridge door open, and jerk open a kitchen drawer I think might have a bottle opener in it. It doesn't. It has junk – a torch, some keys, tape, just miscellaneous stuff like that. I yank the drawer all the way out of its slides and let it fall to the floor.

"Hey," Kai says, although it's barely a protest.

I open another drawer. This one has tea towels in it – I make sure it joins the other one the floor.

"Hey!" Kai says, louder now, as he steps forward.

I go for another drawer. This one has kitchen utensils in it. There's a big knife, as well as a steak knife, which I take out and place on the counter. I could thrust either into Kai and disembowel him. He stops his approach, like he fears that's a possibility. I find a bottle opener, open my beer, leave the bottle opener on the kitchen counter, take a drink, then wrench that drawer to the floor. The sound of all the utensils crashing down is like a cacophony of cymbals.

I go back through the dining room, noticing a smell I hadn't picked up on before because of the fan. It's staleness: the staleness of clothes that haven't been washed, carpets that haven't been vacuumed, and a room that hasn't been aired out. This is what our house grew to smell like after Mom died, and reeked of just before I moved out. Well, that, and Scotch – Dad's drink of choice. The added ingredient here is musk – a cologne, perhaps. It's a good cologne. I can tell that much just by the scent of it. But a good cologne doesn't drown out bad smells; it just creates this weird cocktail of a sickeningly sweet bad smell.

Drinking my beer, I head into the hallway and check the other rooms. The bathroom is tiny – you'd have to sit in the tub – and a crack runs through the glass partition of the shower cubicle. The toilet is small, and the toilet itself low. Then there's a small empty room, which must be a laundry, although it contains no washing machine.

Finally, the bedroom. I expect maybe this'll be the pinnacle of Kai's majesty, but it's like the rest of his place. It's small, the curtains drawn, and has a set of double doors that probably lead into a closet. The bed's nothing special – just a regular double bed with a beige quilt. But it might be a bed on which my wife has fucked.

I see Jane straddling Kai on the bed … although it wouldn't be the measured pace we enjoy. Not after what I saw. I take a drink. A big drink. The Asahi's bitter after the smoothness of the Corona, but it's a nice beer. Half of it goes down in one gulp.

How many ways has Jane fucked him? How many things has she done with him that she's never done with me? How familiar has she become to him? How uninhibited, how *vulnerable* – as Luke would put it – has she been?

I take another drink. Kai's come about halfway down the hall. The open door silhouettes him. Now he steps back, and presses himself against the wall like he wants to clear the way for me to take the door.

"She told me it's over," he says.

I finish the beer, spin it in my hand, and catch it by the neck so I'm holding it like a hammer.

He draws back. I approach him. He flattens against the wall.

"It's really … you know, I'm sorry," he says. "It shouldn't have happened."

I walk past him back into the dining room, and then into the kitchenette. I grab another beer. Open it. Take a drink. Then I stand there, and imagine all the places Kai might've fucked Jane: on the couch, over the coffee table, against the TV cabinet, over the kitchen counter, pushed up against the jamb of the archway in which Kai now squirms.

I shake my head.

Walk back across the dining room. Hurl the empty bottle at the LCD TV. The plan is to shatter it, but my inebriated aim is bad. The bottle smashes against the wall above the TV. Shards of glass spray everywhere.

"Hey!" Kai says.

He advances on me. I spin. He stops. He holds his hands up. That's the extent of his defiance. He doesn't know I accidentally missed the TV. Better that he thinks it was a warning. Of course, I could still smash the TV, but it seems redundant now.

I take another drink of my beer. "I could come back," I say. "I don't know. If I do, I don't know what I'll do to you."

And I mean this because I've taken some schism into a place I've never been, some confused, angry, desperate place that's abandoned all my typical meekness and is driving me into a realm where nothing's certain anymore.

I start for the door. Turn just as I reach it. Kai gapes at me. He's worked it out: I have no idea what I'm doing, but he knows I might snap – all I need is the trigger. He doesn't move, doesn't breathe, as if that inactivity will grant him invisibility.

I leave his shithole.

I drive back up the hill. The setting sun's waiting at the top. It blazes into my eyes.

I head home.

40.

My stomach's grumbling by the time I pull into the drive. There's an acidic taste in the back of my throat. I've drunk too much. I should eat something, but don't think I'll be able to keep anything down. I grab the beer from the cup holder. There's half left. I should tip it out. But I finish it and grimace.

Grabbing the empty bottle and the sledgehammer from the back, I get out of my car. I hoist the sledgehammer over my shoulder, the way a soldier would carry a rifle. He's been a good friend over the last couple of days, even if I didn't need him today. There's nothing I can't do with him. I'm like Thor, the God of Thunder. That's who I've become. Well, except for the *Thunder* part. More like *Blunder*.

I put the sledgehammer away, then look at the emptiness of the garage.

Minutes later it's not empty anymore – I bring my car in, but as I use the remote control to close the garage door, all I can think is I'm fortifying myself in my own home, like I'm preparing for a long siege.

Or maybe it's not a siege but a hibernation.

I stand in the kitchen, yet again unsure what to do with myself. My beer remains on the coffee table. I've barely touched it. The allure's gone out of the drinking. I should stop – that's what I need to do. I have non-specific memories of Dad drinking – non-specific because what was going on became omnipresent. There was always a Scotch, sometimes a beer. Mostly, I'm struck by how bland a drunk he was – he wasn't demonstrative, wasn't abusive, wasn't anything but a cocoon of the man metamorphosing into his eventual death. It's not the first time I've told myself, but I can't keep drinking. I decide to order a pizza, so I fish my phone out of my pocket.

They tell me there'll be over an hour's wait – if not more – on account of it being Saturday night. I mumble indifference, although it makes me think about how the world's moving on while I'm trapped in purgatory. Nobody's waiting for me to get myself in order.

The doorbell rings. I should worry about who it is given the events of the last two days. It could be Kai, maybe with a gun – although that's a bit dramatic. Still, weird things happen when people are driven to extremes, especially when passion's involved. I should've kept the sledgehammer with me.

As I shuffle down the hallway, I decide I don't care. Not anymore. Where do I go from here? It can be Kai with a shotgun. It can be the police come to arrest me over Bianca. It can be Vic on a tirade. It can be Chloe to seduce me. It can be Jane come to collect her things. It can be anybody, and it doesn't matter.

I open the door.

It's none of them.

Maya stands there in a pink blouse, a modest denim skirt, and sandals. Her frame is athletic – not something I've ever been able to tell in her school uniform. Her legs are long and slender. Under her left arm, she holds a big sketchpad.

"Hi, Mr. Gray!" she says. "I hope you don't mind – I looked up where you live. There were lots of Grays, but when I saw 'C Gray' right here in Meadow, I knew it had to be you!"

"You … looked … me … up?"

"You said you'd like to see my other sketches one day. So I thought I'd bring them over. Is that okay?"

She has the enthusiasm of a puppy. I hate to crush it – although yesterday she was too embarrassed to look at me. There's something to be said for the innocence of schoolgirl crushes, but Principal Hetrick's warning – about responsibility – resounds in my mind, not to mention I'm already in enough trouble over Bianca.

I must concern Maya, the way I'm standing here wordlessly. She sniffs, and takes a small step back.

"Have you been drinking, Mr. Gray?"

"I was working outside. In the yard. I've been cooling off with a beer."

Maya smiles. Just like that, she trusts me. No wonder both Principal Hetrick and Stuart are so concerned about the way I handle kids. It would be so easy to lead them astray, and to do so unthinkingly. Perhaps that's what I don't understand about Stuart, that every step he takes is measured against possible risk, regardless of how unwitting it might be, and how paranoid the concern.

"May I come in?" Maya says. She advances, expecting me to stand aside, but I remain unmoved. She stops.

"Maya, that's probably not a great idea at the best of times, but all things considered …"

"All things considered?" Maya blinks, not understanding. I hope then that when Maya starts getting involved in relationships, she avoids any and every sleaze who might take advantage of her, because take advantage of her they will.

"Because of what happened with Bianca," I say.

Maya blinks rapidly, like she's trying to process that.

"Because they think I was somehow involved—"

"That was Anthony!" Maya says, then laughs, before lifting a hand to her mouth, perhaps realizing laughing at something so serious is imprudent.

"*What?*"

"Haven't you heard?"

"No."

Maya shrugs, then looks left and right – as if to check we're not being overheard – before she whispers to me, "They were making out—"

"Anthony and Bianca?" I can't keep the surprise from my voice.

"Uh huh. Somebody told me they ..." Maya mimics smoking a cigarette, but then I belatedly realize she's not talking about a cigarette but a joint. "Anthony brought it and, well, that's Bianca, always trying things. He got all gropy and tried to push it." Maya's face is stoic, like this is everyday fodder in the schoolyard. "She fought him off." She lifts one hand and claws it, then snarls, although it has the ferocity of a kitten. "She scratched his face. But she was pretty messed up until she told police Anthony—"

"Bianca told police?"

Maya nods. "Yesterday afternoon. She started talking and told them everything; said Anthony wanted sex from her for the ..." Again, she mimics smoking a joint. "Her parents took her home last night."

"Maya, how do you know all this?"

"This morning, Bianca called Justine, Justine told Dom, who told—"

"That's okay, that's okay." I should've guessed the school grapevine would be the first with the information. But Anthony?

Of course, there has always been something unnerving about him: lingering glances, lewd grins, inappropriate comments. He seems to have a casual disregard for women. He'll grow up to fuck women the way Kai fucked Jane. I wonder if that's the way Kai feels about Jane. And if she likes being treated that way.

"I knew you couldn't have done anything, Mr. Gray!"

"No …" I want Maya gone now so I can … I can … I don't know.

Something tight and burning has ignited in my midriff, something growing hotter by the moment. Maybe it's reflux. Maybe I'll vomit – just spray regurgitated beer all over Maya's face. Or maybe this is what true rage feels like. I've carried this fear about Bianca all last night and today, and it could've been resolved yesterday *afternoon*. Of course, if it had, I never would've tried to catch Jane earlier at work.

"Have I come at a bad time?" Maya asks.

"Let's have a look," I say, leaning on the door jamb and holding my hands out for her sketchpad. If nothing else, Maya deserves some respect.

Maya looks past me, her gaze landing on the line of anniversary pictures going up the stairwell. "You're married, Mr. Gray?" she says.

"Sorta." I try to be flippant.

"Sorta?"

I open my hands for her sketchpad. Disappointment marks her face. She still expects to come inside and I almost relent. It's Maya, after all. And this is going to be awkward, standing on the front doorstep. Across the road, Josh hauls out his hose to water the lawn. He holds up his hand. I wave back and my decision is made. Life's complicated enough.

"Maya?" I say.

She hands me her sketchpad, and I flip it open to the first page, which shows a picture of an Asian man in profile. He's seen from a low angle – from the floor, maybe. No. From a child's point of view. Maya's drawn him in charcoal and captured the details meticulously – not just physical details, like his little oval glasses and thin mustache, but the hardness of his features, and the furrowing of his brow, as if in disapproval.

"My father," Maya says.

There is a scattering of other portraits – Maya's mother, a younger brother, and younger twin sisters – but her father is dominant throughout, always caught stern, from low, and in an iris. Maya's attention to detail is flawless, but it's how she captures mood, how she represents emotion, which is amazing.

"These are wonderful, Maya. I told you when you showed me the other pad: you have a gift."

"Teachers have to say things like that."

"No they don't. You told me last time you didn't like drawing."

"You remembered."

"Of course. Why don't you like it?"

Maya shrugs.

"Can you perhaps go a little deeper than that?"

"I'm not sure."

"Maybe it's what you're drawing. Your other pad had your neighborhood, seen from windows. This is of your family. Maybe you should get out, go to the beach one day, draw a horizon."

Maya laughs.

"What's so funny?"

"I don't know. The idea, I guess."

"Funny in a bad way?"

"No." Maya shrugs again. "I think it's funny because it's never something I've considered – to go out and draw."

"There's a whole world out there."

"When I was younger, my dad would sit me in front of a vase or some flowers and tell me to draw them. He'd always point me to something in the house. I guess I didn't think there could be anything else."

"How do you feel about drawing a beach or a sunset or a city building?"

Maya purses her lips. "That actually sounds nice. Like something I could do for me."

"Maya, I've always enjoyed drawing, but it's something I wish I pushed myself to do more when I was your age – or I wish somebody had pushed me to do. Don't let this go – at least not until you're old enough to understand whether it's something you don't want for yourself. You'll never have this time again."

I smile at her. Maya blushes, a crimson that rises in her cheeks until she lowers her face and her eyes close – initially, I think it's embarrassment, or even because she's overwhelmed. She shifts from side to side, pivoting at her ankles – a lot like the way Jane did that first night we kissed. And that's when I get the sense that's what Maya's building to – she's going to try and push her crush.

I step back, and fold my hands behind my back. All the hopefulness seeps from her face. Her lower lip quivers. Something passes between us – acknowledgment: she's nurtured this crush, and I've just made sure she knows that's all it'll ever be.

Maya sniffles, trying to stop herself from breaking down entirely. I should comfort her, but it's another line I don't want to risk crossing. I don't know when such simple actions became minefields, or maybe they have been for a while and I'm only now becoming aware of them. Josh waters his rose garden, but casts curious glances in our direction.

"Maya, come on, it's okay." I hold my hand adjacent to her arm.

She lifts her hands to her face, then peeks at me through her fingers. Smiles. She's got a gorgeous smile that radiates from her. There's none of the affectation of so many of the other teens from school who are in a hurry to grow up, who are constantly trying to project an image that encourages acceptance, or perhaps it's not even acceptance but reverence.

"I'm sorry," she says. "I knew I shouldn't do this, but …"

I wait for her to elaborate. She doesn't. I decide not to push it.

"I should leave you alone."

"Maya, if you ever want to talk about drawing or want to show me your drawings, feel free to – any time at school. It's nice to know a fellow artist."

"I will."

But she probably won't. She may never get over her pass today. She'll be polite, smile, say the right things, but she may never recover from the embarrassment.

"I should be going," Maya says, taking her sketchpad from me. "Thanks, Mr. Gray."

"I'm serious about your talent, Maya. *You* have a gift. I hope you nurture it."

"Thanks, Mr. Gray. Goodbye, Mr. Gray."

"Bye, Maya."

She walks down the path from my front door.

41.

I close the door, trying to work out what to do next.

Stuart. I want to call him. After the way he and Principal Hetrick interrogated me, I thought I was – or would become – the prime suspect. They should've told me I wasn't.

Returning to the kitchen, I finish my beer, then grab another.

Stuart can yank me out of class to tell me my kids are noisy, he can stand at the school entrance and censure me for being late, but when he should be telling me, hey, everything's okay, he says nothing.

I sit on the couch, working through my thoughts, telling myself I need to calm down. The last thing I should be is impulsive. But all I do is work through several more beers, and then begin to question whether I actually want to work through my thoughts, or whether I'm trying to find reasons – or mellowness in drinking – to avoid a confrontation.

No, dammit. That's it. I want to talk to him. *Need* to talk to him.

I grab my phone. It buzzes in my hand. A text from Beth:

> Hey, you haven't answered.
> Everything all right?

I think about what I should tell her. But the doorbell rings.

It's my pizza. I pay for it, extravagantly leave the change from the fifty as a tip, then sit on the couch. The pizza's lukewarm and soggy, and ham spills all over my T-shirt and the couch. If Wallace were here, he'd vacuum it up for me. And if Jane were here, she'd complain about Wallace vacuuming it up and get a sponge to clean up before the grease stained. I pick up the ham and throw it into an unused corner of the pizza box.

While I eat, I think about what I'm going to say to Stuart. I'll be diplomatic. Express the same moral superiority he does.

Hello, Stuart.

Hello, Casper. Is there something I can do for you?

I just learned something interesting.

Yes?

As of yesterday afternoon, Bianca identified Anthony Tselikas as her assailant.

Yes, that's right.

Didn't it occur to you to tell me that?

Well—

You and Principal Hetrick had, after all, all but convicted me.

We did no such—

Yes you did, Stuart. And it would've been decent of you to let me know I was clear, instead of letting me go on with this completely unwarranted fear hanging over my head.

You really are—

Look, Stuart, why don't you call me back when you're prepared to apologize, okay?

Then I'll hang up. I won't have my apology, but I'll have my moral victory.

In situations like mine, sometimes that's all you can ask for.

The pizza's tasteless, the process of eating mechanical. I get through about half of it, then close the pizza box. Time for more important matters. I pick up my phone, lean against the kitchen counter – right against Jane's white paper bag – and rehearse everything in my mind once more. I know it won't go down exactly like that. I just need the framework. I can improvise from there.

My heart pounds in my ears. It should be fast, but it's not. It's slow. Deep. It convinces me I'm doing the right thing. I don't know why my mind makes that connection, but it does.

I dial Stuart's number. He answers almost immediately.

"Hello?" he says. "Stuart speaking."

I take a drink of beer.

"Hello?" Stuart says again.

"You cunt!"

"What? Who is this?"

"It's me, fuck you. Me! Thor!"

"Who?"

"Thor! *Thor!*"

"Casper, is that you?"

"Yes, it's fucking me!"

"Have you been drink—"

"Shut up!"

"Mr. Gr—"

"*Shut up!*"

"B—"

"Shut the fuck up!"

Silence. I think he's hung up.

"Hello? *Hello?*"

"Yes, I'm here," he says carefully.

"After the way you and Principal Fucktrick talked to me yesterday, did either of you consider calling me and telling me that I was in the clear?"

More silence.

"Well?"

Nothing.

"Well?"

Nothing. He's hung up.

◻

I ring back. Stuart answers straight away.

"I didn't—"

"WHY DID YOU FUCKING HANG UP ON ME?"

"I didn't. I didn't. I *didn't*. The phone cut out. I think it was yours."

It's possible. I check my phone. The battery's down to nine per cent, but there are three bars of reception.

"I apologize, Casper. You're right. Principal Hetrick or I should've called you. In all honesty, I didn't because I believed the detectives were going to talk to you on Friday afternoon about your kids. I'm sorry. It was an oversight – a serious oversight. But it still doesn't mean that it should've happened."

I don't know what to say. This isn't the way Stuart's meant to behave. He's meant to be sanctimonious. I want to shout at him. Want to batter him down with profanity and anger the way I tried to batter down the wall with the sledgehammer.

"I'm sorry, Casper."

I go sit on the couch. Put my head in one hand.

"I'm sorry."

I'm unsure where this goes from here. *Okay, fine, don't let it happen again?* That's what I'd say to one of the kids. Or I could accept his apology, although I don't know how to do that after everything that has prefaced it. I run my hand through my hair.

And hang up.

Putting my phone on the coffee table, I turn on the TV, and try to find something to watch as I settle. I half expect the phone to ring, but it doesn't.

Beer. That's all I've got now. I need to stop denying it. *Beer.* But once I lift my beer to my lips, the room sways. A mixture of digesting pizza and stomach acid wafts through my mouth. I don't care. Not yet, at least.

I get up, go to the toilet, then stand in the archway to the dining room. The first thing I see – or re-see – is Jane's paper bag on the kitchen counter. I'm always seeing it. The thing has become an eyesore.

I cross to the counter, pick up the bag, open it.

I know what's inside before I see it – I think I've always known, which is why I've tried to ignore it: sure enough, the bag contains a pregnancy test.

Jane and I have gone this route many times before. We'd go up to her bathroom. She'd pee on the stick. I'd wait outside the door – usually seated on her side of the bed. Then she'd come out, eyes brimming. She'd swear we would never get excited again – but we always did. Well, I was always still a little bit leery, but her enthusiasm would always be unbridled.

That one time she *was* pregnant our whole lives changed for that brief period before the miscarriage. We discussed names, talked about how we'd decorate the room, looked at shopping from the point of view of what we'd need for a baby, and we'd even buy the odd stuffed toy.

For a little while, the expectation of the future was perfection.

Now, she's brought home a pregnancy test, which can only mean she thinks she's pregnant. It's been a while since the last false alarm, so this is a shock. I think perhaps we'd even given up – not openly, but with stuff like the IVF where we were meant to be saving, we'd spend loosely, going out, grabbing dinners, and things like that. It's like we accepted it was something that wasn't meant to be.

I crunch the pregnancy test, and fall to my knees. Then I slump against the wall of the kitchen counter. My eyes blur. I grind my palm into my left eye, then my right eye. My chest heaves. A sob grates from my throat. I sag onto my left side, curling up. I can see a stray piece of ham by the foot of the couch. Jane would hate that. And Wallace would've hunted it out.

I smirk and sob at the same time. The tears flow now. Because of my position, they stream from my left eye, down my cheek, and I feel them pooling around the lobe of my ear. From my right eye, they run down the slope of my nose, onto the tip, and drip, like a leaky faucet.

I still feel that swaying. Usually, it's the time I'd swear to never drink again. But I welcome it now. If I don't end up hunched over the toilet, I've drunk enough to sleep.

For a little bit at least.

42.

Jane's back. She's ringing the doorbell. I want to get up and answer it, but can't. The doorbell keeps ringing. My eyes open. I'm asleep on the floor and have incorporated the sound into a dream. The ringing continues. For one desperate moment, I hope it *is* Jane but, of course, she has her keys. She wouldn't need to ring the bell. I sit up. The room tilts the other way, then steadies.

I pull myself up by the edge of the kitchen counter and check my phone. It's 9:45pm, which is later than Jane or I have ever had visitors. Of course Jane's not here. And the way things have been going, it could be anybody at the door.

It's Beth, in a lemon singlet and a pair of tan shorts – the sort of casual wear that's too informal for school, so for a moment the sight of her dressed that way surprises me.

"Hey," she says. "You okay?"

I shrug. I'm still not awake. My mouth is dry. I need water.

"Can I come in?" Beth opens the security door, then recoils on the doorstep. "You don't look so great. Where's Jane?"

I shrug again.

"She's not home?"

"No."

Beth comes in, puts a hand on my back, and starts to guide me down the hallway. I hear her close the door behind me as I trudge along, the floorboards squeaking under the soles of my feet. When we get to the dining room, Beth ushers me to the couch, then retreats to the kitchen and puts the kettle on.

"I could do with some water," I say.

She opens the fridge. "Got enough beer?"

"There was more."

"I can imagine." She finds a one-liter bottle of water and brings it to me, surveying all the scrunched up paper on the floor. "Had a snowstorm in here?"

"I was trying to draw."

"Hmmm."

She proceeds to clean up – gathering the paper and shoving it in the kitchen bin; stacking the beer bottles on the sink; putting the remaining pizza on a plate, which she wraps and puts in the fridge; and even packing the pregnancy test back in the white bag and putting it back on the counter. She could comment on it. Most would. *You're expecting a baby?* But Beth goes back into the kitchen as the kettle whistles.

"Tea for me please," I say. I don't feel like it, but she's going to force something hot down me. I open my bottle of water and gulp from it.

Beth scours the kitchen, rifling through cupboards for mugs, coffee, and tea bags. I could tell her where things are, although now that I think about it I'm unsure. Those things are where they are. I find them unthinkingly. It doesn't matter because Beth's more than capable.

"Stuart called me," she says.

I look up at her.

"He was a bit concerned about you. He said you sounded upset."

I take another drink.

"Not just over this Bianca thing. He said the whole week he's sensed you've been on edge."

Beth brings over her coffee and the tea, puts them on the coffee table, using coasters Jane's left out.

"I've been trying to contact you all day," she says.

"Sorry. I forgot." I take my phone. There are other messages there from Beth, all asking whether I'm okay. "I didn't even see these. I think I slept through them."

She puts a hand on my thigh. The bruise around her wrist is faint. I wouldn't have noticed it if I didn't know it'd been there. I can see in her eyes she wants to ask me what's wrong, but she's too polite to be forthright. She wants me to volunteer the information, and I want to volunteer it. But can't. Not yet.

"These your sketches?" She picks up my sketchpad from the coffee table.

"Yeah."

Beth goes through them. She's seen all of them but the unfinished picture of Jane, which is now the very last page. "This is excellent," she says.

I shrug.

"You need a new sketchpad."

I don't respond. She closes the sketchpad, puts it back on the coffee table, then cradles me until my head's resting on her shoulder. Her hand runs up and down my back.

"Jane's cheating on me."

Beth's hand stops.

"I saw her. I mean, I saw *them*."

"Are you sure of what you saw—?"

"I saw them fucking so, yeah, I'm pretty sure. It was so …"

When I don't finish the sentence, Beth prompts, "What?"

"Violent, I guess."

"Abusive?"

"No, not violent that way. *Primal*."

"Where is she now?" Beth asks.

"I'm guessing she's staying with her friend. Fuck her."

"You don't mean that."

"I don't know." I sniff. "It was one of her workmates. They've worked together for years. Maybe this has been going on all that time."

I move my head to the couch's headrest, and run a finger across my right eye. Beth's looking at me like I'm telling her about a movie I saw. I wish she'd frown or shake her head or whatever the right reaction is because this unconditional acceptance doesn't seem right.

I grab my water and take such a big drink that the plastic bottle implodes. But I need it. Beth picks up her coffee, sips. I get up and search the fridge for another bottle of water. All that remains is the bottle I bought from Sofia's on Monday. I grab it, then sit back on the couch. I'd love to lie down, maybe rest my head on Beth's lap. But that's wrong. Although given the situation, it's funny to still be following rules.

We make small talk then. First it's about Bianca and Anthony. Then about Stuart and what an officious prick he is. Next we run through the rest of the faculty. Small talk becomes nothing talk, and I yawn more and more. But it's good to have nothing to ruminate upon. I try to drink my tea, but it's gone cold. So I stick with the water, finish the bottle in gulps, and abscond to the toilet several times to pee. With how much I've drunk, I'll be up some time during the night, if not several times.

"It's time you went to bed," Beth says. "You've had an exhausting week."

I go to check the time on my phone but the screen remains black. The battery's finally dead. I put it down and look at the wall clock in the kitchen. 11:16. Did I sleep that long? Or, given how much I've drank, did I black out? Neither seems that important anymore, outside of as a warning of searching for obliviousness. Maybe that's what Dad pursued.

"Do you want me to stay the night?"

I gape at Beth. She laughs.

"I don't mean like that. If you want some company – somebody to talk to."

I don't know what to say.

"You've got a spare room, right?"

"Yeah."

"Come on," Beth says. She rises, and tugs me by the hand. "I'll put you to bed."

Beth goes to turn off the lights in the kitchen and dining room, then stumbles back toward me. Her hand finds me, patters on my arm, then closes around my wrist. She leads me down the hallway, and stops at the foot of the stairs.

"Is it up here?"

"Uh huh."

I guide her up the stairs to my bedroom. She enters, but I stand in the doorway, just as I did last night. It's worse tonight. Maybe it's how much I've drunk, or that last night the initial shock insulated me from the complete magnitude of what happened, or just everything that's happened today, but I don't want to enter the bedroom.

Beth looks at me and I'm sure she'll ask what's wrong, but she smiles. "It's okay." She holds out her hand, the way you would when you want to encourage a child.

I don't move.

"*Really.*"

Last night I thought the emptiness would crush me. Tonight, I'm sure of it. Beth comes over, takes my hand, and tries to guide me into the bedroom. My feet dig into the floor the way a dog's do when they don't want to be taken in to see the vet.

"Maybe you should take the spare room," Beth says.

"No …"

I take one little step, then another, and then another, until I get to my bedside. Pulling off my T-shirt, I slide under the covers, drag my shorts off under the quilt and let them fall to the floor. The heat smothers me. It'll make it even harder to sleep tonight.

"You okay?" Beth asks.

I don't answer. The urge to flee burns. I picture myself bolting from the front door and down the street in my underwear. The neighbors will watch me, sprinting and screaming. Somebody will film me. I'll go viral. *Man cheated on runs and runs*, the captions will say. I don't know where I'd go, but the hope would be I could get away from this. But there's no getting away from this. This is *me* now.

Beth clambers onto the other side of the bed and sits with her back to the headboard.

"What …?" I begin. "What're you doing?"

"How about I keep you company until you fall asleep?"

"That might be a long time."

"Amazingly, I don't have anything better to do right now."

I surprise myself with a laugh, but the truth is her presence is a comfort. Not because it's her, or not specifically because it's her, but because her presence approximates Jane's.

I close my eyes to the darkness.

Right now, Jane and I should be enjoying our anniversary night at the Sheraton. We might be sitting on the balcony, drinking champagne and enjoying the view. Or we might be in our room's spa. Or we could be pigging out on room service. Or having sex on the coffee table, like we did a couple of years ago. Or we could be cuddling in bed.

There's a lot of things we could be doing together.

But we're not.

"I tried to smash his TV," I say, because I can't sleep, and the silence in my room makes me think of where I should be.

"What?" Beth says.

"Kai. That's his name. Jane's workmate."

I roll onto my side. I can't make out details, but I can *feel* the concern in Beth's big eyes.

"You went and saw him?" she asks.

"I was drinking. It seemed like a good idea. I don't know what I expected to do to him, but when I got there …"

"What?"

"I don't know." I'm quiet a long time, thinking about Kai, in his pitiful unit, where he might or mightn't have fucked Jane just as he did in that second-floor office. "I didn't want to be the bad guy, I guess. That sounds stupid."

"You're entitled to be the bad guy."

"I think I wanted to be noble."

"You tried to smash his TV, you said."

"Well, there was that. I threw my beer at it. But I missed. From only a few feet away. Isn't that pathetic? It doesn't matter. I wanted him to know that could've been him."

"Really?"

"Maybe that's the way I'm rationalizing it. Maybe the truth is I'm too cowardly to do anything."

"That's not a bad thing."

"If it had been Roger, would you have done anything?"

"If Roger had cheated on me, I like to think I'd be noble, but there'd probably be a bitchfight."

"A bitchfight?"

Beth laughs. "Yep. Hair pulling, scratching, the works."

"So is that the answer?"

"I know we can talk about the right thing to do, but sometimes, you need to react wrong because there's no other way to cope. Sometimes, it's worth letting go and putting yourself back together later."

"Letting go?"

"Uh-huh."

I think about the sledgehammer in the garage.

"I haven't shocked you, have I?" Beth asks.

"No."

"Ultimately, we have to live with what we do, so maybe it isn't so bad you didn't do anything you'd regret."

"Maybe regrets are what tell us we've lived."

"That's very philosophical, but I don't know if it's true. Regrets tend to tell us we've lived wrongly, or we haven't made the choices we should've."

I fold the quilt down to my waist. Already, I'm covered in sweat.

"Hot, isn't it?" Beth says.

"Yeah. I keep waiting for it to break."

"It's unbearable."

We're quiet. Beth's breathing deepens. She might've fallen asleep. Now we're in this situation, it isn't as awkward as it seemed initially – me half under the covers, her on top. It means nothing. Or that's what I tell myself. These are special circumstances. They exist in a pocket outside my real life.

Beth lies on her side, her head on her arm.

"I thought you'd drifted off," I say.

"I think I was close. It's really sticky."

"Yeah, I know. It gets like that once the heat gets in."

She runs her free hand through her hair and sighs. That much hair must be uncomfortable on nights like this. I can feel my own, damp on my scalp.

"Roger and I used to be into bondage," Beth says.

"Sorry?"

"Nothing major. It was very light. Sometimes, he'd tie my wrists to the headboard. Sometimes, I'd tie him – little things like that. Sometimes we'd use sex toys."

I think of the lavender vibrator she left on the pillow.

"Again, nothing major," Beth hurries on. "We experimented. The night I talked to him about getting serious, he said things were fine the way they were. We argued the whole night, slept, then argued again in the morning. He lost control. Said he couldn't risk losing me, and he had to teach me a lesson, so he tied me to the bed and, well … I fought and screamed at him, but he was unrelenting. When you came to see me, he had to untie me so I could come out to meet you."

That explains the bruises on her wrists, but I also remember the buzzing before Beth emerged from her bedroom. And, well … well, the vibrator. Beth seems to read my mind.

"There was other stuff. It doesn't matter; it was all part of the games we played – the way we punished one another—"

"*Punished?*"

Beth smirks. "Maybe that's too strong. The way we *chastised* one another – you know, the way you might tease your partner during sex. Sometimes, we'd drag that out as long as possible, because there's something to the payoff. And it *has* been mild. That's my limit. But looking back, I think Roger wanted to go somewhere I wasn't prepared to – was *never* prepared to. Him losing control … that's when I realized I didn't know him, that while our relationship might've moved forward physically, it never had emotionally."

"You wanted to be like Jane and me."

"I wanted to be what I thought you were."

"Maybe you never really know somebody."

"Maybe. But maybe it's about knowing somebody as well as you can."

"Who would want to?"

"You're married. Didn't you want to?"

"I think I did. But the longer you go, the less there is to know. You lose that allure. It's like reading the same book over and over."

"You're an English teacher. You get a new appreciation for some books when you read them over. And some books you hold dear to you your whole life. Isn't that the way you felt about Jane?"

"Does it matter?"

Beth rests her hand on my shoulder.

"It's not about how I felt about her. I thought I felt right about her. I thought I was doing all the right things. It's about the way she felt about me. Apparently, it wasn't enough."

"You don't know that."

"Why else would she fuck somebody else?"

"I don't know why people do what they do."

"You think you do all the right things. You work, you save, you buy a house and overextend yourself, you get a dog, you look at starting a family. That's the dream, isn't it? That's pretty much what everybody wants. I don't even know why. It's like a generational program. Look at me and Jane. We've done exactly what our parents did, and what our grandparents did. Look at what you wanted to do with Roger. What's the point? it's an endless, meaningless cycle."

"It's not meaningless."

"Right."

Beth's quiet. She's not even breathing – maybe she's holding her breath, like she's preparing herself for what comes next. Finally: "I saw the pregnancy test on the floor."

I snort.

"What?"

"How do I even know it's mine?"

"Did she bring home that pregnancy test?"

"Yes—"

"She wouldn't have brought it home if she didn't think it was yours."

"Or maybe it's convenient."

"What do you mean?"

"We've been trying to have a baby for years. Maybe she fucks this Belgian twat and he impregnates her. Maybe she thinks she can pass the baby off as mine. Then out comes the baby and it bawls like a Belgian."

"Is he Belgian?"

"Belgian or French. Is there a difference? I don't mean between Belgian and French. But as to what he is. He's just a cunt."

"Casper, you're angry and you're hurt; that's understandable. And you'll probably be angry for a while. And hurt. That shows you it's not meaningless. You wouldn't feel that way if it were meaningless."

"Maybe I'm stupid."

"You don't believe that."

"I love her and I hate her."

"That's understandable."

"When Roger came to your mom's place the other night, how did you feel about him? I mean, seeing him again. How did you feel?"

"I didn't tell you everything about that night."

"What?"

"I was home alone at my mom's. She's on holiday."

"So you confronted Roger alone?"

"He doesn't know she's on holiday. I told him she went to the movies."

"That's all you didn't tell me?"

"Roger proposed to me that night. He had a gorgeous diamond ring. Got down on one knee and everything."

"That's what you wanted."

"And it was hard, because he looked good, I felt that way I did when things were good between us, and he said all the right things. He told me he wanted to change everything. That he didn't realize what he'd lost. It would've been so easy to say yes and have everything I wanted."

"When you told me about this on Friday, you said you'd decided you deserve better."

"I do."

"So you told him no?"

"I had sex with him first."

I half sit up. "What?"

Beth pats my shoulder until I lie back down. "I had sex with him because I wanted to dominate him. I didn't want the last contact we had to be what it was – what he'd done to me. So I wanted to subjugate him, although I knew there was a risk because he *is* bigger and stronger than me. If he wanted to get the way he had been that morning, things could've turned nasty."

"So you tied him up?"

"No. I needed him to know I'd beaten him freely. We fucked. Then I told him no. We argued naked in the dining room. He got really angry. Started throwing out accusations. He accused me of having an affair with you – that's why I'd left him, apparently. Instead of facing the reality it was him and only him, he concocted a way to put it on me. That's Roger – never taking responsibility. Given what happened last time, I worried I might've overstepped. He could've done anything. For a moment, I thought he would. He can have the most horrible temper. But then he begged. I mean, literally, he begged until he was almost sobbing. I'd turned around that dynamic we had. It was liberating. That's when I realized that the whole time I'd been with him, the relationship had been on his terms. This proposal was still on his terms. He was still trying to control the situation. To control me. Then it clicked: I deserve better. Even he does. He deserves somebody who'll enjoy being objectified by him. You shouldn't have to change who you are."

"What do I deserve?"

"You don't deserve this, Casper. To be unhappy. It's up to you where things go next."

Beth's still sitting up. "It really is hot," she says.

"I know."

She pulls her singlet over her head, and drops it by the bedside. Her bra silhouettes her breasts and the protuberances of her nipples. She lifts her butt, slides her shorts down her legs, and drops them to the floor also.

"Don't take this the wrong way," she says. "It's hot. It's no different to being in a bikini. And it's dark anyway."

I don't know what to say. It's not *that* dark, given the streetlight always filters through the bedroom window. My erection stirs but, fortunately, it's hidden under the covers. Beth reaches behind her back – she tries to do it surreptitiously, like she's got an itch back there, but I'm sure she unclasps her bra, although she doesn't remove it.

Then she lies back down.

I know it should be awkward, but I keep rationalizing the situation: it *is* hot – hotter up here than it is downstairs. I'm under the covers, she's on top. And she's still in her underwear. I think. There's nothing else sexual about the situation. She's not touching me inappropriately, although part of me wishes she'd cross that barrier because, right now, I need that physical companionship.

We're quiet and stay quiet long enough that I'm sure I drift off. My body jerks. My eyes open. Beth's sitting up, like she was on the move. I can see her bra hanging loosely over her breasts – so she did unclasp it.

She rubs my arm. It's a gesture Jane would make. I wonder if Jane ever made it with Kai. That would cheapen it. Make it common. But after what she did with Kai, maybe that's her.

"You okay?" she asks.

"Yeah. What were you doing?" Maybe she was going to jump me, although I'm not much of a target conscious, so I'm unsure why she'd go for it while I was asleep.

"I was going to the spare room."

"Oh."

She continues to sit there. I can make out the shape of her nipples, long and pointed.

"You can go," I say.

She shakes her head and lies back down. "I can wait."

"You don't have to."

"Casper, it's okay."

"I feel so bad you have to babysit me."

Beth takes my hand and clasps it. "I'm not babysitting. I'm keeping you company. Okay?"

I'm unsure how to answer. I like my hand in hers – that bit of connection.

"Okay?" she asks again.

"Okay."

I'm thankful she declined me. Even with the two of us here, the room's too empty. Maybe this is life without Jane.

"Beth?"

"Hmmm?"

"Can I ask you something personal?"

"I think you can ask me anything at this point."

"Why would she let him treat her like that? What do you see in somebody who you let fuck you like that? Where you have no control, no inhibitions, no nothing? From a woman's point of view, why would she let him do those things to her?"

"I think it's a form of intimacy."

"Intimacy? My friend says it's more like a demeaning gesture."

"I don't know if I agree with that."

"Have …" I want to ask Beth if she's done those things. But I also *don't* want to know because I don't want to see her that way. "How's that work?"

"For me, sex has always been about meeting halfway, doesn't matter what the act itself is. If you can get your partner there, and you take some pleasure from it yourself, it's not only amazing, but intimate because you've bared yourself to one another. Haven't you and Jane ever experimented?"

Our sex life is sedate – me taking Jane on the kitchen counter was about as exciting as it's gotten in terms of anything different lately. We were more spontaneous and adventurous when we first started going out, although that was still just sex around the house, a few times in the car, and once in a side alley after we left a bar and Jane looked irresistible to me. Another time, she went down on me in a cinema, when we were seated right up the back. There were only a few other people in rows further down from us, and the movie was boring. There are other things I've considered suggesting, but been too meek to. I wonder if Jane's felt that way: that we've grown so close and think we know one another so well, we're afraid of suggesting anything new for fear we'll shock – or worse, *repulse* – the other.

"No, not really," I say. My eyes close and I stifle a yawn. "I guess we've settled. Do you think that's why …"

"I don't know, Casper. That's something you'd have to take up with her. As far as I go, you know, I've never had a fling. I've always needed some sort of connection with my partner – I want to know I can give myself to somebody, put my trust in them, let go of all my inhibitions and live in that moment. Then there's nothing as rewarding, nothing as satisfying. Does that make sense?"

"I don't know," I say, although I'm starting to see she's saying the same thing Luke said about vulnerability, but just coming around to it from a different angle. "Perhaps I'm myopic, or not as worldly as everybody else."

"I know it's going to be hard, but you can't keep analyzing it. Whichever way you go, you have to accept it as something that happened."

"And if I can't?"

"You have to."

SUNDAY

43.

My eyes open. The ceiling. That's the first thing I see. Then the light fixture. My mind orients to the reality that it must be early morning. That soft, ghostly luminescence from the streetlights burgles through the window. Outside it's quiet. Sweat dries on my brow. The hair on my arms dries and rises.

I lie there, trying to come to terms with why I woke. My throat is so dry it's hard to swallow. A pain throbs in my head – the anchor every hangover lands to keep you mired to misery. The need to pee is busting from my crotch. Jane breathes heavily by my side. What have we done?

My shoulder and back ache as I get out of bed and tiptoe to the bathroom. The floor creaks, but the house is otherwise still. So is the whole neighborhood. Moonlight through the bathroom window gleams blue off the walls and tiles.

I ease myself free from my underwear and am about to start urinating when something sparkles at me from the bottom of the toilet bowl. I peer closer, thinking I'm hallucinating. No, the sparkle remains.

Then it clicks: the anniversary bracelet.

Everything else falls into place – the events of last night; and that it's not Jane breathing heavily in bed, but Beth.

I kneel unthinkingly, fish the bracelet out of the water, and stare at it lying wet in my palm.

I pee, grab a drink from the faucet to wet my throat, then wash my hands and the bracelet with soap over and over, although I don't know why – it's not like I plan to give it to Jane. But as I keep scrubbing at the bracelet, it hits me: it's like I'm trying to clean the tarnish from our relationship. I plug one of the sinks, fill it with hot water, and squirt some disinfectant in there. The water clouds. I drop the bracelet in, then creep back into the bedroom.

And stop.

Beth is sprawled across the bed, bra tented loosely over her breasts, lace boxers snug and hiked up around her right hip. There's just enough light to caress the details of her body, and reveal the smoothness and tautness of her skin. Her right arm is folded under her head, her other arm stretched out toward my pillow. Her feet angle into the lower corner of the bed on my side. She's a bed hog.

I don't remember when we fell asleep, and it wasn't with the intention of sleeping together. It makes me wonder how easily some things can happen. Was that how it began between Jane and Kai? Just like that? At what point do you decide to start making the wrong decisions? Or is that something you begrudgingly surrender to?

I should go back to sleep – maybe, to be safe, in the spare room.

I climb back into bed.

44.

I toss, turn, then flip back and forth, unable to get comfortable. Nervous energy pulses through me. I sit up, wondering if I should get out of bed and start my day. On the bedside table behind Beth, I see the time on the clock radio: 3:56am. Way too early. Beth sighs. I lie back down and can just make out the details of her face, her eyes blinking.

"Sorry – did I wake you?" I say.

"Hard to sleep."

"Yeah."

Curled up, she slides her hands – pressed together – under her cheek. Those big eyes are doleful. I can't imagine how Roger could do anything but revere her. That's a simplification, but it's a comfortable simplification to make, because she is smart, and funny, and gorgeous. I don't even know why I'm thinking this. Maybe given the vacuum Jane's created, I want to idealize Beth – and she *is* easy to idealize – because I need to believe in somebody.

It's then that I notice Beth's bra has dislodged. I try not to look, and I keep repeating it in my head – *Don't look! Don't look! Don't look!* – but now that I'm aware of it, I also become painfully conscious of our mutual state of undress. It's not the lack of clothes. It's everything we've shared. We're naked to one another.

Vulnerable.

Open.

Beth slides one of her hands free and, with a fingertip, traces the curve of my shoulder. I shiver – I can't help it, it's juvenile and cliché, but I do because she touches me, and it's not to console me like she did downstairs, nor to help me up to bed because I'm so uncoordinated from alcohol and shock, but a simple gesture of tenderness.

The fantasies I had earlier about Chloe resurface, but now with Beth as their star. Only they're not primal. They're not dominant. There's a synchronicity, a union that's significant, that romanticism of a relationship – well, if you believe in fairy tales.

And then what? Beyond the obvious. A narrative unfurls in my head: Beth and me – we have great chemistry, we've always connected, and she supports and encourages my art. I'd treat her one helluva lot better than Roger did, and she'd never treat me as Jane has. So there it is – happily ever after. Just like that.

Beth smiles. "You seem deep in thought."

"Uh-huh."

Beth shifts a little closer, and her hand folds around my shoulder.

Here's where it would be easy to let go. But while there's an undeniable appeal about my fantasy, I can't abandon Jane. I don't want to. I need to know where we go from here, if there is an *us*. Maybe there are no *happily-ever-afters*, but only an ideal you keep working toward, although I guess along the way, there are going to be obstacles and detours and diversions. That's natural.

"Sometimes, it's worth letting go," Beth says. "You know?"

My hand closes on hers. "I know."

45.

It's almost morning when I shower in my bathroom. I stand under the water until it grows cold and I'm shivering, but I brave it until I'm desensitized to it. Finally, I turn off the faucets and lean against the shower wall, dripping, until I summon the energy – or perhaps it's the motivation – to get moving.

In my bedroom, Beth is stretched out, still asleep, the quilt almost artfully positioned to cover her hips and her breasts. I want to get back into bed, or wake her, but instead stand there, and what replaces the urge now is this deification of her – this would make such a beautiful sketch: there's no pretentiousness about it; it's not contrived – she's just beautiful and defenseless and fully trusting.

That's what relationships are: trusting your partner won't fuck you over. Luke got that part right.

I get a fresh pair of underwear, shorts and a T-shirt and get dressed on the landing.

I throw the towel and all of yesterday's clothes into the hamper in the laundry. Wallace's basket sits in the corner, along with one of his squeaky toys – a rat – and a frayed rope toy. I need to ring the vet first thing.

I take the basket outside and give it a good shake. Wallace will need it now he can't hop onto the couch in the study. Then I take it back inside and set it by the couch in the dining room. Before picking him up, I'll have to shop for the playpen we'll – *I'll* – need for his recovery.

I grit my teeth. Vic really needs to answer for what he's done.

I make and eat breakfast, then wash the dishes and clean up around the house, throwing the bottles in the recycling bin outside, which has to go out tonight. Cleaning up makes me feel like I'm getting things in order. It's a good feeling.

"Hey." It's Beth. She comes in, back in her singlet and shorts. Her hair is tousled. It looks good on her, like she's been wild. The thought stirs me. I squash it down.

"Hey," I say.

We stand there wordlessly, unsure how we fit together now. I should offer her breakfast, although I want to be moving. I can't be still too long. That's what led to yesterday's debacle.

"I planned to go to the spare room," Beth says, "but guess I drifted off."

"Want some breakfast?" I say. "Coffee and a two-egg omelet maybe?"

"Sure." Beth smiles. "That'll do."

I get to work in the kitchen, grabbing two eggs from the fridge and cracking them into a bowl. I throw a dash too much salt in after them, and then pour Beth a glass of juice. I bring it over to her when she sits on the couch.

"Thanks," she says.

I go back into the kitchen, put the kettle on, put some oil in a frying pan and let it heat over the stove while I beat the eggs with a fork.

"You look better," Beth says.

"Life goes on, right?"

"You'd be excused for thinking it doesn't."

I pour the eggs into the pan. It's not so much an omelet as two eggs beaten into a consistent texture. The kettle boils, and I make Beth her coffee – white with two sugars, which I know from school. I also make myself another tea.

"If you want to use the shower or anything," I say, when I bring Beth her coffee, "feel free."

"I should probably get going after breakfast."

"Okay." I'm both relieved and disappointed.

"I really need to start looking for a place."

"Got any prospects?"

"There's a few I've marked down. What're you going to do?"

"I have to pick up Wallace today. I also need to buy him a playpen to keep him contained while he's healing."

I flip the egg in the pan, then search for my phone. It's on the coffee table. I pick it up, but it's dead. I plug it into the charger in the kitchen. The phone buzzes, happy to be back on the juice, although it'll need a little more time before it reboots. I check the time on the wall clock. It's 8:24.

"Poor little dog," Beth says.

I slip her omelet onto a plate, and bring it and a fork over.

"Thanks."

I sit next to her – well, not next to her, but on the couch. As she eats, I grab my emaciated sketchpad.

"Have you ever painted?" Beth asks.

"Not for years."

"You should."

"I'm having enough trouble drawing, although ..."

"What?"

I don't know if I should tell her.

Beth grabs my wrist. Gives it a shake. "Come on."

"Just the way you looked in the morning when I got up, I thought that would make a good sketch."

She smiles – I haven't embarrassed her. Then she shrugs. "Maybe that's something to do."

But that gets me thinking about Jane, about Jane posing for me – was our relationship a lie then? Was she fucking Kai? How could she suggest something like posing while she was fucking another man? It's easy to think relationships are black and white, that people are wholly good to you or wholly bad, but they can actually be both simultaneously.

I lower my head. It all seems so insignificant now. Beth puts her hand on my back.

"Casper, you *are* a good guy. You didn't deserve this."

"Maybe it's me."

"Why would it be you?"

"People grow apart."

"Have you felt that?"

"Not on my side, but …"

Beth sets her empty plate down on the coffee table, which gets me thinking about dinner, and that gets me thinking about calamari – my signature meal whenever we go out. Unless it's not available, like that night with Stephen and Renée – the night Jane went up and sang karaoke. She wanted me to come up but I was … I was so many things. Meek. Embarrassed. Cowardly.

"Maybe I bore her," I say.

"Do you really believe that?"

"I don't know what to believe anymore."

"You're *not* boring. Like, if you were Stuart, yes. You? no."

I laugh – I can't help it.

"You're questioning yourself," Beth goes on. "That's natural. And you'll probably do that for a while over a lot of things, if not over *every*thing. But maybe this is about her, not you."

"Do you believe people can change?"

"Everybody *can* change. But they have to have self-awareness."

"Was Roger self-aware?"

"No. Everything Roger does is with a view toward controlling a situation because he can't bear to be out of control. He tries to micromanage everything, although …"

"What?"

"That night we argued, when he was begging, there was a point I think the thought of losing me opened his mind up to possibilities he'd never considered before."

"What possibilities?"

"Marriage, kids, all that. I think he caught a glimpse of that in his future as something he wanted. You know, from the heart, instead of it being a measure of stature or a way of keeping me compliant. It's like when people who smoke a pack-a-day for years have a heart attack and realize what all that smoking's done to them. I'm sure beforehand they know smoking is bad. But when their minds open up to the reality, that's when they change."

"So all you need is a near-death experience?"

"All you need is the capacity to look inside yourself. Everybody I know is so much on autopilot, like the way Stuart patrols the hallways at school, or Stan complains about his marriage during the staff breaks but does nothing about it, or the way Roger's so career-oriented because that's what he's been taught to pursue. That's why I like art. It's not automatic. You don't sit there and say, 'I'm going to draw a house', or whatever. Sure, some people do. But the great artists reach inside themselves. They shrug off everything they know, everything that's been programmed into them through upbringing and relationships and everyday life, and they produce something original, something only they can produce. That's when I think people are special. I mean, it doesn't have to be art – it can be anything. But it's when they go inside themselves in that way." Beth laughs, sips at her coffee. "Sorry. I've gone off."

"No. It's … I like that."

"That's why I encourage you with your art. You're good – you probably don't know or believe *you're* good because you can be diffident, but you *are*. And if you ever need a model …?" Beth smirks, and now she does come across a little self-consciously, so she hurries on. "I guess, though, you're asking if you can rebuild your trust in Jane, right? That she'll change and won't do this again? That things can be like they were?"

"Yeah."

"I don't know."

Beth hugs me tight at the front door. She kisses me once, but soundly, on the cheek before she pulls away.

"I can stay if you want," she says. "I mean … for support."

"It's okay – I appreciate it, I really do, but I need to start working through this. And there's Wallace."

"If you need to speak to somebody, you call me. Don't hesitate. Just do it. Okay?"

I nod.

"You better, because I *will* check on you."

"I will."

Beth hugs me again. I open the front door.

"Bye," she says, although she lingers.

"See ya."

We stand there, looking at one another, before she flashes a smile, and starts away.

I close the door.

Alone again.

46.

Closing my eyes, I sit on the couch, absorb the vacuum of the house, and take a deep breath. And then, it's like the house is imploding with me at its epicenter, crushing me. Perhaps Luke is right. There may be no fixing things. Maybe all you're left with is the wreckage and the postmortem.

Tomorrow, I'll have school. That'll keep me occupied. In fact, I should call Stuart and apologize for last night's tirade – not that he deserves it, but I could've handled that better. *And* soberer. That's something to do. I need to buy Wallace's playpen. Pick up Wallace.

It seems hardly enough to fill an hour, let alone a day.

I wash the dishes, and put everything away in the dish rack as it hits 9:00am. Grabbing my tea, I take a sip, then call the vet. I don't recognize the voice of the nurse who answers. We have a short conversation. I introduce myself and ask about Wallace. She tells me Wallace is fine and he'll be okay to come home at midday. I thank her and press whether I can come earlier. No – midday's the earliest. I thank her and hang up.

That gives me three hours to kill.

Better get the next bit of unpleasantness out of the way.

I pace back and forth in the kitchen as Stuart's phone rings in my ear, then open the fridge and almost grab a beer out of habit. It's tempting, but right now I still need to get my head around Stuart. Perhaps he's not home. Or maybe he's still asleep in bed. I begin formulating a response to leave on his voicemail, but then he answers.

"Hello?" he says.

It's now I realize I have nothing formulated to say at all.

"Hello?"

I cough to clear my throat. "Hi, Stuart, it's me."

"Casper?"

"Um … yeah." Surprised. Like I have to confirm it even to myself.

"What can I do for you?"

His voice is as even as always. There's no recrimination, no expectation, nothing but Stuart being Stuart. Anybody else might respond warily, or indignantly, or with a sense of indebtedness. I would. But Stuart seems to be more magnanimous than that.

"I wanted to apologize for last night." I say it before I lose the courage. "As you might've picked up, I've—"

"Casper, it's all right."

"But—"

"It's all right."

"I—"

"It's okay."

Quiet. I find his graciousness hard to reconcile.

"I understand you've been having difficulties, and we *should've* informed you immediately about the Bianca situation. That *was* unpardonable. I'm happy to tell you she's fine. You're right; Principal Hetrick and I queried your handling of the situation, but if I'm hard on you, Casper, it's only because I believe you have it in you to really make a difference to kids' lives."

"Thank you, Stuart."

"But you need to consider the repercussions of any actions you take."

"I'll try to be better."

"We are a role model for these children, after all."

Ah, here's the old Stuart!

"We set the example for their behavior," he goes on.

"I understand that now."

"That's excellent, Casper. Why, you remind me of myself at that age."

I'm unsure how to take that. "Thank you, Stuart."

"Is there anything I can help you with?"

I almost laugh at the offer – well, not the offer itself, but at everything I need to remedy. It all seems beyond help.

"I'm fine, thanks, Stuart."

"Then I will see you at school tomorrow morning."

"Tomorrow morning."

"8:45."

"8:45." I close the fridge door finally.

"Have a pleasant Sunday, Casper."

"You, too."

He hangs up.

I sit back on the couch, still tempted to have a beer. The apology to Stuart has bought some small peace of mind. Now I have to move onto whatever's next. What I should do is go to Westfield, buy a playpen, then catch a movie. That'll kill the morning. I could grab lunch, and finally pick up Wallace.

Perhaps I should call Beth. She *did* offer. Although I hate to be an imposition. She'd say I wasn't, so I start pulling her name up on my phone. No, this is all avoidance of the empty house. Or maybe it's me wanting to hang out with Beth, with somebody who'll be strong for me because I can't be strong for myself.

I shoot to my feet, and grab Wallace's basket from where it sits by the couch.

47.

I crash out the front door and freeze. My car's gone! It's not on the nature strip where I always park it. Across the street, Josh is washing his car and Karen is pruning the roses in her garden. I take one hurried step forward with the intent of running across to ask them if they saw anything. But then it hits me: I put the car in the garage.

A door bangs open to my right – Kirit and Pia charge out of their house, their mother Tarika calling after them. I open the garage door before the kids can see me. If they see me – particularly because I'm holding Wallace's basket – they'll ask about Wallace, and I can't get into it.

I put Wallace's basket in the passenger seat of my car, then get in the driver's seat and stare at my eyes in the rear-view mirror, like I'm expecting some revelation. My heartbeat's a herald to some unimaginable battle I'm yet to face. But there's nothing.

Nothing but me in this car.

I start the engine.

I've no sooner reversed from the garage, the garage door sliding closed in front of me, when there's a thump at the window. I slam on the brakes, sure I must've hit something. A hand splays across my driver's window – a hand that's meaty and grimy and calloused. It slides down and yanks the door open.

Vic.

"Put the car in park and get out," he says.

My foot judders, a reflex to hit the accelerator. But I check myself, put the car in park and pull on the handbrake, although I don't kill the engine.

I have to slither out of the car, since Vic doesn't give me much space. He towers over me, his greasy coveralls stinking of petrol and grease.

"What've you been doing with my wife?" he says.

"What?"

"Chloe – you know, Chloe? Always chatting to you. Always nice to you. Always smiling."

Different fears fill my head – ranging from Vic knowing I watched her while she was sunbathing to possibly believing I made an advance on her. Is this why he hates me so much? Not because of Wallace, or not *just* because of Wallace, but because he feels Chloe has something for me, even if it's only sympathy? Is this his own insecurity?

"I don't know what you're talking about, Vic—"

Vic grabs me by the scruff of my T-shirt and swings me away from the car, my feet dangling briefly above the ground.

"Did you tell her I hurt that shit of a dog of yours?" he asks.

"Vic, I really can't do this—"

Vic shakes me, literally shakes me, like he's trying to jangle the answers out of me. "She got upset at me," he says.

"Vic, please—"

"Over your fucking little mutt."

"Vic, this isn't a good—"

"She wants me to pay for his vet bill."

"Well, you did—"

"Fucking animals cost fortunes."

"Vic—"

"*Vic*," he mimics me. "*Vic. Vic! Vi*—"

I shove him the way I shoved Kai. Vic's grip on me breaks as he stumbles back a step, his face shocked that I've offered any defiance. His shoulders rise and fists clench, veins on his neck and temple bulging.

"*Don't* push me."

He thrusts his hands into my chest. It's as good as a punch and knocks the breath from my lungs as I stagger back into the car. Pain erupts across my chest and back, but instead of registering in my brain as something to heed, it incites the anger in me. I leap, propelling my hands into Vic's chest. It's like hitting a brick wall, but he teeters and his face hardens.

"You fuck!"

Vic swings a punch at me, a right hook that comes flying up from his hip. My reaction is purely reflex, or perhaps it's instinct cultivated from all those years of plucking Luke from the dozens of fights he got involved in. I duck, the blow sailing harmlessly over my head, the momentum throwing Vic off balance. As I come up, my right knee fires into his groin. A pocket of breath explodes from Vic's mouth and he collapses to his knees, gasping.

I spin with the intent of diving into my car to make a getaway. But the rage that's been building incinerates my fear, incinerates my natural instincts, and ultimately incinerates me. Vic is momentarily defenseless. I have the advantage.

And he's going to fucking know it.

When I spin back, it's with a punch – the first punch I've thrown at anybody in a real situation. But I've seen Luke maul people. And when we were younger, we would train and box and impersonate any fight movies we might've seen at the time, because that's what teenagers do.

So the punch, as clumsy as it might be, as misdirected as it might be – I aim for the square of Vic's cheek but hit him flush in the nose – lands fully and jars my hand. But there's a satisfying crunch as Vic's nose shatters and he falls and curls into a fetal position.

I kick him then, landing my toes in his left ribs. Whatever breath was left in Vic's lungs belches like a fart from his mouth. "Is this what you want, Vic?" I ask, and punctuate it with another kick. "Is this what you want?"

I do it again and again, I don't know how many times: first the question, then the kick, until he's cowering, holding his hands up in front of his mottled face partly to shield himself, and partly in supplication to me. His nose bleeds, his eyes grow bleary and, most of all, he shrinks in on himself.

My own breath is ragged, rage burning away until I'm left only with a self-consciousness – a hyper-consciousness. Vic wheezes on the ground, blood trickling from his right nostril. I run a hand through my disheveled hair, and push it back over my head. Josh and Karen are unmoving across the street. Tarika holds Kirit and Pia close to her. I'm sure the curtain in the front window of Vic's house flutters. Surely Chloe couldn't be home, or she'd come out.

I thrust a finger in Vic's face. "You are paying for Wallace's surgery, you fuck, or I will take this wherever it needs to go – cops, courts, whatever."

The thought again of what's happened to Wallace incenses me and I cock my leg back. Vic now holds his hands up purely in surrender. I want to punt his head like it's a football – punt it into the next suburb. But he's pathetic – this bluster of a man who bullies his way through life. I lower my leg. Get into my car. Josh waves in acknowledgment, then nods, as if in approval.

I pull the car out onto the street.

As I drive away my arms tremble. I grip the steering wheel tighter. Vic could retaliate, or press charges, although the neighborhood could attest to the fact that he started this altercation, just as he started the previous one. And if what Vic said about Chloe is true, she's likely to verify what Vic did to Wallace – well, hopefully she would, even after what I've done to Vic.

What I've done to Vic.

There's an unreality there. But also a satisfaction. I stood up to Vic. I did *more* than stand up to him. Maybe the anger was fueled by a combination of things, and maybe my actions weren't even wholly conscious, but, on this day when I want to be putting things right, I put Vic right.

In recognizing that, though, I also recognize that I snapped. I can't afford to lose control. That's what Dad did. I can't do the same.

I pull the car over to the side of the road and take a deep breath. What I'd love is a beer or two. The temptation is undeniable. I stamp down on the thought. I can't discipline the fear of losing control by losing control through drinking, even if the prospect of facing another day of this is terrifying.

The tremors grow violent, like a quake moving through my body and I tighten my grip even further on the steering wheel and close my eyes. The simple reality is this could be it, this could be my life. Maybe this is who I become in the aftermath, in life post-Jane, where her affair has obliterated everything I once knew and took security in.

I need to keep my mind moving. I can't stop. If I stop, this is what happens.

I open my eyes and hit the accelerator.

48.

I park close to the entrance, stroll into Westfield, and take in the faces of the few Sunday morning shoppers, wondering what else is happening in their lives. I see a twenty-something blonde in pink shorts and wonder if she's having an affair, even though I don't know if she's even in a relationship. I see a group of teenagers and wonder if any of them are capable of a sexual offence. Everywhere I look there's somebody — old, young, male, female — and I question what might be happening in their lives that they keep to themselves. Everywhere there're secrets. Nobody's who they seem on the surface.

I want to scream at them to beware, that their secrets will see them undone. That their secrets will hurt those around them. But what good would that do? Nobody's fully honest, not even with themselves. It's a case of living through a filter. But maybe that's all we are — a projection of who we let ourselves be, and how we try to have people see us.

Pushing onwards, I wander aimlessly, not even aware if Westfield has what I'm looking for, but right at the opposite end of the complex I spot a store called Baby Mart. Of course. I'd earmarked this place during some of Jane's previous false alarms. I'd forgotten it was here. Or perhaps I'd blocked it out.

There are other people in the store: several pregnant women who look ready to burst, mothers with kids or infants in prams, and even a handful of couples — just people building families. I pause to watch them as the wondering returns — wondering how intact these families are, how truthful, how *true*. Nobody knows the secrets you keep until it's too late.

I hunt through the aisles, things that mightn't have meant anything before now taking on an entirely new context due to Jane's pregnancy. There's a pram we might need. And a gorgeous crib. There's a cute mobile with dangling birds. Things jump out at me, explode, like fireworks demanding my attention. Everything is too bright. The store rocks. Dizziness fills my head.

And then, there it is: in the corner of the store, the sight of an assembled sample playpen orients me. I stumble over to it. Lean on it for support. It'd be perfect to contain Wallace and later, of course, it'd be perfect for the baby, so it has a double use. Well, that is, if Jane and I remain together, although if we don't I guess I'll need my own things for when I have custody – *if* I get custody.

I almost crumple to one knee and choke back a sob as a new reality impacts me – the separation of everything we own. The house would be sold. We'd keep our respective cars. Savings would be split – or I think they would, although Jane's made more than me over the years. What about Wallace? Where would he go? He'd be confused alternating between two households. I'd keep Luke as a friend, but what about Stephen and Renée? Stephen is my friend, Renée is Jane's; they met at our wedding. Who keeps them? Do they go one way or another? I don't know how this works.

"Are you all right, sir?"

It's a salesgirl, her round face untarnished in its adolescence. Her concern doesn't seem to be directed to my wellbeing, but to what protocols she'd have to follow should I collapse in the store. She probably doesn't even know. I should collapse to find out.

"I'd like one of these." I tap the playpen.

She points to an adjacent shelf where the playpen sits unassembled in long rectangular flat packs. I grab one, hoist it out, mumble my gratitude, and head off.

I'm shaking when I get to the cashier, and a chill crawls across my skin that isn't the air-conditioning. I want to drop the playpen, bolt to my car, race home, and lock myself in the house, although even the house is foreboding in itself. I plant my feet until I can feel the tension in my ankles cramping into my calves.

I buy the playpen, leave Baby Mart, and march from the complex, shoving the playpen in my back seat. I check the time on my phone: 9:34. Still almost three hours before I have to pick up Wallace.

Three hours.

I climb inside my car, which has baked in the sun. Rolling down the window doesn't help. Sweat's already pouring off me. I need to get moving, if only to get out of the sun.

Home's not an option. When I pick up Wallace, at least he can accompany me back. I won't be alone. He'll keep me occupied. He's a little dog, but his presence is big enough to fill the emptiness that occupies the house now.

Or so I tell myself.

Starting the car, I pull out of the parking lot.

49.

I walk into The Andion, stride up to the bar, and take a stool. It feels good in here with the air-conditioning, the ferment of beer, and the chatter of the patrons who've either come for breakfast or to gamble on the horses. It's alive and filling and yet thoroughly routine. There's security in that.

"What'll it be?" the bartender asks.

"Beer."

The bartender nods and pours a beer while I pull a ten from my wallet and lay it on the bar. I shouldn't be drinking, I really shouldn't. How many times have I made this vow since this began? But I don't know what else to do. I don't want to fall back on Beth or Luke. There's nothing more to thrash out with them. It's only what's left inside my head.

"Here you go." The bartender puts my beer down in front of me and takes the ten.

"Keep the change," I say.

He murmurs his thanks, and moves on.

I pick up the glass. It's cold in my hand – refreshing after being cooked in my car. I'm reminded of the days and nights that Stephen, Luke, and I would drink ourselves to oblivion – that'd be our aim. I can't take it that far. There's still Wallace to consider. And I'm driving, even if I did drink-drive yesterday. But yesterday was the exception. And stupid. I can't make stupidity the rule.

Somebody calls for a Scotch, a voice that sounds familiar. I lean forward to peer around the other patrons seated at the bar and see, at the very end, Roger. He's dressed in a suit and shirt, but the top two buttons of his shirt are undone, and his tie dangles from his pocket. He's unshaven, although his stubble is splotchy. Every part of his image that has been so carefully cultivated has been unpacked to reveal the mess he's become.

I jerk back – not out of alarm, but surprise that Roger and I are in some form of synchronicity, both deserted by our loves, albeit for different reasons. I take another peek in time to see the bartender deliver the Scotch to Roger. He has a pile of money on the bar, which the bartender draws from unbidden. Roger swirls his Scotch, and takes a sip. He's probably been at it a while, if not here then elsewhere.

I pause in the act of lifting the beer to my lips, holding it there like it's a microphone, and I'm about to make a speech.

This is the cliché, sitting in a bar, nursing one's wounds, although it's a *good* cliché, a *proven* cliché, one that's born from fact – drinking mightn't help but it does medicate temporarily. Like it's doing for Roger. Like it did for me yesterday. Like it did for Dad.

I set the beer back down, wondering if Dad thought this, whether he thought he had it under control, or whether at some point he surrendered and accepted he was going to drink until he knew no more, or possibly until he himself was no more. Maybe it wasn't even a surrender but a conscious choice, a course he dedicated himself to.

Then it became his existence – all he was. And for what? I think about Luke's story of seeing Dad crying in a toilet cubicle at my wedding. Drinking might've dulled the pain, might've helped him escape its intensity, but drinking didn't eclipse it. He never truly forgot. I guess some things you can't. Some things you need to deal with because, otherwise, they're what get you in the end.

Rising abruptly from my stool, I think about how easy it would be to follow this path. Me. The quiet one. The meek one. The one who not only never stood up to anybody or anything, but who never stood for anything either.

There's another habit that's grown to dictate my life: the diffidence. And, while I've always known it's there, I see it as some cancerous part of me – this organism that's grown, that's always sought the easiest way out of issues because that hasn't taken courage.

I charge from the bar and into the toilets, doubling over the sink. My breath comes in big, uneven gulps, and giddiness pulses through my head until I'm sure I'm going to throw up. Jane cheating on me is horrible. But me playing the victim until that personifies me is worse.

Lifting my head, I look into the mirror, seeing that my face is pale, and my eyes are wide. But is that because of this? I dread this is how I've always looked, but I'm only *now* seeing it. This is what it took. Like Beth said – the way people need major trauma to truly confront who they are.

Vic, though – I stood up to fucking Vic, although that wasn't necessarily a stance against his bullying, but just a trigger that detonated all the shit I'd been burying, all the fear and resentment and embarrassment I've accumulated over the years, and which amalgamated into a rage just waiting to be tapped.

The door slams open. Filling the doorway, maybe trying to be as foreboding as some wild west gunslinger, is Roger. He stumbles in, no doubt trying to be menacing given the way he sneers and rolls his shoulders, but which comes across as comical.

"I thought it was you," he slurs as he nears me.

I tense, preparing for another confrontation. The altercation with Vic has hardly hardened me so I'm cavalier, although the closer Roger gets, the drunker I realize he is – his eyes bleary but glassy, and he stinks, although not just of scotch, but of sweat and something nastier that might be vomit. This isn't just the result of some morning drinking session. I wouldn't be surprised if he's been drinking for days.

He lifts his hands and claps them on my shoulders. My gesture to ward him away dies in mid-motion because I see a tear stream down his cheek. He collapses to his knees, his kneecaps making a sickening crunch on the floor, and knots his hands into the hem of my t-shirt.

"Please," he says, his voice warbling like somebody trying to refrain from sobbing. "She respects you. You can help me get her back."

This is what Beth said he did with her – this begging bit, and as he now begins to cry, I truly believe he's sincere in his contrition. How long will it last though? How long before he gets comfortable? How long before he just goes back to being the condescending dick he always is?

"I'll do anything for you," he says. "Whatever you want. Money? Help me, and I'll give you money." He must see my distaste, because he hurries on, saying, "You want to know I'm for real? What'll it take?"

"It's not my decision to make, Roger," I say, although there's some possessiveness involved too. I don't want to risk Beth going back to him even for a second.

"I *can't* lose her! I can't. I don't know what I'll do without her."

I want to tell him I know that feeling.

"You want me to humble myself?" Roger says.

"I think you've done that already."

"You want me to sink further? Prove how genuine I am?"

Roger prostrates himself, and I feel his lips pucker on my naked toes – it's a hell of a day to have chosen to wear sandals. I skitter back, his face sinking to the floor, his arms stretched out until it's like he's bowing.

"I can't help you, Roger. I can't—"

My intention is to say, *I can't even help myself,* but he lifts his head, his eyes wide and hard, anger snapping him back into some sort of focus.

"You fucked her, didn't you?" he says. "That's why you won't help me! You want her to yourself! You fucking bastard!"

His right foot digs into the floor the way a sprinter about to set off would, and he propels himself forward. Maybe if he was sober, he'd spear me with a tackle to the hips but inebriation, exhaustion, and despair unbalance him, and instead of sailing through the air, he stumbles, tries to regain his balance, stumbles again (at which point I neatly sidestep him), and crashes into one of the porcelain urinals.

His chin strikes the rim hard enough that the porcelain emits a guilty *clunk*, and his faces pitches into the basin, sinking into a handful of urinal cakes, and a small pool of piss that hasn't drained from whoever used it last. He splutters then, like he must've swallowed, or almost swallowed some, spraying it back onto the face of the urinal.

I reach out to help him – his face has a fine sheen of piss, and blood's streaming from his chin – but he waves me away, and sinks his head onto the urinal's rim for support.

"Leave me alone," he says, his chest heaving once, twice, like a car reluctantly starting, and then he's freely sobbing.

I don't look at him as a cautionary tale – as pathetic as I can be, I can't imagine ever being this pathetic. But he does make me think about how you truly find out who you are when you're confronted with shit you're not ready, or equipped, to face.

"Let me get you a taxi," I say, leaning forward, but again he flails one arm.

"I said leave me alone!"

And that's enough for me – he deserves no further pity nor decency, and I think even my entreaty to help him is probably some holdover from school, because I'd immediately try to help any student who needs it. But there's no helping this. It's something I understand now. He has to fix this himself – even if it's too late for him and Beth.

I leave the toilets, opening the door and bumping right into Jean Jacket. He steps back, then holds up his hands in a mollifying gesture. His gaze goes from my head to my toes and back again. He grins that easygoing grin. I feel nothing now – not after everything that's happened since we last spoke. This might've been a game for him, but I know now it's not one I need to keep playing.

"Hey, buddy," he says. "How're you doing?"

"I've been better, Bruce – you know?"

"Yeah, I know, I know. Noticed you were edgy. Sad to see it. Really. So, what do you say?" Jean Jacket tugs at the baggy in his pocket until I can see the corner of it. "And you wanted to forget, right? That was *your* thing." He shakes the corner of the baggy a couple of times. "*Right?*"

"I don't want to forget, Bruce."

Jean Jacket's face is blank, maybe surprised by my temerity. But then he nods, and points his finger at me. "You're okay," he says.

"Thanks, huh?" I say. "You might want to try the guy in the toilet."

"You mean the *toilets*," Bruce says, pointing at the door.

"I mean what I said," I say, clapping him on the shoulder.

I start away, feeling his eyes following me.

And then hear the toilet door open and close.

50.

Driving, I run a hand across my bleary eyes, then flick the radio's volume until it's so loud it pounds at me and I can't hear my own thoughts. I think I'm driving aimlessly, but eventually find myself arriving at Finchley Photography, which isn't far from Web Myriad.

I park the car on the street and sit there, unsure why I'm here. Usually, the routine would be our anniversary dinner on Saturday night, a night at the Sheraton, then in the morning the photo to tie up the anniversary. Jane would have the photo up before the week was out – I'd clumsily bang in a nail, then hand her the picture, which she'd hang with a smile. I'd stand a couple of steps beneath her on the stairs, hands around her waist to hold her steady.

Maybe I'm here because I want to challenge the observance of this ritual, which has operated unfailingly the last six years, despite whatever events have preceded it. It was a cornerstone of our relationship, one that I imagined would accompany us into our old age – if we could find room to hang all those pictures. Now where do I stand? Where do Jane and I stand? I rub the left shoulder of my T-shirt across my forehead.

I pull the key from the ignition and get out of the car.

The door buzzes when I open it. The lobby is large and red carpeted, with low-hanging lights that sway in the breeze that slips in as I do. Pictures are everywhere. I think that's one of the reasons *why* the lobby's so spacious – to accommodate them all. One wall's dedicated to family portraits, another to couples, one to kids, and the one behind the ornate, arched marble counter has pictures of celebrities. A narrow hallway – and even this contains pictures – leads to the bathrooms.

I take a seat on the bench and hear clicking coming from the studio, light flashing through the seams of the door – Oscar Finchley busy at work. I check my phone: 10:14am. Leaning forward, I plant my elbows on my knees, and examine the way the red carpet is pixilated with flecks of black.

I smell her approach – her strawberry fragrance a touch too rich, which usually has my sinuses almost gagging in protest, but now smells familiar and secure. Since the door didn't buzz, she must've come from the bathrooms. She sits down close enough to me that I can feel her warmth. Or perhaps it's her shame.

I don't look at her.

Silence.

Perhaps she's expecting recriminations or accusations or condemnations. My mind is awash with all of them, angry things I want to say, hurtful things, *final* things, but there's no composure to articulate them, strength to voice them, or conviction that that's the direction I want to take.

"Words are the only things I have," Jane says finally, her voice low, "and they're not going to be enough. But please take them for what I want to convey, and know that I can never fully relay the depths of how genuinely I mean this: I'm sorry."

Of course. What else would she say?

"It's not that anything's lacking between us," Jane says. "It's not that I've lost any feelings for you. You haven't done anything wrong." She sniffles, and I hear rustling – perhaps she's running a hand across her eyes. "Nothing's missing."

"And yet," my voice is a croak, "*Kai*."

"Kai and I have been friends since we first started working together. Lately, it … went too far. I think it was something that happened because it had none of the pressures of our lives, it had none of the concerns of trying to have a baby or making a home together. It was a thoughtless escape, free and oblivious and stu—"

"How long?"

"What?"

"How? Long?"

"A month." The words barely spill from her lips.

"So … what? You did it every day? Like before he brought you home? When he picked you up—"

"Casper, no—"

"A month full of lies every day, every hour?"

"Is this – ?"

"Tell me! How often – ?"

"Five times!" Jane struggles to contain her sobs. "Okay? Five times."

Five times. It's a weird statistic that I need. Maybe it shows me they haven't fucked so frequently it's become a blur, and that she remembers each time implies that's she cataloged those episodes out of … what? Shame? Or orgasmic nirvana? I see her comparing my years of inadequacy against Kai's orgasmic pillaging.

Cupping my hand over my mouth, I squeeze my lips until they hurt to create a block against the tears. This is, in part, still my fear talking. I don't know why the logistics are so important – it's not like if it were X number of times it would be unacceptable, but Y number of times is okay. Maybe knowing is a way of trying to sift a truth out of a mess that's unsearchable.

"From the very first time, I broke it off," Jane says, "I knew I'd fucked up and … I don't know, Casper, I don't know – I promise. Every time I hated myself more and more. Every time I told him that was it. And … I don't want to make excuses. I don't know why I let it happen repeatedly. Finally, I told him that was it – I mean, *really* it. I finally reconciled what I was doing, and what *he was doing* – that he had no respect for me, or what I had at stake."

"So that's why it's over? Because of the way you found out he feels—?"

"No! That's not what I meant. I just … I just … I knew this had to be done regardless of what he felt. But it just helped me understand the importance of what I have with you."

Have.

Her hand begins to come down on my shoulder. I recoil, sit back on the bench, and run my forearm across my misting eyes. Still, I don't look at her. I *can't.* I don't know what I'll see.

"When?" I say.

"I'm sorry?"

"When did you tell him it was finally it?"

"Casper, why – ?"

"Because I *saw* you. On Friday. I came to work. To *your* work. I *needed* to talk to you. And I saw you," I clench my hands – they're shaking – and wedge them into my lap, "and him."

"I was leaving early … because *I* wanted to talk to you." Jane's breathing deepens. "He chased me to that second floor. I can't explain everything. I lost myself telling him it was over. Maybe I had a temporary breakdown, like a blackout – I'm not trying to rationalize what I did. You and I have been trying so hard to build our lives, I think sometimes we forget just to be us. We get lost in the everyday minutiae of who we are and what we want, that we forget to be free. That's what I was with Kai – or I thought I was … until Friday. On Friday, I surrendered out of self-loathing more than anything. To find out there was nothing there. To find out he meant nothing. To find out to him I was nothing more than sex, and I was sacrificing everything I had with you out of … well, not just stupidity but because I lost sight of what's important – what's *truly* important."

I don't know what to say. Luke suggested she'd shift blame, that somehow it would become my fault, but she hasn't done that, so that's something. Still, everything's so neat. Rehearsed. Qualified. Methodical – other than for the times I've pushed her for details, when I've forced her from her script … although I can't blame her for having one. It's what I would've done, and she hasn't lacked sincerity. But it's only been two days.

"So just like that?" I say.

"Just like … what?"

"I still don't understand how you go from friends to crossing the line – not just once, but again and again. And again. And *again*. I …"

I think of Beth looking at me, the way she touched me, and the way I thought our friendship was better in some ways than the friendship at the heart of my marriage. I don't have to accept what Jane's telling me, I don't even have to understand how it works, but I can accept it happens.

"What, Casper?" Now Jane does squeeze my hands.

I shake my head. I don't know what to say. When it becomes obvious to Jane that's the way it's going to stay, she resumes.

"I quit. I rang Henry and told him I had to leave, effective immediately."

"And Kai?"

"What about him?"

"What contact have you had with him since Friday?"

"He messaged me on Saturday night to say you came over – well, he messaged after he tried to call repeatedly." Jane gulps, choking on the words. "I didn't answer. I … thought of you, going there … driving you to that sort of anger … I don't know what I've done …" The last is almost indecipherable, lost in a wail that she bites on, until her breath is a rasp trying to stifle the cries.

I finally turn to her, unsure what she expects from me. Her hair is frazzled but tied back, make-up not entirely disguising the redness of her eyes. Her crying is making her mascara run. She wears a denim skirt and a white blouse that are too big for her, and a pair of sandals. The clothes aren't hers – she hasn't had an opportunity to go home and get changed, so the clothes must be Sarah's. Sarah's much more buxom than Jane, which explains why the clothes don't fit properly.

"The pregnancy test?" I ask.

Jane blanches. She's going to tell me it's Kai's. Restlessness coils into my legs; I feel it in my hamstrings, like the muscles have become too tight and need me to get up to relax them. I could spring right out of here – right through the ceiling and aim for the stratosphere to escape this.

"I took a test at Sarah's. I had an appointment with a doctor yesterday morning. I'm pregnant. Six weeks."

Six weeks – a pointed time reference, given she told me she's only been with Kai over the last month. How convenient.

"I'll do whatever you want to prove that," Jane says quickly, reading my doubts. "It's yours, it's yours, it's yours, I know, it is. I'll take a blood test. Whatever you want. But it is."

I say nothing. What is there to say? I want to believe her. *Need* to believe her. That's the only way there's any chance for us. But it's more than that. This is about trust – what I've lost.

"I wanted to call you," Jane says. "I wanted to call you on Friday night. Then on Saturday morning. Then Saturday afternoon. I was so afraid you wouldn't take the call, or that you'd hang up on me, or tell me any number of things you have every right to say to me and not give me the chance to apologize. In the end I stayed in our hotel room last night, hoping you'd show. I sat there, and counted down the minutes. I stayed up until 4:00am. I knew it was next to impossible you'd come that late, but I stayed up all the same, thinking about you, thinking about you all alone in the house, thinking about what I'd done to you. Then I came here, thinking the same thing."

I want to be numerous things simultaneously – relieved, angry, incredulous, comforted, *comforting*, condemning. They jostle for some form of individualization. I wait for something to take prominence and determine my response. But they're all equal.

"Why did you come here?" Jane asks.

"I don't know. I could say something, *tell* you something, but I don't know if it's the truth or the way I've rationalized things. I want to hug you, tell you I love you, and that I forgive you."

Jane's face softens and her eyes brighten. She begins to lean forward.

"But I also want to shout at you, swear, and tell you you're a fucking bitch for doing this."

Jane freezes. Teary eyes blink frantically.

"I want to take solace in your words, what you've *told* me, but I also want to tear them apart, throw them in your face. I don't know where I go from here, where you go, where we go, what's meant to happen, what could happen, or how things unfold. I don't have answers. You know me. I'm not ... a strong man."

"Casper, no, you—"

"No, Jane, I'm just me. *Just* me. And – and as much as it sums up my life – I don't know where to go. I think somebody's always been leading me – my parents, Stephen and Luke, then you. I don't know what to do."

The door to the studio opens. Oscar Finchley emerges first. Everything about him is thin – his slicked back sandy hair; his mustache, which almost seems penciled on; and even his anemic smile. A smartly dressed family of four follows, although only the mother wears it well, her curled hair unmoving, her make-up – particularly the blush and lipstick – overdone. Her son is perhaps eleven, and already pulling his shirt from his pants while whining for ice-cream. Her daughter, probably in her early teens, the swell of femininity budding, demands over the top of her brother that she's meant to be dropped off at her friend's. The father, middle-aged, belly hanging over his belt, sweat glistening on his temples, agrees unthinkingly to both of them, although he probably just wants to go home and unwind with a beer in front of the TV.

The mother exchanges formalities with Finchley: readiness of their portraits, how it went, whether her daughter had smiled enough (Finchley assures them she was fine while the daughter scowls) – the typical babble of families. I see it all the time on parent-teacher nights or at school functions.

They're archetypes that are perpetuated in media everywhere and make me wonder, outside of some biological imperative to procreate, why people follow this pattern of generational reproduction. I only ever hear parents complain about everything they lose when they have kids – time, freedom, peace of mind. And, as Luke said, families specialize in fucking you up.

This could be me.

But in thinking that, I see myself rocking my baby to sleep, pacing with it as it cries in early mornings; reading to it, playing with it, teaching it to feed Wallace; I see myself in the pool teaching it to swim, at parks on the swings, and tucking it into bed. I see myself introducing it to the books I love. I see taking pride in its achievements – when it's acting in a play at school, or learning to play piano, or excelling in sport. I don't know its sex. Nothing tells me. I just see us together and in that sight I'm sure the world is right.

Well, it would've been.

Finchley escorts the family out, then frowns at Jane and me – I'm not sure whether it's how strung out we look, the way we're dressed, or he's simply surprised to see us given the way I responded to him yesterday.

"Jane, Casper, I'll be a couple of minutes," he says.

Jane nods and Finchley goes back into his studio.

Today has been a day of fixing things – Wallace with his surgery; apologizing to Stuart; the Vic and Roger encounters; and even leaving that beer on the bar and having that chat with Jean Jacket. But I don't know how to fix this, or if indeed it is fixable.

I stand up. Jane catches my hands.

"I want to come home," she says.

I yank my hands from hers and fold my arms across my chest. Don't look at her. But I can imagine her eyes brimming and tears streaming down her cheeks until they drip from her jaw.

"I don't expect you to forgive me. We don't even have to sleep in the same bed. I'm not expecting it to be like it was – not right away. But I'll prove myself to you."

"How can you prove yourself? How?"

"I ..." Jane lowers her gaze to her toes.

"How?"

Jane sways there, like Bianca did when I questioned her about Jean Jacket.

"*How?*"

Jane looks up at me.

"Because that's the wall I keep hitting – what happens next?"

"What happens next is we try. It doesn't have to be the way it was. It can be anything – anything we want to make it. *Anything.*"

Desperation strains her face, her eyes unblinking, and what worms its way into my mind, oily and undeniable, is she's talking about sex. She's offering me what she had with Kai – something untamed and boundless, meant to convince me she's giving herself to me wholly. Maybe I'm misreading it, filtering her offer through what I saw. Can this ever again be pure? Can it ever just *be*?

"On Friday I realized why you stare at that blank page in your sketchpad for hours on end," Jane says. "Our lives are nothing but endless possibilities. I lost sight of that. Let me prove myself to you. Let me prove my commitment to you, to *us*, to the future we can build together."

"I don't know if I can ever trust you again."

"I understand. But I can't convince you otherwise unless you give me the chance."

My eyes flit to her belly. Rise up her body. To her teary face. So many times over the years, this is when I would've reached out to cradle her in my arms. The instinct is there to do it. But I don't want to. She can cry. She deserves to cry. But I still want to hold her.

I think about my sketchpad, about the excitement I had drawing her, what her gesture meant to me, and how for the first time in a long time I found the inspiration to draw. No, wait, there was Bianca during Beth's art class. But even then, it was only because Bianca had reminded me of Jane. Now my sketchpad sits at home with that incomplete picture, every effort after it ditched, every subsequent page torn out, scrunched up, and thrown away. Maybe that's what my future would be without Jane: nothing. Well, nothing but me. Maybe this isn't even about Jane anymore, or about us, but me – what I want for my life, what I want for my future, and who I want to be.

The week's events scatter through my mind, like they've been crammed into a box that's been upended. I don't like what I see, the way I've handled things, the way I've been – things that are reflective of my life in general. I like today. This morning. That's where I need to stay, and in staying there, I need to factor in what happens next.

Nothing else exists now but this decision. I've spoken to everybody, I've pontificated, I've obsessed about it, but now it's only me and what I need to do. I don't want to end up like my dad, mourning what was, or become like Roger, lamenting what could've been, and yet how do you repair the seemingly irreparable? The choice I have to make terrifies me. But maybe that's a good thing – like Jane told me during dinner that night at The Andion: usually, the path we're meant to take is the scarier one.

"You can come home," I say, "but I don't know where it's going to go."

She jumps to her feet and her arms go wide, as if she's going to throw them around me. But she stops herself. I lower my arms from where they're crossed against my chest.

"But if you think this is going to be a smooth transition," I say, "you're kidding yourself."

"I know."

"Maybe I'm kidding myself."

"I'll prove you're not."

"It might never work."

"I understand."

Finchley emerges from the studio. "Ready?" he asks.

51.

I stand by Jane, my body tense, my arm around her but barely making contact. My smile is strained, but can't look much stupider than the clueless smiles I've forced the last six years, and it does me the courtesy of erasing the perpetual shock I usually wear on my face in these photos – or at least I think it does, because I don't feel the usual bemusement. Jane's smile is genuine – not one of happiness but relief, and tinged with trepidation, like she knows it might come apart at any moment. We must look farcical dressed the way we are – at least compared to years gone by.

"Let's get this started," Finchley said.

He begins snapping pictures.

52.

I drive to the vet, and enter with Wallace's basket tucked under my right arm. The nurse, Rebecca, greets me with a smile and comments on what a gorgeous Sunday morning it's been. I'm not sure what to say to that.

I want to take care of the formalities first, so I slide my credit card out of my wallet.

"Oh, no need for that," Rebecca says.

"Sorry?"

"A Chloe Booth came in this morning with her husband," Rebecca says.

"What?" I threatened Vic that he should be liable for the cost, but I didn't think he'd actually pay it. Of course, he wouldn't have. Chloe would've made him. I feel almost guilty about her gesture.

"They paid for everything. Mrs. Booth said her husband was inadvertently responsible – he said he backed out of the drive and hit Wallace."

"Oh." My guiltiness evaporates. I'd like to hit Vic with my sledgehammer.

I slip my credit card back into my wallet, and put my wallet away.

Rebecca gives me some medicine for Wallace to take daily – an anti-inflammatory, a painkiller, and an antibiotic. We arrange another appointment for Tuesday for an examination.

When we're done, Rebecca takes me out the back while giving me all the same advice she did when I visited Wallace postsurgery. I assure her I have it under control and that I've bought Wallace a child's playpen.

We enter the back room. Wallace lies on a cot, head pointed away from me. The moment he hears us, he lifts his head to look back over his body. His ears flip back. I can imagine the expression says, *Help – I don't know what's happened to me.* But then his ears pull back and his mouth drops open, like he's grinning.

He scrambles to get up. I tell him not to, hold him so he stays where he is, and scratch his belly. I'm sure his eyes beam with gratitude. His tail quickens, like a propeller building speed. I scratch him behind the ears and gently ruffle his chest. He licks my hand.

I put Wallace's basket down on the cot.

"Want to go home, boy?" I ask.

His tail quickens.

53.

I pull into my street, one hand on the steering wheel, the other patting Wallace, who lies in his basket on the passenger seat. The air-conditioning is blaring, blowing into my face and sending a chill through my T-shirt and down my chest. Wallace's fur flutters, like somebody has a hair dryer to his muzzle.

It seems everybody's out, like they've gathered to welcome Wallace home. There are neighbors I know only peripherally, who I might only ever exchange a wave with, others I know by sight but have never spoken to, and a few I don't even recognize.

I should feel nervous coming home, but all I feel is disconnected, like I've stepped outside myself, and I'm watching everything unfold as a spectator, witness to some film that's only of the mildest curiosity to me.

As I near my house, I see Chloe is out watering her lawn, wearing little shorts, a singlet, and a visor, her ponytail sticking out the top. She waves as I pull into the drive. Kirit and Pia throw a ball back and forth in their yard while Tarika prunes some potted plants lined up by the flowerbed. Her husband, Chapal – a small, balding man I rarely see – is hanging them up on the veranda.

I get out of my car, and hurry around to the passenger seat. Josh and Karen are across the street, washing Josh's car. Karen's car is also out, like they're planning to do that one next. They wave to me as I open the passenger door. I wave back.

Then I slowly lift Wallace's basket from the car, careful to support the underside. I debate taking the child's playpen, but it's too much to carry. I need to be sure I don't jostle Wallace, let alone drop him.

"Oh, the poor thing," Chloe says, approaching as she continues watering the lawn. She tickles Wallace under his chin. Wallace licks her hand. "I hope he'll be okay."

The curtains in her front window flap – Vic. My heart thumps once in my chest before it settles. I glower in that direction – or hope it comes across as a glower.

"I can't thank you enough for the vet bill," I say.

"Don't be silly. I should be thanking you for not taking this further."

"Really, Chloe, I can't tell you how much I appreciate it."

"You're welcome."

"It's so much—"

"It cost whatever it cost. I also want you to know you have every right to take this matter further, if you like. You should." Chloe casts a pointed look at the window. "But we won't be."

"It's okay."

"Just be sure." Chloe runs a hand up and down my arm. "Make sure he's okay."

"Thanks, Chloe. I should get him inside."

"See you around, Casper. Maybe by the pool one day."

As I approach the house, Kirit and Pia ignore Tarika and charge toward me, jumping up on tiptoes to look into Wallace's basket. They are wide-eyed and their mouths hang open.

"What happened to Wallace?" Kirit says.

"He broke his leg."

"How?" Pia asks.

"He had an accident."

"Is he going to be okay?"

"I hope so."

"Can we pat him?" Kirit says.

"Maybe just gently – we don't want to give him too much excitement."

Kirit and Pia stroke Wallace's head like he's a house of cards that might collapse under their ministrations. The astonishment doesn't leave their faces.

"Kids!" Tarika says. "Come back here! Let Mr. Gray take Wallace inside."

"Can we come visit?" Pia asks.

The question is indiscriminately pitched – it could be at me, or at Tarika. Chapal, on a stepladder, pauses in the act of hanging a pot plant. He shrugs at me, like he's telling me that it's my call.

"Sure," I say.

"See you, Wallace!" Kirit says.

"Bye, Wallace!" Pia says.

They run back into their yard as I unlock the front door of my house.

54.

Wallace pants as Jane bounces down the stairs. She's changed from Sarah's clothes into her own, and now wears shorts and is buttoning up her blouse.

There's silence between us. I don't know what to say. Neither does she. Fortunately, Wallace's presence saves us. He wags his tale frantically, excited to see Jane for the first time since Friday morning. Jane coos over him and scratches him behind the ears. He laps up the attention.

I set him alongside the couch, then grab the playpen from the car. I'm no handyman, but can follow a set of instructions. Pulling everything out of the packaging, I lay it out, then get to work, cursing every now and then when I get something wrong.

At one point, Jane brings me a beer and, without thinking, I take a drink and set it down on the coffee table. For the next half an hour, I continue assembling the pen, interspersed with gulps of beer and wiping my sleeve across my brow. It could be just any other day.

Wallace seems bemused once I've caged him in. Jane brings his bowls and sets them down by his bed. He gazes quizzically at her. She scratches him under the chin, then rises to stand next to me. Absently, I move to put my arm around her back.

And stop.

"Ex …" *Excuse me.* That's what I was about to say. *Excuse me.* Like Jane's some stranger or first date I'm trying to make a good impression on.

I flee upstairs.

In my bedroom, I change into a fresh T-shirt, then sit on the corner of the bed. Although the house is just as quiet as it has been, I can *feel* Jane and Wallace downstairs, but it's not the same as it was. I close my eyes, trying to find some familiarity, like I'm trying to identify the name of a song whose tune I can't shake from my head. There's no answer – nothing but that ringing in my ears.

Going into the bathroom, I pee, then go to the bathroom sinks. One is filled with white water, and it takes a moment for it to click this is where I left Jane's anniversary gift to disinfect.

I wash my hands in the other sink, then pull the plug out of the filled sink. The water drains away to reveal the bracelet. I rinse it under some hot water, dry it with a towel, then retreat to the bedroom. I threw the bracelet box but have no idea where it landed.

Kneeling, I press my cheek to the floor and scour the bedroom. There's a shadow by the rear bed leg. It's the box. But there's also something else behind it, something long, flat, and rectangular.

I pull it out. It's a gift, wrapped with a ribbon – Jane's anniversary gift. I tap it. It sounds like a wooden box. I shake it. There's lots of minute rattling inside. I ponder what it is. Then, as my hands tremble, I decide it doesn't matter. Holding this gift makes me think of our lives together, of the way our anniversaries have been the heartbeat of our marriage.

I slide the gift back under the bed. Take the bracelet box and put the bracelet back in it. Close the box, and slip it into my pocket.

When I enter the dining room, Wallace tries to get up. I hurry across to him, and pat him, encouraging him to stay down. He licks my hand. I smile at him. He really is a good dog.

"Want something to eat?"

Jane's in the kitchen, making a tuna sandwich. I shake my head as she comes into the dining room. We move to sit on the couch at the same time. Jane sits in the middle, like she wants to get close to me. I lean on the armrest, like I'm trying to gain space away from her.

"I'm sorry," she says.

I don't know what to say.

She nibbles at her sandwich. I grab my beer and scull what's left of it for fortitude. The tension is unnatural, a reaper hovering over our relationship. There's no way we'll survive the day, let alone any attempts at reconciliation, if it remains.

"Here," I say, grabbing the bracelet box from my pocket and thrusting it at Jane.

Jane hurriedly swallows the bite of her sandwich and puts the plate on the coffee table. She takes the box, opens it, her eyes both widening and tearing.

"This is gorgeous," she says. "Thank you."

Usually, she might lean over and give me a kiss, but now all the protocols have changed. We stare at each other awkwardly. I feel almost like I should offer a handshake. I shoot to my feet.

"Gonna take the bins out," I say, starting for the door.

"Hey."

I stop.

"I got you something, too."

The silence that follows is so long that I'm starting to put a foot forward when Jane talks again.

"I'll get it?"

I turn my head and offer her the smallest smile. "Surprise me," I say.

55.

As I head outside to the bins, my phone beeps. I yank it from my pocket. It's a text from Luke:

You okay?

My fingers move to the screen, but I stop. I don't want to be glib – not now. Luke deserves better, given the way he's stood by me. But in thinking that, I realize that I'm unsure there's *any* satisfactory answer. I throw the empty beer in the recycle bin, drag both bins to the curb, and try to work out that simple question.

Am I okay?

I lift my face to a cloudless sky, although the day cools with the promise that this belated summer's finally breaking. The neighborhood teems with life around me – I've always heard it, always seen it, but never really registered it. Now I recognize how rich and alive and unique every sight and sound is. Kirit and Pia shriek and whoop, then charge from their yard down the street to join some other kids, who run around chasing a ball. Opposite me, Josh and Karen now wash Karen's car, vigorously attacking it with soapy sponges as they chat and smile – I can't hear what they say, but I *feel* their happiness, their contentedness, and that sense of belonging. Chloe continues to water her lawn; she notices me looking and flashes a smile – she might even wink, although I'm not sure if I imagine that, and I find myself almost winking back. The door to her house opens and Vic – nose swollen, eyes blackened – stands there, sees me, then darts back inside and closes the door.

And that's when it hits me, and I think the simplest thing I could possibly think: *fuck it*. It's that easy – that easy to fit in, to move forward, to create a place I want in this world, to create *the* world I want. The labor itself might be hard – and there will be obstacles and detours and diversions – but the rest is just the way I approach it, and I've been timid and indecisive for too long.

Jane said she got *why* I stared at my sketchpad – because those blank pages are implicit with endless possibilities. But I've been focused on that one crumpled sketch of Jane. There are plenty of other blank pages – although that's not quite true, I realize belatedly. I tore every page out of my sketchpad. I don't know if that's meant to be a commentary on where I am or not.

No, I can't let that define me. I need a new sketchpad. That's the undeniable truth. I'm starting new with a whole pad full of blank pages and I can fill them with whatever I want.

Then, almost as if on cue, my phone dings with another message – Beth:

> Just touching base. You all right?
> Want to catch up a little earlier
> tomorrow? We can talk about you
> sketching me. ☺ X.

I type three letters back to Luke:

> Yep

And to Beth, I start to write:

> Sure!

Then I stare at that single word.

Four letters.

Four letters but so many possibilities.

Given what's happened today, should I be catching up with her? More than that, should I be sketching her?

My heartbeat grows just a little bit faster.

I begin to delete that single word, thinking I should text her an explanation as to why the sketch mightn't be the best idea. But then I stop that, too. I'm reacting out of fear and meekness. Beth deserves better – much better.

And I deserve better, too.

I'm not sure what *right* is, and decide I need to think about this a little more.

Shoving my phone in my pocket, I go back into the house.

ACKNOWLEDGMENTS

So, when the opportunity presented itself to re-release this book, I thought I'd look through it again.

If you've read this book before (thank you), you'll notice it's just a little bit different, the way directors sometimes tweak their movies and release a Director's Cut. The changes aren't major. But I think they improve the book.

That's not to say the book was incomplete when it was first released in 2017 by Pantera Press; it was the very best I could do at that time. But, as you get older, hopefully smarter and maturer (some people might debate that in my case), you look at things differently.

So, thank yous, a combination of old and new:

- Pantera Press, who first took a chance on this story when other publishers were telling me they really liked it, but didn't feel they could sell it: Ali Green, Marty Green, Susan Hando, Madeleine Konstantinidis, James Read, John and Jenny Green, Katy McEwen, Elly Clapin, and especially my talented, dedicated editor Lucy Bell, and anybody I might've missed out.
- my proofreader, Desanka Vukelich, for polishing that final manuscript.
- Blaise van Hecke, my most faithful, patient, and nurturing alpha reader. I miss your insight.

- Bel Woods, Ryan O'Neill, Laurie Steed, and A. S. Patrić, for their input and support. When you write, it's always useful to have a cadre of like-minded writer friends.
- the 2013 Hachette Manuscript Development Program: Bernadette Foley, Vanessa Radnidge; author Charlotte Nash; and the other writers chosen that year: Kim Lock, for her fabulous feedback; J. M. Peace who loved the story and helped with police procedural issues (if you're wondering *what* police procedural issues, well, they're no longer there because I learned how unlikely they were); Sarah Ridout, Mhairead MacLeod, Laura Elvery, Kathy George, and Kim Paul; and the Queensland Writers' Centre who coordinated the Program.
- my old writing group: Beau Hillier, Jasmine Powell, Gina Boothroyd, Deb Graham, and Blaise van Hecke (again), for reading some of the early chapters as I was reworking the book.
- my old football friend Peter Panayiotou, for acting as an intermediary with his talented vet daughter, Mel, and answering my endless veterinary questions. If there's any errors here, they're no doubt mine.
- Barry Carozzi, who answered all my questions about being a high school teacher, from routines, to classes, to responsibilities.
- my agent, Sally Bird, for believing in this book.
- Rosie Giuliano, for the fantastic new cover!
- and ECG Press, for rebirthing this book into the world.

And, finally, thank you to you, the reader, for picking up this book. I hope you enjoy it.

BOOK CLUB QUESTIONS

1. What would you do if you found something incriminating in your partner's possessions?
2. What can you do to stop long-term relationships from becoming stale?
3. How would you handle a neighbor bullying you?
4. Casper wonders about who people are and how they behave behind closed doors. Do you ever think about the lives of your neighbors?
5. What sort of relationship do you think Vic and Chloe have?
6. What do you think happened between Beth and Roger?
7. What would you do if somebody hurt your pet?
8. Can you have a close inter-gender friendship?
9. Do inter-gender friendships run the risk of developing into something more?
10. Both Luke and Beth talk about boundaries not existing in sex when you're in love – do you believe that's true?
11. Does adultery only occur due to a lack of something in an existing relationship, or could it occur regardless?
12. Could you forgive your partner if they cheated on you?
13. Beth stays the night with Casper, and it's ambiguous what happened. What do you think happened?
14. Casper and Jane's lives haven't gone according to plan. Does anybody's?
15. What do you think became of Casper and Jane and their relationship?

ABOUT THE AUTHOR

Les Zig has always loved to lose himself in stories – from reading *Dennis the Menace*, *The Adventures of Tintin*, and *Asterix* as a kid, to *The Lord of the Rings* as a twelve-year-old, fantasy fare as a teenager, and (as he fell more and more in love with reading) anything he could get his hands on.

He believes stories have a universal appeal, that readers can live vicariously through characters, can soar with their triumphs, can wallow in their miseries, and find exhilaration in their adventures.

His novels and stories often focus on troubled, flawed characters trying to find a place in the world, which is reflective of his own journey with mental health challenges.

When he's not writing, he's thinking about writing.

Other novels by Les Zig …

ECG Press
Any More Complicated Than That
Prudence

As Lazaros Zigomanis …

MidnightSun Publishing
This

ECG Press
Song of the Curlew
The Shadow in the Wind

Busybird Publishing
Pride